NIGHTMARE

'THE DETECTIVE STORY CLUB is a clearing house for the best detective and mystery stories chosen for you by a select committee of experts. Only the most ingenious crime stories will be published under the THE DETECTIVE STORY CLUB imprint. A special distinguishing stamp appears on the wrapper and title page of every THE DETECTIVE STORY CLUB book—the Man with the Gun. Always look for the Man with the Gun when buying a Crime book.'

Wm. Collins Sons & Co. Ltd., 1929

Now the Man with the Gun is back in this series of COLLINS CRIME CLUB reprints, and with him the chance to experience the classic books that influenced the Golden Age of crime fiction.

NIGHTMARE

A STORY OF CRIME
BY
LYNN BROCK

WITH AN INTRODUCTION BY
ROB REEF

COLLINS
CRIME
CLUB

COLLINS CRIME CLUB
An imprint of HarperCollins*Publishers*
1 London Bridge Street
London SE1 9GF
www.harpercollins.co.uk

This Detective Story Club edition 2017

First published in Great Britain by W. Collins Sons & Co. Ltd 1932

Introduction © Rob Reef 2017

A catalogue record for this book is available from the British Library

ISBN 978-0-00-813777-9

Typeset in Bulmer MT Std 11.5/12 pt by
Palimpsest Book Production Ltd, Falkirk, Stirlingshire
Printed and bound in Great Britain by CPI Group (UK) Ltd, Croydon CR0 4YY

INTRODUCTION

Lynn Brock's *Nightmare* is not a regular Golden Age offering. Its bleak atmosphere bears comparison with noir fiction and the disturbing, almost absurd, hopelessness of its main characters reminds one of protagonists in plays by Samuel Beckett. From a purely formal point of view, *Nightmare* is most comparable to the fiction structure of inverted detective stories like Francis Iles' *Malice Aforethought* or Freeman Wills Crofts' *The 12:30 from Croydon*. In all these books, published in the early 1930s, one can follow the genesis of a murder shown from the perspective of the perpetrator. They all paint a gloomy picture of the human condition, but while Iles and Crofts develop sophisticated studies in psychology in their tales, Brock seems to motivate his *Nightmare* from an even darker and deeper source.

To those who know Brock's more traditional Colonel Gore detective novels, this ambitious book will come as a surprise. For all the others not so well acquainted with the author, it seems appropriate to start with a brief biographical outline.

Lynn Brock was a pen name used by Alexander Patrick McAllister, an Irish playwright and novelist born in Dublin in 1877. He also published using the pseudonyms Henry Alexander and Anthony P. Wharton. Alexander, or Alister as he was known in the family, was the eldest son of Patrick Frederick McAllister, accountant to the port and docks board in Dublin, and his wife Catherine (née Morgan). Educated at Clongowes Wood College, he later obtained an Honours Degree at the Royal University and was appointed chief clerk shortly after the inception of the National University of Ireland. At the outbreak of the First World War, McAllister enlisted in the military. On July 21, 1915 he went to France, where he served in the Motor Machine Gun

Service of the Royal Artillery. Wounded twice, he returned to Dublin in 1918 and resumed his occupation as a clerk of the National University of Ireland. He married the same year. Once retired on a pension, McAllister and his wife Cicely (née Blagg) settled in London before later moving to Ferndown near Wimborne in Dorset where he lived many years and died at the age of 66 on April 6, 1943.

In Dorset, McAllister wrote his first detective novel at the age of 48 under the pseudonym Lynn Brock. This work, *The Deductions of Colonel Gore* (1926), became a huge success. Many of his later novels featuring his title hero-detective were often reprinted and widely translated. His complex plots and witty style won the praise of Dorothy L. Sayers, T.S. Eliot and S.S. Van Dine. Against this background, his publishers at Collins had perfectly justified high expectations for *Nightmare* (1932), which they advertised as 'one of the most remarkable books we have ever published.' Yet they would be disappointed. *Nightmare* never saw a second edition, and it was Brock's first crime novel not to be published in the US.

Though not a success in his time, *Nightmare* is still a fascinating story and, from the perspective of literary history, his publishers' statement seems to be not entirely wrong. Reading *Nightmare* not as another psychological crime novel with a missing twist at the end but rather as a tragedy of the human condition itself allows interpretation of the work as what may be the first philosophical crime novel. For this reason, it may be considered a milestone in crime fiction.

To explain this seemingly surprising hypothesis, it is necessary to take a closer look at McAllister's career as a writer, which did not start with the first Colonel Gore mystery in 1926. McAllister first made a name for himself twenty years earlier when his play *Irene Wycherly*, written under the pseudonym Anthony P. Wharton, became a big success in London and on Broadway. In 1912/14, his celebrity reached its peak when *At the Barn* (later made into a silent movie called *Two Weeks* in

1922) was staged in theatres on both sides of the Atlantic. Many plays and premieres followed, the last of which was *The O'Cuddy*, staged shortly before his death. However, neither of these could revive his earlier fame.

Why is it then worth considering his career as a playwright? Because it shows his intellectual origin as a writer. Lynn Brock, one of the author's alter egos, was much more akin to George Bernard Shaw, T.S. Eliot and Frank Wedekind than to Agatha Christie, Anthony Berkeley or Freeman Wills Crofts. As with many turn-of-the-century pre-Freudian artists and writers, McAllister was deeply influenced by the philosophy of Arthur Schopenhauer. In Schopenhauer's principal work *The World as Will and Representation* (1818), the philosopher describes life as a dream motivated by an essence called 'Will'—a mindless, aimless, non-rational urge at the foundation of everything including our instinctual drives. The world as 'Will' is an endless striving and blind impulse, devoid of knowledge, lawless and meaningless. There is no God, and there is neither good nor evil. The 'Will' causes a world of permanent struggle where each individual strives against every other individual in a 'war of all against all', and where daily life is suffering, a constant pendular movement between pain and boredom with misfortune in general as a rule. This world-as-representation is a nightmare for all individuals, staged by the 'Will' for his eternal self-involved entertainment.

It is this nihilistic and gloomy worldview that motivates Lynn Brock's *Nightmare*. Bookended by the appearance of a gramophone playing music—the only art that, according to Schopenhauer, shows the metaphysical 'Will' itself—the story follows the tragic misadventures of Simon Whalley and a handful of other characters trapped in an ominous house community revealing the 'war of all against all' and individual suffering in a nutshell.

Though Whalley's life bears some resemblance to McAllister's biography as a playwright, the whole tale has a surreal quality.

There are no distinguishable villains or heroes. All of the characters are driven by the same sinister force towards an abyss of despair, gently oscillating between daydreams of fresh starts and the inevitable nightmare-like realization of the impossibility of those intentions. All of the protagonists are doomed but Whalley, worst-hit by the cruelty of some of his neighbours, succumbs to the pressure and prepares himself for murderous revenge. The following events are predictable, and the ending is as gloomy as the setting of the story against the backdrop of the Great Depression.

What makes *Nightmare* truly genuine is its subtext. The plot not only unveils the motive of the crimes committed, it leads one to the metaphysical core of the human condition itself. Throughout the book the characters develop an uncanny consciousness of their nightmare-like existence in an endlessly striving and meaningless universe. They feel that 'Life itself is a silly faked-up old story', a 'bitter, merciless struggle'. They anticipate that 'everything that has been is for ever' and one 'might have to start all over again at the end of it'. Such half-hidden maxims of Schopenhauer's philosophy make Lynn Brock's *Nightmare* an extraordinary and notable contribution to the Golden Age of crime and detective fiction, and it is to be hoped that this new edition might help to bring it up for discussion again.

ROB REEF
March 2017

TO MY WIFE

*All the characters and incidents of this novel are entirely
fictitious.*

CHAPTER I

1

IT was a sullen, sultry afternoon in early June—the unsatisfactory June of 1931—and after lunch Mr Harvey Knayle, who hoped to play tennis at the Edwarde-Lewins' after tea, had retired to his bedroom for a nap. At half-past three he still lay there on his bed, slumbering soundly in the twilight of down-drawn blinds, clothed, beneath a gay dressing-gown, in gay pyjamas. For Harvey Knayle had reached an age at which an afternoon nap was a thing to be taken seriously and with all possible ease and comfort.

He was a fresh-coloured, clean-shaven, spare little man of fifty precisely, with thinning, carefully-groomed blonde hair, a high forehead, a longish aquilinish nose, good-humouredly sardonic lips, and a cleft chin. The combined effect of these details was agreeable, restful, and unobtrusively distinguished, as became the personal appearance of anyone bearing the name which was his.

For the Knayles were one of the oldest families in Barshire and intricately linked with many others of the same standing all over the west country. It is true that the particular branch of the family to which Harvey Knayle belonged had declined considerably, financially, during the past century. None the less, as things had fallen out with the help of a war, the little man who lay there sleeping peacefully, with one cheek cupped in a well-shaped hand, his knees tucked up, and a smile of child-like content upon his face, was separated by but three lives from a baronetcy, one of the largest estates in the county, and an income of fifty or sixty thousand a year. There was no likelihood whatever that he would become the actual possessor

1

of this dignity and affluence. But it was a source of mild gratification to him that a large number of people—without ill-will towards the three healthy obstacles—quite sincerely hoped that somehow, some day, he would. Meanwhile he had an income of something over two thousand a year from sound investments, hosts of friends, excellent health, and an unfailing interest in the game of life. More especially, as will be seen—this was one of the many reasons of his social popularity—in the games played by life with other people.

For, in point of fact, his own existence had been perfectly uneventful. From Oxford he had returned to his father's house near Whanton and for a few years had lived the life of a country gentleman. But at thirty he had quickly wearied of unadulterated rurality and had migrated to Rockwood, Dunpool's most select residential suburb, where, on the frontier between town and country, he had lived ever since in bachelor content. There he had found new friends and had still been within easy reach of old ones. He danced satisfactorily, was a sound bridge-player, a reliable and good-tempered performer at tennis and golf, a sometimes brilliant shot, a good horseman, and a keen fisherman. He knew everyone in the neighbourhood worth knowing and knew everything worth knowing about them. If not a brilliant conversationalist, he was an excellent listener; if he rarely strove to say an amusing thing, he never said a malicious one. Finally he was a Knayle. And so the past twenty-five years of his life (during the War he had acted very efficiently as Adjutant of a Remount Camp close to Rockwood) had flowed tranquilly along a rut of comfortable sociability, pleasantly varied by annual trips abroad. He had found during them plenty of time to take an interest in other people—an occupation which was, indeed, the principal pleasure of his life.

It is necessary, in view of subsequent events, to define his position on that drowsy afternoon, geographically, with a little greater accuracy.

The bedroom in which he lay was situated on the ground

floor of a large four-storey house—its number was 47—in Downview Road, one of the main arteries of Rockwood. The house, detached, and formerly, like its fellows, the dignified and undivided residence of a succession of well-to-do tenants, had come down somewhat in a post-War world and had been converted into four flats, the upper two of which were reached by a steeply-pitched outer staircase of concrete built on to one side wall. At the moment the basement flat, beneath Mr Knayle— one went down a little flight of steps from the front garden to its front door—was let to a Mr Ridgeway, a solitary, elderly man, apparently without occupation. The first-floor flat, above Mr Knayle, was occupied by a Mr and Mrs Whalley. And the top flat, above Mr Whalley's, was tenanted by a Mr Prossip, his wife, and his daughter.

Mr Knayle, as has been said, liked Rockwood. It was, of course, two hours by rail from London. But, though he ran up to London very frequently and had many friends living there, he was always glad to get out of it. Dunpool, he admitted, though it was still the sixth city of England, was a dingy, untidy, shabby-looking place, solely interested in the making of money, doggedly provincial in outlook. But Rockwood was picturesque, dignified, quiet, had agreeable literary and historical associations, and was notoriously healthy. There was a pleasant variety in the people one knew there—the commercial magnates of the city, people connected with the county families, retired Service people of all sorts, the men from the college and the university, people who moved about the world and did all sorts of things. It was true that a good deal of shabby gentility was hidden away in lodging-houses and boarding-houses, and that, since the War, many houses where one had dined and danced had been converted into flats in which curious-looking people lived now. But curious-looking people were everywhere now. One could always avoid seeing them. On the whole Mr Knayle thought Rockwood as good a place as any to live in. At any rate, everyone knew who one was.

At half-past three, as he had arranged, Mr Knayle was

awakened by the entry of his servant, Hopgood, and opened his eyes—bright blue eyes—permanently a little surprised, but with a birdlike quickness of movement and fixity of gaze. They watched Hopgood let up the blinds, observed that outside the windows the gloom of the afternoon had deepened to definite menace, and closed themselves again with resignation.

'No tennis this afternoon, I'm afraid, Hopgood. Looks rather like a thunderstorm, doesn't it?'

Hopgood, a neat, stolid, oldish man, turned to face his employer. He had been in Mr Knayle's service for many years and was permitted, upon reasonable occasion, a reasonable liberty of speech.

'Well, all I can say, sir,' he replied, his usually colourless voice tinged with acidity, 'is that if there is one, I hope a good old thunderbolt will plop into the top flat of this house.'

Mr Knayle, opening his eyes again, smiled sympathetically upon his retainer's grimness of visage and, divining its cause, cocked an ear to catch a remote wailing which had of late grown familiar.

'Mr Prossip's gramophone busy again, I hear.'

So far Hopgood, emulating his master's stoicism, had refrained from complaint of the annoyance to which they had both been subjected for a considerable time past. But, having made up his mind to complain of it, he had entered the room determined to do so, after his fashion, thoroughly.

'Busy, sir?' He produced from a pocket a befigured slip. 'I'd like to ask you, sir, if you have any idea how many times that gramophone plays that same old tune in the day?'

'None whatever,' replied Mr Knayle placidly, inserting his neat legs into the trousers with which Hopgood had supplied him. 'Have you?'

'Well, I've been working it out this afternoon, sir, timing it and taking the average. Say it takes four minutes to play the tune—including stops—though there's not many stops once it starts. Very well, that's fifteen times it plays it in an hour. In the morning it plays it from eight o'clock to ten o'clock. In the afternoon it plays it from half-past one until four. And at night it plays it from ten to eleven. That's five and a half hours a day. If you multiply that by fifteen, sir, you get it that it plays it eighty-two times in the day. And it's been doing that now for seventeen days. What I make of it, sir, is that since they began that silly game up there in the top flat—last Saturday week it was—their gramophone has played that same blessed old tune fourteen hundred times.'

He put away his memorandum with lips tightened impressively and helped Mr Knayle into his coat.

'Quite a number of times,' Mr Knayle agreed. 'Involving quite a large amount of labour for someone—I should surmise some more than one.'

'They all have a go at it, sir, I reckon. But it's that brazen young trollop of a maid of theirs that does most of it. I hear her running out of her kitchen to start it up when it stops.'

'Why hear her, Hopgood?' asked Mr Knayle soothingly. 'Or it? I don't.'

'You may say you don't, sir—but you do. How can you get away from it, with the noise coming down through the well of the staircase like through a flue? I believe they've put the gramophone right over it, on purpose.' Hopgood's voice, approaching now its real purpose, invested itself with respectful reproach. 'I wonder you don't make a complaint to the landlord, sir. It's disgraceful that a quiet gentleman like you should be worried this way from morning to night. The fiddle was bad enough by itself; but this—well, it's sheer torture, sir, that's what it is, sheer downright, cold-blooded torture. Any other gentleman would have complained long ago.'

But, while he surveyed his completed toilette in a long glass critically, Mr Knayle put a kindly foot upon this attempt to stampede him, and scotched it firmly.

'Never allow yourself to be worried, Hopgood. And never, never let other people know that they can worry you. I admit that the same tune played fourteen hundred times begins to pall a little. But it might have been played twenty-four hundred times. The sound is hardly audible down here—unless you listen for it. Let us console ourselves by the reflection that other people are having a much worse time of it than we are. A great help, that—always.' He looked towards the windows. 'Yes, there's the rain. I had better get off, I think. Has Chidgey brought the car round?'

As Mr Knayle drove off in his smart coupé to spend the afternoon with his friends, the Edwarde-Lewins, he glanced up casually towards the first floor. But there was nothing to see there. Perceiving a showy-looking young woman in coquettish apron and cap standing at one of the windows of the top flat smoking a cigarette, he smiled. The lease of his own flat would expire in September, and he had all but decided, before falling asleep that afternoon, to write that evening to the landlord giving him the agreed three months' notice that his tenancy would not be renewed. He would be away for the greater part of those three months, so that the persistency of the Prossips' gramophone, which, he was resolved, should not trouble him in the least, was of no concern to him.

He was quite determined that it should not trouble him in the least. During the past few months, he had noticed, a lot of people whom he knew—quite good-tempered, placid people, formerly—had developed a marked tendency to allow little things to worry them and make them irritable. He had noticed in himself a tendency to attach too much importance to trifling annoyances—a lost golf-ball, or a dud razor-blade, or a little tactlessness on the part of a friend—and had occasionally found it necessary to check it with some firmness. He assured himself now, therefore, that though stupid and childish and, of course, annoying for Mr and Mrs Whalley (a pity, though, that Whalley should allow himself to take it so seriously) the dogged perseverance of the Prossips' gramophone struck him as rather amusing.

As, of course, it was.

Seated beside Mr Knayle, his chauffeur, Chidgey, had also glanced up to the windows of the top flat and smiled faintly. He knew all about the Prossips' gramophone and thought it a game. His smile faded almost at once, however, and his rather pleasant face became gloomy. The gear-box and the back-axle of the car should both have been refilled last week. He had not refilled them last week, nor since. He couldn't explain to himself why he hadn't, except that it was a messy job and that he had felt disinclined to do it. He had been with Mr Knayle for three years and had always taken anxious care of the two new cars which his employer had acquired in that time. It worried him that he had had this funny feeling lately that he didn't want to do jobs about the car that were a bit troublesome and messy—a sort of feeling that it wasn't worth bothering about doing them.

2

At all events Agatha Judd—the brazen young trollop of the top flat—was quite sure that the gramophone's persistency was amusing—the most priceless lark, in fact, that had so far diverted her light-hearted existence.

As Mr Knayle's car disappeared from her view round the curve of Downview Road, once more the gramophone blared triumphantly the long-drawn closing note of 'I can't give you anything but love, Baby'. The needle slid off the record and the abrupt succeeding silence aroused her from her never-wearying contemplation of the passing traffic. But the disturbance caused her no resentment, though for two hours past, without intermission, at intervals of a few minutes, precisely similar disturbances had called her away from her window. Jamming a cigarette between her full, bedaubed lips, she flitted with hurrying eagerness out of the kitchen and along the little central corridor of the flat to where the gramophone stood on a small landing or platform at one side of the three steps descending from the corridor to the hall-door. Having started the needle once again upon its pilgrimage over the worn record, she wound up the instrument recklessly and then stood for some moments listening, her bold hazel eyes narrowed to exclude the smoke of her cigarette.

She was a slim, shapely girl of twenty-four or five and, despite her hardy allure, her powdered skin, and her salved lips, a noticeably good-looking young creature, obsessed by her own personal appearance, inefficient and lazy, equipped with the mentality of a Dunpool slum-child of ten, and possessed by a never-flagging determination to extract a bit of fun from life. At that moment, as has been said, despite the unavoidable monotony of the means, she was extracting a quite satisfying bit of it. As she stood listening, blissfully unaware of the grim fate whose scissors were already opening above her sleek little head, she smiled with vivid pleasure.

Stooping to the gramophone again—it rested on the bare boards of the little landing, whose carpet had been rolled back— she laid a finger against the edge of the record, increasing and relaxing its pressure alternately. The melody dissolved into hideous ululations, wailing and howling in dolorous insanity. She laughed softly while she continued this manipulation for a minute or so and then climbed over the balusters—relics of the former interior staircase of the house, removed at the time of the conversion—which enclosed the landing on two sides. Bracing herself, she sprang into the air and descended upon the boards with her full weight. The hollow, echoing reverberations which resulted—for the flooring beneath her high-heeled shoes consisted merely of match-boarding—widened her smile. She reproduced it with deliberation half a dozen times, then wound up the gramophone again, restarted the needle, climbed back over the balusters and, crossing the passage, entered the flat's sitting-room.

In there Marjory Prossip, a heavily-built, sullen-faced young woman of thirty, sat bent over the construction of a silk underskirt. She turned her large, elaborately-waved head as Agatha entered and rose silently from her chair. For a moment of preparation the two faced one another in the middle of the room, then, together, they sprang ceilingward and descended upon the carpet with a violence which set the windows a-rattle. This athletic feat having been repeated several times, Miss Prossip reseated herself with her work and Agatha returned humming to the kitchen, pausing along the way to start the gramophone once more. No word had passed between them. Agatha had not troubled to remove her cigarette from her lips.

For five minutes, measured by a clock upon which she kept a watchful eye, Miss Prossip plied her needle industriously. She rose then and, joined by Agatha, hopped on one foot along the corridor, into a bedroom at the end of it, around the bedroom three times, and then back along the corridor to the sitting-room, where, rather blown, she resumed her sewing. No slightest change of expression manifested itself in her sulky, sallow face while she performed these curious gymnastics, which she executed with the solemnity of a ritual. In the agile Agatha, however, the awkward heaviness of her broad-beamed superior evoked a special gaiety. As she hopped behind Miss Prossip's labouring clumsiness, she giggled happily.

Another five minutes passed and again Agatha entered the sitting-room, having again attended to the gramophone. Miss Prossip arose and faced her silently. Then, together, they sprang ceilingwards.

Some time later Mr Knayle had the curiosity to make some enquiries about Miss Prossip. He learned that she had always been regarded by people who knew her as of perfectly normal intelligence and general behaviour, had been educated at the local High School, (a celebrated one) where she had been considered by her mistress a rather clever girl, if somewhat difficult and moody, was passionately fond of music and played the violin with talent, and, in general, had been considered a perfectly normal and sensible person. Mr Knayle himself had frequently encountered her in the front garden and exchanged 'good mornings' and 'good afternoons' with her. His personal estimate of her, until the outbreak of the present hostilities, had been that she was a perfectly sane, if exceedingly unattractive, young woman. Slightly more intent observation of her, in the course of the past few weeks, had afforded him no reason to revise this opinion. Nothing that he ever subsequently learned about her or her family history ever afforded him the slightest reason to revise it. And so the fact is to be accepted that Marjory Prossip was an intelligent, well-educated, well-behaved, industrious, quiet girl of thirty, an accomplished violinist, and very fond of the kind of music which abhors tunes and never says the same thing twice.

3

In the sitting-room of the first-floor flat, directly beneath those four prancing feet, Simon Whalley sat at a small oval table near the open windows. He was tallish, black-haired, grey-eyed, like Mr Knayle, clean-shaven, in his middle-forties and rather noticeably thin. The well-cut lounge suit which he wore fitted him excellently and yet had the effect of having grown a size too large for him. On the table were an ash-tray, half full of cigarette ends, and a writing-block. Three sheets had been detached from the block and lay crumpled-up on the carpet beside his chair—a severely un-easy chair, imported from the dining-room. On a fourth sheet, beneath the carefully-written heading 'CHAPTER XVII', he was drawing with a fountain-pen a design of intricate and perfectly unmeaning arabesques.

Over this task, which had occupied him for the past half-hour, he was bent in concentrated absorption, thickening a curve here with nicety, rounding off an angle there, finding always a new joining to make or a new space into which to crowd another little lop-sided scroll or lozenge. At regular intervals, automatically, his left hand removed a cigarette from his lips, tapped it against the ashtray and replaced it. Whenever he lighted a new cigarette from the old one, his eyes made a curiously methodical and concerned journey round the room, beginning always at the window-curtain to his left hand and travelling always round to the armchair, which stood just beside the oval table, at his right. As they made this circuit slowly, they examined each object upon which they rested with an anxious intentness. From the armchair they glanced always to a small, stopped clock on the mantelpiece and then returned, slowly and reluctantly, to the writing-block.

The room was a large, rather low-ceilinged one, quite charming to the cursory eye with its biscuit-coloured wall-paper, bright carpet and curtains and rugs and chintzes, rows of dwarf book-cases, easy chairs and bowls of roses. It was sufficiently high up to escape serious molestation by the noise of Downview Road's voluminous summer traffic. Its windows looked out across the road, over the wide, pleasantly-timbered expanse of Rockwood Down. It was a friendly, cheerful, comfortable room, and Whalley hated it and everything in it with a hatred that was all but horror.

As he sat elaborating his futile design, his mutinous brain, refusing stubbornly to perform the functions which had once been its delight and relief, persisted in exploring, for the hundredth-thousandth time, the emotion of nauseated distrust and apprehension which the room now evoked in him whenever he entered it or even looked into it. No aim directed this vague, depressed analysis; no satisfaction or hope of remedy resulted from it. It proceeded always, however, he had observed—for it had long ago become a subconscious activity, so persistent as to attract his uneasy attention—along the same line.

It began always with the furtive, secret dinginess and decay that underlay the room's superficial brightness and freshness— began, oddly, always with the same window-curtain.

Pretty curtains. But they had been up for two years now.

When you shook them you found that they were thick with dust. They had faded a lot. There was a small tear in the left-hand one, at the bottom. Bogey-Bogey's work.

The windows. It must be two months at least since the windows of the flat had been cleaned. Seven-and-six . . . but they must be done. A nuisance, the window-cleaner, in and out of the rooms with his bucket and his sour-smelling cloths and his curious watching eyes. And then there was that broken sash-cord. And the cracked pane.

The roll-top desk. Lord, what a litter it was in! All those pigeon-holes . . . full of dust and rubbish. What an uncomfort-able brute of a thing it was to sit at. Much too high and too narrow. And your legs were always cramped. He had paid fourteen pounds for it, and had never succeeded in writing a sentence at it . . .

The chintz covers. They had faded badly, too. All of them wanted cleaning, especially those of the armchairs, which were perfectly filthy . . .

A leg of that arm-chair wanted repairing.

The rain last winter found its way through the wall up there, above the fireplace, cracked the plaster, and stained the paper. That watercolour below the stain had begun to mildew and blotch . . .

The fireplace would have to be seen to before the autumn; its back had burnt out, and a lot of the tiles had cracked. The chimney must be swept, too, before the autumn. That would mean that the whole room would have to be turned topsy-turvy in preparation for the sweep and cleaned right out when he had finished. A woman would have to be got in to do that job. Ten shillings. And the room unusable for the whole day.

The carpet. All right until you looked closely. Then you saw that it was dotted all over with little stains and thickly covered with Bogey-Bogey's hairs. It would have to come up and go to the cleaners, also. And one couldn't use the room without a carpet.

The Crown Derby set on the Welsh dresser. Thick with dust. A two hours' job to collect it, piece by piece, and carry it out to the kitchen and wash and dry it and carry it back and arrange it on the dresser again. He had smashed a cup last time he had done that job, three or four—no, it must be six months ago—before last Christmas—and spoiled the set. Clumsy brute, always smashing things. It had worried him ever since, whenever he had looked at it, to think that the set was a cup short.

The portable . . . God, how he hated the wireless now—the fatuous voices of the announcers—the maudlin, insatiable music . . . Music . . . God—

All those infernal dusty, stale, useless old books. Three or four hundred pounds worth of rubbish—one probably wouldn't get five pounds for the lot if one tried to sell them and get rid of them. Neither he nor Elsa had opened one of them for years. And what a business it had been moving them about. What a business it would be when they would have to be moved again. And they would have to be moved again.

The settee. Ruined by the dog's paws. That must be re-covered—for the dog's paws to filthy again.

The rugs. All faded, all soiled and stained and ragged at the fringes. More work for the cleaners.

That armchair. The springs gone and a castor off. He had been intending to fix that castor for over a year.

Expense—disturbance—trouble. And all for nothing. Everything was wearing out—going. Nothing would stop its going. In a few months, after all that fuss and upset, everything would be dirty and dingy again—older—shabbier. Hopeless to try to keep things decent with clouds of dust coming in from the road all day long and a dog messing about from morning to night and no servant. Hopeless—mere waste of time. Time— God, how the time flew away. The sitting-room alone took a couple of hours to do—even scamping the job. And next morning it looked as if it hadn't been done for weeks.

And yet one couldn't live in a piggery—one couldn't allow

Elsa to. All those confounded things must be cleaned. All those confounded small jobs must be done and paid for.

For that matter, the room would have to be done up very soon—ceiling, wallpaper, and paintwork. All of them were in a bad way, and would be definitely shabby if they were let go until the spring. If the sitting-room was done, the passage and the bathroom would have to be done at the same time. One job must be made of the lot—one upset. More argument and discussion and difficulty with that surly, tricky brute of a land-lord—more worry. Probably he would refuse again to do the work. Even if he did consent to do it, it would mean all sorts of nuisance—the greater part of the flat out of action—workmen about it all day long—noise, smells, mess. Elsa and he would have to sleep and meal at an hotel or somewhere. More expense. And one or other of them would have to be about the flat while the workmen were in it. Lord, what a nuisance.

How pretty the room had looked when they had settled down in the flat two years ago. How sure he had felt, that first afternoon in April, 1929, when he had seated himself at the just-delivered roll-top desk, that, in that friendly, comfortable, peaceful work-room, his brain would come back again, tran-quilly and obediently, to the playing of its old tricks.

That damnable, cheerful-faced clock on the mantel-piece. How many hours of bitter defeat and impotent self-reproach it had hurried away, eagerly, irrevocably. For two years of hours, each a little swifter than the last, each a little nearer to panic-speed, it had hustled him and bustled him and mocked his flurry and his failure. Cursed, smug thing . . . Extraordinary how loud its faint tick had grown—how long he had failed to detect its power to irritate and distract him—how instant had been the relief when, one afternoon six weeks or so back, a sudden impulse had caused him to jump up from his table and stop it. On that afternoon he had written nearly a whole chapter—the chapter which for over three months had refused to begin itself. In the following three weeks he had succeeded in writing four more chapters, turning out four thousand words a day, still with some difficulty, but regularly. The spell had seemed broken at last. For that brief space the sitting-room had worn again the guise of its old encouraging friendliness. He had taken to hurrying in there after lunch, leaving Elsa to wash up unaided.

And then this damnable, idiotic, maddening trouble with the Prossips had begun—just when there had seemed at last, a hope . . .

He turned his head towards the door of the room. A thick portière was drawn across it and, actually, the sound of the gramophone was a faint and remote whining. No portière, however, could shut out its real torture, the malice of its persistency; for Whalley's ears that faint, distant whine was a savage, raucous clamour, hammering at their drums. For a little space he remained, half-turned in his chair, listening to it with rigid intentness. Then, as a heavy thump shook the ceiling above his head he flung down his pen furiously, sprang to his feet, and stood with both hands clenched before his face, glaring upwards.

The paroxysm of anger passed almost instantly—before a second thump followed the first. But he remained for a space surprised by its violence and by its sudden complete obliteration of his self-control. It had produced in him for a moment an absolutely novel sensation—a sensation of being on the point of surrendering his will and his consciousness to some overpowering, hostile, dangerous force. A little like the sensation when one was just about to surrender to an anæsthetic—but much more violent—much more eager to leave behind all the things one knew. A dangerous sensation. For a moment he realised he had been upon the point of shouting—bellowing like a mad animal. He discovered that his legs were trembling a little at the knees and that his hands were still raised absurdly in the air, clenched in front of his face. When he dropped them he looked at them—he had a trick of looking at his hands—he saw that their palms were moist with perspiration.

Ridiculous. Grotesque. Shaking legs and sweating hands. That sort of thing would never do. That sort of thing, he must remember, was just the sort of thing those sluts upstairs hoped he *would* do—allow the business to get on his nerves and shout and slam doors and bang things about. Thank Heaven he hadn't shouted. Shout? Good God, he had never shouted at anyone in his life. All along, since this annoyance had begun, he had kept a close watch on himself, a tight grip on his temper. He had gone out of his way to shut doors quietly, to speak more gently to the dog. No slightest symptoms of resentment, he flattered himself, had rewarded those idiots in the top flat for all their trouble. No doubt they kept watch up there, too—listened—always hoping for some sound of anger or retaliation. Well, they had waited in vain—they would wait in vain.

Now, why on earth had that one particular thump had that strange effect upon him. They had been thumping and banging away up there for nearly three weeks now. He had heard hundreds of thumps. At least a hundred times a day, he supposed, he had heard a thump somewhere above his head. There—they were at it again now. But he was able to smile now—felt no anger whatever, merely an inclination to yawn. Yet that one particular thump, no louder than the rest, had swept away from him all knowledge of himself save a desire to shout madly. Funny. Too many cigarettes, probably. The afternoon was stuffy. And, of course, the thing *had* been going on for three weeks now.

The fountain-pen had rebounded from the surface of the table when he had thrown it down and, falling on the carpet had marked it with a small inkstain. An agitated dismay seized him. He clucked, hurried to the roll-top desk, reduced its disorder to chaos with searching hands, found at last a small piece of blotting-paper in a drawer and hurried back to go down on his knees over the stain. The ink had soaked into the pile of the carpet swiftly, however, and the blotting-paper proved of little avail. He picked up the pen with another cluck, and examined its nib solicitously. It had been Elsa's first gift to him on the first day of their brief engagement—a pledge of the victorious future it was to have won for them. He smiled wryly as he rose to his feet again; there had been no victories.

Luckily, the pen had escaped damage. Laying it on the table, he tore off the bescrawled sheet of the writing-block and, having collected the crumpled debris from the carpet, rolled the result of his afternoon's work into a ball and dropped it dejectedly into a waste-paper basket. One more afternoon gone—one more defeat—

Thump.

Furiously his face, its pallor flushing darkly, jerked upwards towards the ceiling. He shouted ragingly, ludicrously.

'Stop it! Stop it, blast you! Stop it, I say!'

4

In the top flat, as if upon an awaited signal, Bedlam had broken loose. Trampling feet were charging from room to room; doors were banging; furniture was hurtling about; a whistle was screaming; a tray was beating like a war-drum; a bucket was rolling backwards and forwards along the passage. For just an instant after he had realised in stupefaction that his own voice had uttered those three cracked, strangled cries, Whalley had hoped that the noise of the traffic might have drowned them. There had been just an instant of silence save for the traffic and the whine of the gramophone. But then exultant triumph had burst forth above him, preluded by a first long-drawn blast of the whistle. The whistle was new. The enemy had made special preparation for the celebration of victory.

As he stood at the centre of the room, dismayed by his folly, he heard the handle of the door turn and saw the portière ruck and sway inwards as the door opened a little beneath it. He made no movement to draw it aside; for the first time his eyes were unwilling to meet Elsa's. Lest she should edge her way in, he wiped his face hurriedly with his handkerchief in a vague attempt to obliterate its disturbance. His voice essayed bored amusement.

'Having rather a field day upstairs, aren't they?'

'Beasts. Did you call?'

'Call? No.'

'Oh, I thought I heard your voice.'

'No.'

It was his first lie to her—curt and clumsy. He eyed the portière uneasily, glad that it hid him from her clear, steady gaze. There was no suspicion in her voice when it spoke again, but it waited just too long before it did so. She knew that he had shouted, and that he had told her a lie.

'You can't possibly work with that awful row going on. Let's take Bogey for a walk before tea.'

'It's going to rain. It's raining already. Besides, I must do the kitchen.'

'But you did it not a week ago, dear. Don't bother about it today. Let's chance the rain and go out.'

Yes. She had heard him shouting like a lunatic. He was certain now. Well, bad enough that she should know that he had shouted, but . . .

He hurried to the portière, pulled it aside and saw the slight, adored figure framed in the aperture of the partially opened door. Her unfathomable, enfolding smile fell upon his ruffled spirit like morning sunlight and banished all its anger and defeat and bitter self-reproach. He caught her in his arms and kissed her passionately before he blurted out his confession.

'Yes. I did call out. I shouted up to them to stop—like an infernal ass.'

She patted his arm, offering him just excuse.

'It really is rather awful this afternoon. But we're going to keep on laughing at it, aren't we, dear? Let's go out. The kitchen can go for days still, quite well. And it's such a job.'

He hesitated, for a moment disposed to yield. But just then, startlingly, the offensive upstairs developed a new activity. Behind Elsa, as she stood facing him in the passage, was the little landing—corresponding to that upon which the Prossips' gramophone rested—covering in the well of the former staircase. Two of its sides were fenced in by surviving balusters, the other two by ugly partitions of painted boarding, the handiwork of the jobbing contractor who had carried out the 'conversion'. One of these partitions formed the back of the Prossips' coal-cellar, the greater part of which descended into the Whalleys' flat. This frail wall, consisting of a single thickness of match-boarding like the landing's floor, had suddenly been assailed by a wild bombardment, alarming in its abrupt violence. There was no need to speculate as to the nature of the enemy's ammunition; each furious blow upon the boards was followed by the unmistakable sound of broken coal falling. Already, where the tonguing of the boarding had split away in places, tricklings of black dust had begun to find their way through, to fall upon the rug covering the Whalleys' landing.

They stood for a little while staring at this visible invasion which, trifling as it was, held an outrage infinitely more acute than the total volume of all the outrageous noises which had assailed their ears during the past weeks. Elsa laughed at length. But for the first time her sense of humour had failed her, and her laugh was, she knew, a failure.

'Idiots. Well, they'll have plenty of slack for the winter. I must rescue my rug.'

She stole on tiptoe to the landing and rolled back the rug out of danger, then stole back to him. 'I shan't be a moment getting ready.'

Her husband did not appear to have heard her. He was still

staring at the trickling coal-dust with a frowning, calculating absorption that made her catch at his hands anxiously.

'You're not going to do anything, Si? Don't. It will only make things worse.'

He came out of his brooding reverie and laughed harshly.

'Do anything? Yes. I'm going to wash the kitchen floor.'

'Let me help you to move the things out. I've finished all my darning.'

But he twisted away from her, freeing himself from her hands impatiently. 'No. Don't worry me, Elsa. Just leave me to myself.'

Incredulously her eyes followed him, hoping that he would turn back to her. His hands—Simon's hands—the gentlest, tenderest hands in all the world, had pushed her off—pushed her off quite roughly—so roughly that one of her elbows had struck the balusters behind her sharply. Oblivious of the deafening uproar that raged within a few feet of her, she strove with that unbelievable fact, refusing to believe it, trying to find excuse for its devastating reality. An intolerable sense of separation and loneliness fell about her like a dark mist. She became conscious of a little nervous tic beating at the corner of her mouth. With a determined effort she smiled, bracing her whole body with a deep breath.

The coppery glare that announced the near approach of the storm, passing in through the kitchen windows, reached her and detached her vividly against the darkness of the little unlighted passage. When Whalley turned at the bathroom door to ask: 'Tea at a quarter to five—will that do? I shan't finish until then,' he saw her so, illuminated as if by a baleful spotlight. The whistle was blowing again now—in the coal-cellar, apparently—and its shrill screaming blended with the blare of the gramophone and the thudding smash of the coal in an orchestra of almost stunning viciousness. The small, trim, beloved figure, despite its erectness, seemed to him suddenly forlorn—menaced. A little chill passed between her and his eyes and made her indistinct. His heart missed a beat.

Absurd. He turned about again. Her 'Of course, dear. Any old time,' had been whispered along the passage to him laughingly. Unusual lighting effects had always affected his imagination strongly . . . his invincible, idiotic instinct to dramatise. As for shivers and palpitations, *they* were familiar enough. He went on into the bathroom, which he used also as his dressing-room.

When its door shut Mrs Whalley returned to the bedroom in which she had been working and, having arranged a number of freshly-darned socks and stockings in neat pairs, put them away in her work-basket, walked slowly to the wardrobe and halted before the long mirror set in its central door.

All her life, in moments of loneliness—before her marriage she had had many of them—she had found comfort and company in her own reflection. It confronted her now—at first reassuringly, extraordinarily unchanged by the strains and stresses of the past two years. Two tiny creases, one beneath each long eye (her eyes looked even longer than usual today, she noticed, and, because her jumper was jade and the light was dull, were bright bronze-flecked emerald) were only detectable when she bent forward until her nose all but touched the glass. There was no other line or wrinkle in the fresh smoothness of her skin, no trace of flabbiness or heaviness along the clean sweep of her jaws, about her resolute chin, or at the corners of her lips. Thank Heaven for that. She had always detested flabbiness of any sort. Her lips (she had never had any need to touch them up) had retained their warm red. Her teeth, save for an occasional stopping, had never given her any trouble. Her hair, without any doubt whatever, had grown brighter in colour and much thicker since, at last, Simon had consented to its cropping four years before. No danger of stoutness for her—another good fortune to be grateful for; she was thinner and lighter than she had been at eighteen. Making allowances for short hair and short skirts, that old, tried friend in the mirror had altered hardly at all in twenty years. If at all, for the better. She had been very lucky.

But as she continued her scrutiny, a vague distrust grew in her. There *was* some change today in that now detached and aloof image. Her eyes narrowed themselves as she searched for it. Where was it? What was it? Elsa of the mirror refused comfort and company today. Had withdrawn. Had—what? It was as if an Elsa who had been had suddenly stopped being and was looking out at someone else—someone different—someone who, she knew, would be very different. What was it? She frowned. After all—ultimately—one was quite alone—

She turned away from the glass and, moving to the narrow space between the two trim beds, stooped and raised the rug which she had spread over Bogey-Bogey's basket that, as was his desire, his afternoon sleep might be enjoyed in darkness. Bogey-Bogey appeared, a silken-coated black cocker, curled in a warmly-smelling knot. He had not been asleep; his tail was wagging slowly and his lustrous eyes were wide open. They regarded her with solemn reproach and then, revolving fearfully towards the uproar of the passage, refused to be enticed back to her. Nor would he raise his head from his paws. Even a kiss and the magic word 'Walky-walk' evoked from him merely a yawn and a slight increase in the tempo of his tail.

A little sharply, Mrs Whalley routed him out of his basket.

'Now then, young man. Pull yourself together and get that tail up.'

But Bogey-Bogey's nerves had been sorely tried recently and the new noise in the passage daunted his small soul beyond trust even in his mistress. He yawned again miserably, and then retired under her bed, reducing himself several sizes. In a vain attempt to dislodge him from this retreat, she struck her nose forcibly against the bed's iron underframe. A little warm gush of blood descended her chin and when she scrambled to her knees she saw that her jumper—a recent, long-considered purchase—was grievously stained. As she rose to hurry to the wash-stand and sponge away this defilement, holding her already saturated handkerchief to her nose, a crashing peal of thunder, apparently directly above the house, joined itself to the Prossips' orchestra. Bogey-Bogey yelped shrilly. Mrs Whalley realised that she had a violent headache.

'Well, well—' she said aloud and, to her dismay, was suddenly overcome by a gust of dry, choking sobbing. She went on, however, towards the wash-stand, her head thrown back as far as it would go, her free hand guiding her. The jumper must be saved, because it had to last her through the summer. If it was to be saved, the blood must be sponged off at once. Most urgent necessity. Simon, who was liable to come into the bedroom at any moment now that he had abandoned the attempt to work, must on no conceivable account know that misfortune had befallen his birthday gift to her. Any damage done to anything upset him so, now. *His* hands—Simon's hands—had pushed her away.

At that moment, as it happened, four other people who resided in various parts of No. 47 Downview Road were thinking about Mrs Whalley.

Upstairs, Marjory Prossip, who hated her passionately, was hoping, while she plied her industrious and skilful needle, that at some time in the immediate future—probably that very afternoon—that conceited, stuck-up little green-eyed thing in the first-floor flat would receive an extremely unpleasant surprise. Her heavy face brightened to a faint animation. What a bit of luck that that little beast of a dog had been alone.

In the ground-floor flat, the elderly Hopgood, who in bygone days had received many a half-crown from Mrs Whalley's father, and who regarded her, with a rather melancholy tenderness, as one of his last links with a past of incredible brightness now vanished for ever, was thinking about her rubbish-bin.

The rubbish bins of the other tenants were kept in the front garden, imperfectly concealed in a recess under the bottom flight of the outside staircase. Mr and Mrs Whalley, however, preferred to keep theirs on their landing of the staircase, outside their hall-door. Lately the Corporation's scavengers had been kicking up a fuss about having to go up to the landing for the bin, and, upon their last call, had refused point-blank to do so. To Hopgood's indignation, they had been impertinent to Mrs Whalley when she had remonstrated with them. As he smoked his pipe and waited for his tea-kettle to boil, Hopgood decided that he would himself carry down Mrs Whalley's bin to the front garden each Monday and Thursday afternoon and carry it up again when it had been emptied into the Corporation cart.

Pleased with this solution of Mrs Whalley's little difficulty, Hopgood proceeded to the brewing of his tea. He had been really shocked by the way in which the Corporation men—two great, hulking, grinning young louts—had spoken to her and looked at her. Especially the way they had looked at her—looked at her legs—looked her all over, grinning—as if she was one of the young sluts they messed about with. People of that kind, Hopgood had noticed—messengers, vanmen, bus-conductors—in fact, the lower classes generally—had suddenly become markedly uncivil and aggressive lately. He had thought a good deal about this, and, for some reason which he could not quite explain, he was somehow uneasy about it. Things had got queer, somehow. All those things in the newspapers now—wars and disasters and revolutions and suicides and murders. Everything had got queer, somehow, this year. It was pleasant to see a lady like Mrs Whalley tripping in and out with her little spaniel—a bit of the old times still left—something you could look up to and feel sure about . . . Looking at her legs . . . The swine.

Below him, in the basement flat, the lonely Mr Ridgeway was also meditating a small service to her. In his dark, damp-ish-smelling sitting-room—only the upper halves of its windows rose above the level of the front-garden—he was re-reading once more a letter which he had written three days before.

'Dear Mrs Whalley,—I am returning, with gratitude, the books which you so kindly lent me some time ago. I have read them with much interest. Please accept my apologies for having kept them so long. But I am the slowest of readers.

'Since our last meeting I have heard from a medical friend who is specially interested in your husband's trouble. I enclose some cuttings which he has sent me with reference to a new extract from which excellent results have been obtained, and hope your husband will be persuaded to give the accompanying small supply of it a trial.

'Yrs sincerely,
'Ambrose Ridgeway.'

He laid the letter down and sat back in his chair, a stoutish, untidy man of fifty-five or so, with a rather gross and bloated face which had once been handsome and was still redeemed by a pair of very fine eyes. Presently, he told himself, he would shave and put on a clean collar and shirt and his good suit and go up the steep steps to deliver his note and his two small parcels. Perhaps it would be she who would open the door—more probably her husband. Though, in the afternoon he tried to work—poor devil.

Presently, though. There was plenty of time, and not often something to look forward to.

His eyes rested upon the medical journals from which he had clipped the cuttings several days before. They still lay open upon a small table, grey with the dust of Downview Road. Misgiving grew again in him. Was it wise to associate himself in any way with medical matters?

After some meditation he tore up his letter, dropped one of the parcels into a drawer, and then stretched himself on a sofa, covering his face with a dingy handkerchief. He would write just a note of thanks, returning the books.

But presently. There was plenty of time. It was raining. Tomorrow would do just as well.

Harvey Knayle also was thinking just then of Mrs Whalley, in whom, as we shall see, he took an interest of a somewhat complicated kind. He was standing in Edwarde-Lewin's study, whither they had retired to discuss, before tea, a projected fortnight's fishing in Ireland, and, while his host fumbled in a drawer, he was telling about the Prossips' gramophone.

'What's the law of the thing, Lewin?' he asked, jingling his loose silver. 'How many times may the chap in the flat over you play the same tune on his gramophone continuously before you can take legal action to make him stop?'

Edwarde-Lewin ceased for a moment to be a genial sportsman and became a discouraging solicitor.

'You can't stop him,' he replied curtly. 'He may play it all day and all night if he wants to. You have no legal redress. Unless you can prove malice.'

'Now, how does one prove malice?' enquired Mr Knayle.

'Just so,' snapped Edwarde-Lewin, and immediately resumed his geniality and his fumbling. 'Now, where the deuce did I put that confounded letter—' He remembered that he had perused, personally, Mr Knayle's agreement at the time of his last moving. 'But the lease of that flat of yours is nearly up, as well as I remember. Noisy place, Downview Road, now. You won't stay on there, will you?'

To his own surprise, Mr Knayle suddenly abandoned a decision at which, upon prolonged and anxious consideration, he had all but arrived that afternoon.

'Oh yes, I shall stay on,' he said quite definitely. 'I'm used to the noise now. Noises don't worry me. Besides, I like the look-out over the Downs. No houses opposite. Oh yes. I shall stay on.'

Edwarde-Lewin found the missing letter and proceeded to read it aloud. Mr Knayle, however, although, as has been said, he was an ardent fisherman, looked out at the already soaked tennis-courts and went on thinking about the real reason which had decided him to keep on his flat in Downview Road.

5

While he shut the bathroom door, Whalley looked at his wrist-watch. Five past four. He had been sure that it was not yet a quarter to. The kitchen floor always took an hour and a half to do—two hours if one washed the skirtings and the other paint-work. He couldn't hope now to finish before half-past five. This alteration of a quarter of an hour in his plans threw him into a flurry. He changed feverishly into the old trousers and dilapi-dated pullover in which he did his housework and, hurrying to the kitchen, began to move its movable furniture out into the passage.

Once a week for the past eighteen months he had performed this detested task—the most detested and most troublesome of the drudgery to which circumstances had doomed him. Like that of all others, its procedure was now stereotyped—a sequence of merely automatic gestures requiring no least direc-tion from will or judgment or even consciousness. He began it, as always, by carrying out the two chairs into the passage and, as he did so, his impatience, already fatigued, rushed on ahead in desperation, foreseeing every dull, familiar detail of the labour before him, every smallest necessary movement, every trifling difficulty, every unavoidabe compromise with the ideal of a perfect kitchen floor perfectly washed.

After the chairs, the small table by the right hand window to be carried into the passage—far enough along it to leave room for the other things to follow it. Then the three baskets in which Elsa kept vegetables and fruit. Then the little cake-larder, which stood on the floor because the walls wouldn't hold nails securely. Then the set of shelves on which the sauce-pans and pan stood and hung. Some of them would fall and kick up a clatter. Then the small table by the sink. Then the basins stacked under it. Then the kitchen bin. (That would have to be washed out with hot water and disinfected when it had been emptied into the big bin outside the hall-door). Then the bread-bin and the flour-bin and the three empty biscuit tins under the big table. Then the big table itself (it had to be turned side up to get it through the door and even then its legs had to be screwed through one by one). Then all the small oddments kept on the floor along the walls, because there was no other place to keep them—unused things, most of them—obsolete trays and grids belonging to the electric-cooker—old boxes and jam pots and tins—kept because they might be useful some time.

The sweeping, then—the same old places that took so much time to get into with the sweeping-brush, the same old snags that caught its loose head, the same old stoopings and twistings to get the same old dust and dirt out. Then the dustpan to gather up the dirt. The dustpan to be emptied into the bin. Then the bucket to be rooted out of the cupboard under the sink (it always jammed against the sink's waste-pipe) and taken to the bathroom and filled with hot water from the geyser. The scrubbing brush and floor-cloths and soap to be collected from the bathroom cupboard. The bucket to be carried back along the blocked passage to the kitchen, very slowly, lest the water should splash over—

At this point, while he hurried from kitchen to passage and back again, his eyes, at each return, fixing themselves for a moment frowningly on the dresser-clock, he began again the old, never-decided debate as to the wisdom of washing the linoleum covering the floor—an expensive, inlaid linoleum which had been a special pride of Elsa's in the days of the kitchen's first freshness. Someone had told Elsa that linoleum ought to be washed—with a dash of paraffin in the water. Someone else had told her that it ought to be washed with Lux. Someone else had told her that it ought never to be washed on any account, but done with polish. He had tried various polishes. Certainly the linoleum had looked better when polished—it always looked grey and dull after washing. But the polishes all left a greasy surface in which dirt lodged. Anyhow, the last tin of polish was practically finished now. The linoleum would have to be washed today—

A vibration—and then a new noise rose in pitch and, piercing a way through the uproar of the Prossips' offensive, became the strident clamour of a plane, flying very low, over the house. It came into view—was illuminated by a blinding flash of lightning—went on its serene, unswerving way, undismayed by the crashing peal that followed. Whalley's eyes watched it until it disappeared over the tree-tops. He smiled bitterly at a vision of its pilot—young, fearless, efficient—a man doing a man's job while *he* washed the kitchen floor.

Twenty past four—and practically nothing done yet. He fell upon the miniature dresser upon which the pans and saucepans were arranged and lifted it towards the door. A pan and two saucepans fell noisily to the floor. As he deposited his burden in the passage, the bombardment in the Prossips' coal-cellar ceased sharply and the whistle fell to silence. Footsteps had hurried from the top-flat's sitting-room; the gramophone stopped. While Whalley stood, vaguely debating the reason of this sudden cessation of hostilities, the bell of his own hall-door rang.

After a brief hesitation—for he disliked being seen in his working-clothes by anyone but his wife—he descended to the door and, opening it, saw his landlord, Mr Penfold, standing in the rain beneath a streaming umbrella. The sudden lull upstairs was explained. By unfortunate chance, the enemy had observed Mr Penfold's approach—no doubt had seen him—from their sitting-room windows, alight from a bus opposite the front garden's gate.

There had been trouble with Penfold—a truculent individual, by avocation a commercial traveller, who had inherited Nos. 47 and 48 Downview Road from an aunt deceased some few years before. The Whalleys had moved into the flat rather hurriedly, accepting a merely verbal assurance that it would be 'done up' in the following spring. But when the following spring arrived, Penfold had refused to remember having given any assurance of any kind as to doing anything. There had been interviews and, subsequently, correspondence, in the course of which he had passed from evasion to incivility and from incivility to impertinence. Finally Whalley had had the kitchen, the dining-room, and the bedroom repainted and repapered at his own cost, and had consoled himself by the fact that he had never since seen his landlord's face.

It was a large, heavy-jowled face, out of which a pair of cunning little eyes looked at him now with unconcealed hostility. Without moving any part of it visibly, Penfold said at once:

'Afternoon. What's this I hear about that dog of yours?'

'I've no idea,' replied Whalley. 'Do come in, won't you?'

Ignoring the invitation to enter, Penfold surveyed the old trousers and pull-over at his leisure and sniffed. Then, taking a fresh stand with his square-toed boots, he transferred his gaze to the cover of the rubbish-bin.

'Oh! You've no idea. I see. Well, I'll give you an idea, then. I have received complaints from the other tenants of these flats that your dog has been molesting them—attacking them and causing them annoyance and nuisance.'

'Who has complained, Mr Penfold?'

'Never you mind.' Penfold's hand swept the question aside. 'That is what I am informed. And I'm satisfied that I'm correctly informed. So we won't argue about the point.'

'I haven't the slightest intention of arguing about it,' Whalley retorted sharply. 'Or about anything else. If you have any complaint to make, put it in writing and I'll pass it on to my solicitors—if I think it worth while doing so.'

Highly amused, Penfold threw back his head and guffawed. He turned then and feigned to depart, but stopped and delivered his ultimatum over a shoulder.

'Now, listen here, Mister Whalley—as you're talking about solicitors. According to your agreement, you are permitted to keep a dog in this flat only on the condition that it causes no annoyance to any of the other tenants. Your dog has caused such annoyance. It attacked one of the other tenants savagely. Jumped up on her and tried to bite her hands. It alarmed her so that she was obliged to remain in bed for two days with a heart attack. I give you notice now to get rid of it immediately. If you fail to do so before this day week, I will instruct *my* solicitors to take action to compel you to keep to the terms of your agreement.'

'You can start taking them now, damn you,' snapped Whalley.

Again Mr Penfold surveyed the old trousers and pullover exhaustively as if expecting to extract from them an explanation of his tenant's childish ill-temper. He sniffed again, then, and turning away irrevocably went down the steps with threatening slowness and heaviness. As Whalley slammed the hall-door, a voice, humming with exaggerated blitheness above his head, informed him that the interview had had an audience. He made his way slowly back along the crowded passage towards the kitchen, revolving wrathfully this latest manœuvre of the Prossips.

The crude but effective ingenuity of it exasperated him—all the more because its malice was feminine and, he knew, had aimed itself more especially at Elsa. For Bogey-Bogey, though he tolerated a master, had but one god and was entirely the property of his mistress—her inseparable companion and, as the Prossips could not have failed to learn from the daily observation of the six months for which they had occupied the top flat, the light of her eyes. They had struck at her most vulnerable point—at his, because the blow was aimed at her.

Savage attack.

The facts were that one day about a week before, Bogey-Bogey, the gentlest and best-tempered of creatures, had escaped into the front garden and, encountering Mrs Prossip and her

daughter there, had, after his inveterate habit of doing the wrong
thing, rushed at her joyously and jumped up on her skirts. The
Prossip girl had jabbed him savagely with her sunshade and he
had fled back whimpering to Elsa, who had witnessed the
incident from the kitchen and had hurried out to his rescue.
She had met the female Prossips on the steps, but they had
made no complaint at that time. It had obviously taken them
some days to discover that Bogey-Bogey had placed a new
weapon in their hands and to induce that brute Penfold to wield
it for them. Not that he was likely to have required much induce-
ment—swine. God! What a face—what eyes.

Victoriously, refreshed by its rest, the gramophone resumed
its blaring. He walked slowly back along the passage until he
stood almost directly beneath the sound, and stood looking up.
Its position could be calculated almost exactly.

Out of the question, of course, to think of parting with
Bogey-Bogey . . . unthinkable. Probably the threat was merely
spiteful bluff on Penfold's part. Though he was quite capable
of trying to carry it out. Of course, he couldn't carry it out. Still
. . . suppose they had to turn out of the flat . . .

Yes. One could calculate the position of the gramophone
almost exactly. The landings of the two flats, of course, corre-
sponded precisely in size and position. The Prossips would
have placed the gramophone where it could be most conveniently reached by anyone who had to go to it repeatedly, either
from the kitchen or their sitting-room, close to the balusters,
two steps down the little stairs from the passage to the hall
door. For, of course, they had to lean over the balusters to get
at it and would do so where their rail, following the fall of the
stairs, first became sufficiently low to place the gramophone
within comfortable reach.

He decided upon a knot in the under-surface of the Prossips'
match-boarding. Just there. A line through that knot—say, from
the centre of his own landing—ought to pass through the near
side of the gramophone. If a hand was restarting the needle,

and if a face was bent over it as it did so, the line would just about catch them both—some part of both of them. It would have to be a little oblique, of course—yes, starting from the centre of his own landing—that would be just about right . . .

Wasn't there something in the agreement about the landlord being able to take steps to recover possession of the premises if the tenant violated any of the terms of the agreement?

One would be able to time it exactly, too. The footsteps would come hurrying—stop—count one—and then the face would be bent over the record—the bullet would rush up at it out of the record, smash into it, stop its sniggering and grinning.

Perfectly simple. The only difficulty was that the bullet might strike the motor of the gramophone and get deflected, or stopped.

He continued to stand, looking up, calculating absorbedly. One couldn't possibly do it, of course. The risk would be too great. No one would believe for a moment, knowing of the quarrel with the Prossips, that it had been an accident, though there *was*, if you came to think of it clearly, no reason why he shouldn't just happen to examine his old service revolver one day out in the passage of his flat and why it shouldn't just happen to go off. That sort of thing was always happening . . .

And, if one could do it safely, of course, it would be so perfectly simple.

Once more the gramophone's blaring ceased. Once more footsteps hurried to it—stopped. Once more the accursed torment began. Five o'clock? What the devil had he been thinking about—standing there like a fool? Too late to do the floor now.

He began to carry back the things which he had carried out of the kitchen, replacing them exactly in their former positions. Tomorrow or next day they would all have to be carried out again.

6

It is clear that Mr Knayle was right and that Whalley was taking this silly, childish feud with the Prossips altogether too seriously. The curious thing is that Whalley had been living on a sense of humour for the greater part of twenty years.

CHAPTER II

1

In August, 1918, as he lay in the white, stunning peace of the hospital-ship which was carrying him to England, a matter which for four years had appeared to him of no practical importance whatever began to invest itself with a faint interest. Suppose that rumour at last spoke the truth and that the incredible was to be believed. Suppose that the Boche *was* finished and that peace was coming some time within the next six months, what was Simon Whalley (Capt., D.S.O.) going to do for the rest of a life which, after all, might continue for a considerable time.

The shrapnel wounds in his head and shoulder were not very serious, he had been told; but it would probably take a year at least to make the shoulder a serviceable one again. It was at all events a possibility that, so far as he was concerned, the War had finished. If it had, what was going to happen him next?

He was then thirty-two years of age. With the exception of some remote Lancashire cousins whom he had never seen and a married sister in the Malay States, he had no living relatives. There no longer existed anywhere in the world for him any place which he could regard as home. He had been called to the Irish Bar a few years before the War, but he had never received a brief—had, even in his student days, regretted that he had committed himself to a legal career—and had now no least intention or desire to resume the old weary, fruitless hauntings of the Dublin Law Library—if there was still such a thing. For that matter he had now no desire to return to Ireland. His parents (his mother had been Irish; his father, retired with a crippled leg and the rank of Major, after Spion Kop, the solitary descendant of an English family which had transferred itself from Lancashire to Co. Meath in the eighteen-fifties) had both died during the War. His brother had been killed in it—a fate which had also overtaken a dismaying number of the contemporaries who had been his more intimate friends both in Meath and in Dublin. Things had changed in Ireland—they were likely, it seemed, to change very greatly. The old days over there were gone—for good. Whatever was going to happen to him, he foresaw, would probably happen to him somewhere else.

Upon his demobilisation he would receive a bounty, he supposed, of two or three hundred pounds. A sum of nearly six thousand pounds stood to his credit in the Bank of Ireland, on deposit. His mother's few thousands had gone to his sister—his father had died with an overdraft. There was no source from which he could hope to augment his limited capital, save his own abilities. These, upon consideration, appeared so unpromising that, by the time a stretcher carried him on to Dover Pier, he had dismissed all but one of them as quite unreliable.

An English public school had made of him an average public schoolboy, decently educated and decently proficient in games. The University of Dublin had given him an entirely useless Honours Degree in Classics. Apart from his law studies he had received no special training in anything. The world, he had already divined, would shortly be very full of smatterers looking for jobs—and of trained men who would crowd them out of them. There was schoolmastering—but his classics were already half-forgotten and no longer held a spark of interest for him. There were the colonies; but even to the colonies he had no talent or aptitude to offer beyond average health and physique and intelligence, discounted by the fact that he was two years past thirty. But one means of acquiring some more money, reasonably quickly, appeared within his possible reach. He had already written—shortly before the War—a couple of comedies, one successful, one very successful. The most hopeful occupation of his immediate future appeared to be the attempt to write others.

Nearly five years—four of them crowded with the almost entirely physical experiences of the War—now separated him from that brief, completely detached period of his life during which he had been a writer of plays. Looked back to now, it still remained utterly unaccountable, utterly dissociated from the rest of the past—a phenomenon as isolated and self-contained as an attack of measles or a passing interest in chess or wood-engravings. Neither his father's family nor his mother's—both had belonged to the small landed gentry class for several generations back—had had any known association with the theatre. His own previous interest in it had always been of the most casual and spasmodic kind, the interest merely of the average theatre-goer who regards it as one means of passing an occasional evening more or less agreeably. Until his twenty-fifth year he had never spoken to any person directly connected with it, never read the text of any play of later date than the eighteenth century, never—with the exception of schoolboy essays—attempted or thought of attempting, literary composition of any sort. The desire to write plays, together with the ability to write them, had both presented themselves to him abruptly at an almost precisely definite moment of a particular night. He could recall the moment quite clearly. He had just then been passing the brightly-lighted entrance of the Shelbourne Hotel and, before he had reached the darkness beyond he had decided that he could write a play and that he would begin to do so before he got into his bed that night.

That had been in the September of 1911. A very popular actress-manager had paid a visit to Dublin with a comedy which had played in London to crowded houses for eighteen months. Whalley had gone with some friends to see her at the Theatre Royal and had been disappointed in the piece, which had appeared to him weak and quite unamusing. It was as he walked towards his rooms in Mount Street, after parting with his friends, that the idea of writing a comedy really worthy of Miss Louie Storm's talents had suddenly suggested itself to him. Within ten days the project had been carried into execution. Within three months the piece had been accepted and produced in London with brilliant success.

This first improbable adventure as a playwright had made him, for a fortnight or so, something of a celebrity. It had not, however, brought him in much money. The syndicate—three Jews—which was then backing Miss Storm, had quickly discovered his entire inexperience in the matter of dramatic authors' contracts. The agreeable, clever young man from Ireland, who was so surprised and amused that his play had been accepted, had been without difficulty induced to accept a flat three per cent. The total sum which he had received in royalties from the eleven months' London run of *That Mrs Mallaby* had been a little under fifteen hundred pounds. The ease and quickness with which this sum had been earned, however, had consoled him for the too-late acquired knowledge that he had been treated shabbily. He would strike while the iron was hot, write another play, and employ an agent to drive a much better bargain with one of those eager managers who, he had gathered, were only waiting to scramble for his next masterpiece. This prospect was all the more agreeable since his father's financial affairs had recently fallen into unexpected embarrassment—as far as could be elicited from that charming but impulsive and simple-minded gentleman, through rash investments embarked upon under no more reliable guidance than a desire to obtain fifteen per cent. instead of five. The recent paternal remittances had been grievously reduced from their former generosity. Whalley had bought himself a typewriter, taught himself to use it, given up frequenting the Law Library, and settled down confidently to the composition of his second play.

The writing of the first had been a matter as simple and as effortless as walking or talking. Its plot, ready-made and divided neatly into three acts, had taken him something less than an hour to evolve and had required no subsequent adjustment or alteration whatever. Its characters had been born with its plot in that single hour of travail, clear-cut and definite. Patches of its dialogue, even, had already shaped themselves as he had scribbled down hurriedly a table of the scenes of each act, showing merely the characters on the stage during each. From this very simple scenario he had proceeded at once to the actual writing of the play, the only difficulty of which had been the inability of his pen to keep legible pace with his eager thought. From first to last the whole business had been joyous, absorbed, unhesitating, and care-free—a swift, certain progress to a certain goal. Before sending the manuscript to the typists, he had made a clean, revised copy; but most of the trifling emendations at first inserted in this version had subsequently been repented of and the original word or phrase restored.

This happy experience had not repeated itself. It had taken him six months to find an idea for his second play and, even then, the idea had for a long time refused to reduce itself to three acts. The writing and re-writing of the piece had, with intervals of loathing abandonment, taken another five months, in the course of which the dialogue, the characters, and even the plot itself had undergone countless revisions and remodellings and repolishings. A well-known agent had, it was true, placed the play almost immediately with another leading lady backed by Israelitish money, upon quite satisfactory terms. But a further seven months had elapsed before *The Vanity Bag* had been produced. It had had a mildly successful run of six months or so and had produced for its author royalties amounting to eight thousand pounds.

With this reward, Whalley had told himself he had every sensible reason to be satisfied. Eight thousand pounds had fallen into his hands just at a moment when they were urgently needed. He had by this time emerged from a rather prolonged phase of vague disillusionment and self-distrust, spent several months abroad, returned then to the ordinary habits and interests of his life, resumed his vigils in the Law Library, lowered his golf handicap, and recovered his normal cheerful and untroubling outlook. Humdrum and, so far, unencouraging as Law had appeared to him, it had seemed on chastened consideration to offer a more secure future than playwriting. Briefs would come—he had now money enough to live on until they did. If he wrote another play or other plays in his spare time, well and good. But playwriting would remain strictly a sideline—the possibly profitable amusement of an amateur. The business of his life must be the profession to which he had been trained.

And so, as abruptly as it had begun, his career as a dramatist had ended. He had never made any subsequent attempt to write anything—never felt the least impulse or desire to do so, though his father's means had now become seriously straitened and it had been necessary to lend him twelve hundred pounds, with little prospect of the loan's repayment. Occasionally the sight of his typewriter's dusty cover, stowed away in a corner of his sitting-room, had caused him a smile of amused reminiscence. When, from time to time, his agent had written as to the likelihood of another play, he had sometimes experienced a momentary pang of regret for opportunities neglected. His reply, however, had always been that he had been frightfully busy lately.

Then the War had happened. He had received a commission in October, 1914, and had gone into the trenches for the first time in February, 1915, near Fleurbaix. Subsequently he had been wounded three times—twice severely—gassed, and blown into the air by a mine, had suffered from trench-foot, lice, a particularly loathsome kind of itch, cold, wet, occasional attacks of blind fear, and, towards the end, an intolerable fatigue and boredom. As the hospital-train rolled smoothly up through Kent, he told himself that, for him, at all events, the War had been a damned silly, tiresome business and that he was damned glad to be out of it—if he was out of it. The best of it had been the marvellous cheerful patience of the men. The worst of it had been that of all the countless jobs that had fallen to him to do, there had been no chance or possibility of doing a single one properly and thoroughly. He had inherited from his mother a punctilious conscientiousness which had always insisted upon the exact performance of detail, and the eternal, unescapable scamping and shirking and botching which he had seen going on around him for the past four years had irritated him profoundly. That, despite himself, he too should always have been compelled to scamp and shirk and botch, had been in the end an exasperation. Yes. He was damned glad to be done with it all.

However, parts of it had been interesting. He had met some wonderful human beings, and, without undue complacency, he could feel satisfied that he had done his bit as well as the next chap. He knew that he had been a smart, smart-looking, efficient and reliable officer, satisfactorily plucky, popular with the men, if a little suspect of his fellow T.G.'s on account of his passion for thoroughness, his lack of interest in whisky and smut, and his capacity, on occasion, for mordant retort. If he had not felt the part, he had contrived to play it not too badly. He supposed that, some time, it would give him some satisfaction to look back to that.

He made an effort to turn his thoughts again towards the future, but there was only a past from which he had escaped. What had he been thinking about? Oh yes—those two old plays he had written . . . donkey's years ago. Awful tripe—especially the second one—as well as he remembered. Plays . . . after *that* . . .

His memory suddenly recalled vividly a very large packing-case which he had seen just before the Christmas of 1911 in a corner of a room at Miss Storm's theatre. The room had been the office of Miss Storm's official reader, a bored, sardonic young man who had raised the lid of the packing-case and exhibited its contents with a grin. It had been filled to over-flowing with tattered typescripts—hundreds of them—churned, it had seemed to Whalley, deliberately, into hopeless confusion. 'The Great Unactable', the sardonic young man had explained, and had torn a page from someone's Act II to light a cigarette with at the fire.

The kind, considerable purr of the train was delicious. Whalley shut his eyes upon that chilling memory and went asleep.

2

After a fortnight in London he was transferred to Ducey Court, the residence of a large estate a little distance outside Rockwood, converted temporarily into a hospital for officers. A few minutes after he had been deposited in one of the cots of a small upstairs ward, the door of the room re-opened and a slim girl in V.A.D.'s uniform appeared, bearing a laden tea-tray. While one hand had reclosed the door behind her, her long steady eyes took stock of the new arrival gravely and then smiled. In that moment, they were both ever afterwards agreed, they both fell in love.

With this artless *cliché* they were compelled, ultimately, to rest content, though, naturally, they made afterwards the usual attempts to define exactly what had really happened to them in that miraculous instant. At all events, whatever had happened, they both knew beyond all thought of doubt, had been waiting from the beginning to happen and would go on happening until the end. This decided, in a little over a week—with a total actual acquaintance of less than twenty-four hours—they resolved to marry one another, and did so—Whalley's shoulder having made unexpected progress—in the week following the Armistice.

Elsa Barnard was then twenty-five. As regarding family ties, her isolation was almost as complete as Whalley's own. Her mother had died during her childhood. Her father—of Barshire family and, like Whalley's, a soldier—had rejoined his old battalion at the outbreak of the War and been killed in the third week of it. Two brothers and no less than seven cousins had been swept away in the following four years. A married sister and a widowed and childless uncle—her mother's elder brother—in whose house and charge she had lived since her father's death, were her only living relatives.

Whalley was duly introduced to them, received with cold politeness, and, after some cross-examination, given to understand that they both washed their hands of Elsa's unwisdom in marrying an individual of whom she knew nothing save that he had a disabled shoulder, no occupation, no friends in England, and no prospects save a hope that he might write plays. They both attended the quiet little wedding, however, and Mr Loxton, the uncle, gave the bride away, having previously presented her with a cheque for a hundred pounds.

The Whalleys spent their short honeymoon at a little Surrey inn under the lee of the Hog's Back. Towards its close they discovered, just outside Puttiford, the adjoining village, a tiny seventeenth-century cottage whose tenant, desiring to spend the following year abroad, agreed to let it to them, furnished, for twelve months, beginning from the following January. This impetuous arrangement completed, they returned to Rockwood—Whalley to Ducey Court for further treatment pending his demobilisation, and Elsa—no offer of hospitality having been made either by her uncle or her sister—to the house of some friends. As she no longer attended the hospital and as his hours of escape from it were still strictly limited, they saw, for nearly a month, very little of one another. During that period of intolerable separations he found ample time to realise what he had done—and what he had to do. The first realisation amazed him; the second transformed his amazement to stupefaction.

Into the paradise in which Elsa and he had strayed for the past two months the serpent £ s. d. had been permitted to make but one brief intrusion. On the afternoon on which they had become engaged, as they returned slowly towards the hospital along one of the drives of the park, they had halted to watch the deer drifting in the September sunshine.

'It doesn't seem of any real importance, somehow,' Elsa had said. 'But I suppose we shall have to eat and wear clothes and live in some sort of a house. I've been taking it for granted that you have some money, Simon. I have none, you know—just fifty pounds a year my mother left me. Poor pater died without a red.'

He had laughed and said, with perfect confidence and tranquillity, as his arm had drawn her slenderness closer to him, 'I have a fountain pen and about six thousand pounds to buy ink with. We ought to be able to write quite a lot of plays before all that ink is used up, you know. If you really feel that we shall want to eat, one winner ought to supply us with a square meal a day for ten years or so. Naturally, we will write the winner first. Don't tell me that you've begun to repent already, Elsa. I've used the fountain pen, you see. They'll never take it back at the shop.'

There had been no further discussion of ways and means. In those few airy words of his he had disposed of all the stupendous difficulties of their future. It was amazing. Not once during the past two months had he caught a glimpse of the chill, dangerous actualities that lay in wait outside his warm, tender, sunlit dream. He had lived spellbound by all the marvellous, lovely, gracious things that were Elsa—her eyes, her hair, her smile, her voice, her way of holding her fork, her skill in shaving him—ten thousand lovelinesses. In the bright aura of courage and confidence that surrounded her he had basked—content, self-complacent, blind to everything beyond. All things had seemed possible, easy, certain. Amazing, for, all his life, he had always foreseen difficulties. Amazing.

Well, the music had to be faced. No more airy talk of writing plays—some time or other. He must throw off the spell—shut himself out from it, tear his mind out of its lazy happiness and start it out on the cheerless, lonely quest for an idea. Now—at once.

He found a deserted, dark little room beyond the operating-theatre, filled with stacked cane-bottomed chairs, and, escaping from the cheerful clamour of the wards, retired there in the mornings as soon as the masseuse had finished with his shoulder. Sometimes he sat there for three hours on end, staring at the dusty chairs, and smoking cigarette after cigarette. Nothing came of these seances, however. His mind appeared capable of two functions only—spasmodic reminiscence of detached experiences during his War service, and impatient eagerness to be with Elsa again. After ten days of this fruitless discipline, he abandoned it and spent his mornings wandering about the park. He had never been able to think constructively, however, out-of-doors or when moving about. Having decided that there was no hope of settling down to work until he had a quiet, comfortable room to work in, he became rather irritably impatient for his demobilisation, which, for some unknown reason, had been postponed.

On one of these morning promenades he had for the first time an experience which was subsequently to become familiar to him—a sudden sick dizziness, accompanied by a sensation that every drop of blood in his body had turned to lead. His legs sagged under him. He came to a stop struggling with an onset of violent depression, bodily and mental. These curious disturbances, however, passed away almost instantly. He attributed them to a too hearty breakfast and the coldness of the December morning, continued his walk, and had forgotten all about them before he reached the hospital.

A week or so later he had another attack of the same kind after his bath. Altering his diagnosis, he cut down his smoking for some days. There were more important things to think about than little attacks of dizziness and shivers. His long-delayed demobilisation had been rushed through and he was a free man once more. And Mr Loxton, relenting of his inhospitality, had invited Elsa and her husband to become his guests until their departure to Surrey.

Mr Loxton had weighed a good deal on Whalley's mind lately. He was a squarely-built, brusque man of sixty-two, a prominent figure in the public life of Dunpool, one of the leaders of its commercial plutocracy, and still the active senior partner of the most important firm of iron-founders in the west of England. He lived in an imposing house in the outskirts of Rockwood, entertained lavishly, got up at six o'clock every morning, neither smoked nor drank anything stronger than water, and never spoke without stating a fact or asking someone else to state one. He was childless; after her father's death Elsa had lived with him, managed his house for him, and been regarded by him, generally, as a daughter. One did not desire Mr Loxton's death; but some time, probably within the next fifteen years, he would die. The reasonable supposition was that he would leave some considerable portion of his money to his two nieces. The thought that his own unsatisfactoriness as a nephew-in-law should have endangered Elsa's personal prospects had worried Whalley seriously since their return to Rockwood.

Mr Loxton, however, was geniality itself during the short visit. After dinner on Christmas Day he held up a glass of water and abandoned the 'Whalley' to which 'Captain Whalley' had already been softened.

'Well, Simon, my boy, here's to those plays of yours. Don't forget that I'm to have a box whenever you have a first night.'

And on the last day of December, just before they started for Surrey, he handed Elsa a cheque for five hundred pounds.

'I expect you'll want a car of some sort, young woman. If that isn't enough let me know. If it's too much, spend what's over on a perambulator.'

Elsa's sister, Mrs Canynge, remained, however, cold. Her husband—he was, Whalley discovered, the managing director of the firm of Loxton & Ferrier, Ltd.—took the trouble to display a marked incivility. Elsa's personal friends, however, were all charming to him. Amongst them was a cheery, pleasant little man of thirty-seven or so, named Knayle, of whom he was to see more later on, and who, he learned, had known Elsa all her life. Mr Knayle, whom she called 'Harvey', addressed her as 'Elsa'—apparently as a matter of course—and was much interested to learn that her husband had written *That Mrs Mallaby* and *The Vanity Bag*, both of which he remembered having seen and greatly enjoyed. He invited them to tea at his flat and proved the most entertaining and sympathetic of hosts.

3

They arrived at the cottage at Puttiford in the dusk of a frosty afternoon. It was a veritable homecoming. The red curtains of the little latticed windows were all lighted up. Silhouetted in the porch stood the maternal woman from the village who was to 'do for' them. They went into the cosy little sitting-room, and found a crackling fire of pine logs and a sumptuous tea awaiting them. Hand in hand, like two happy children, they stood looking about them silently until Mrs Hidgson had finally withdrawn, then, attracted by the hooting of an owl just outside one of the windows, drew aside its curtain. Whalley's best efforts, however, failed to open the window, and he drew the curtain across again with a puckered frown. During tea he was a little abstracted and, half-way through the meal, rose to make another trial of the window, equally unsuccessful.

'Always the way with these picturesque old houses,' he said, returning to her. 'The windows won't open—or, if they open, they won't shut. I wonder if there are any tools in the place. We must get that window right straight away.'

And immediately after tea, before he unpacked, he hunted down an aged screwdriver, repaired its haft, and eased the jammed sash. From her chair before the fire Elsa watched him with amusement and some surprise. Afterwards, however, they spent an evening of rapturous contentment.

Elsa revealed herself as the most capable of cooks and managers. Mrs Higson proved the most efficient of 'doers for'.

The little house was kept as neat and bright as a new pin. Its equipment—including gas-supply and indoor sanitation—was entirely satisfactory. The local tradespeople were obliging. The Guildford shops were but half an hour away by bus. London could be reached in an hour and a half. Puttiford's delightful common and golf-links began at the front door. All the loveliness of Surrey lay around them. They bought a small car, joined the golf-club, made friends with the score or so of agreeable people who were their neighbours, and ran up to town every week for a theatre or a concert. Everything, in fine, connected with their cottage was delightful except that, after a couple of months, Whalley discovered that he couldn't write plays in it.

On the morning of the second day after their arrival he shut himself up in the tiny room between the kitchen and the sitting-room which he had arranged as his own special sanctum. Its one little window faced north, however; the sun never came into it; it was rather damp, and it had no fireplace. The oil stove smelt and he put it out, chilled down, became oppressed by the smallness and darkness of the room and the busy clatter of the kitchen next door. He adjourned to the sitting-room; but a clothes-horse draped with airing-sheets had been drawn across its fire. After half an hour of disjointed musings, he went out and inspected the garden, which, he decided, would want a lot of tidying-up. Then he remembered that his foot had caught in the bedroom carpet when he had entered it on the preceding night. Failing to find either tacks or hammer, he went off to the village to procure them. On his way he met the genial secretary of the golf-club and was easily persuaded to return to the cottage, collect his clubs, and play a very pleasant eighteen holes.

In the afternoon Elsa and he went for a long walk, returning just in time for tea. After tea he remembered the tacks and the hammer and hurried off to the village. The bedroom carpet, he discovered, required tacking down all round. To do this it was necessary to move most of the furniture. Descending to the sitting-room he found Elsa in the firelight.

They sat there until it was time to change for the meal which they had decided to call supper. Afterwards he retreated again to his sanctum and for nearly an hour sat there, endeavouring to entice his thoughts away from their endless retracings of the past four months. They refused, however, to submit to any control—jumped to and fro, from his first walk with Elsa to their walk that afternoon—to the car they would have to get—to Mr Loxton and the unlikelihood of his living beyond seventy-five—to his own father's death at sixty-eight—back to Elsa. Some day—incredible, desolating horror—one of them would die and leave the other. Every moment that he lived must be lived for her—with her. She was alone now—in there in the sitting-room. He had left her alone for a whole hour. But he must leave her alone—sometimes. It was impossible to think except of her when he was with her. And yet . . . that hour had gone from them. Yes—there was a deuce of a lot to be done in that garden. But the garden mustn't be allowed to interfere with the things that really had to be done. Nor golf. It had been a very jolly game that morning—that iron of his at the seventeenth had been rather a beauty. Pleasant chap, the secretary. He had said that his wife would call. He mustn't forget to tell Elsa.

He went back to the sitting-room and kissed Elsa passionately. They were drowsy after their long walk and went off to bed before ten.

The days slid away. The weeks began to slide away. There was always something to be done—something that had been done to think about. Sometimes for a week on end the one thing that must be thought about—that must be done—disappeared completely from view. Then, as they returned from a walk or a drive or a mild bridge-party, an abstracted silence would fall on him, and he would quicken his pace, or speed up the car. Arrived at the cottage he would hurry into the little sanctum, light the oil-stove and a pipe, and seat himself with Elsa's pen and a writing-block. Mrs Higson's curiosity was aroused by the elaborate designs drawn on the crumpled sheets which she found in the sanctum's waste-paper basket. She had believed that the master was a literary gentleman, but formed now the conclusion that he was an artiss or something.

No other tangible result was produced by these spurts of industry which gradually became more and more widely spaced. Whalley, of course, explained to Elsa humorously what happened to him when he shut himself up in his lair.

'I sit down and think that I have got to think of an idea for a play. I immediately stop thinking about anything for a bit. Then I begin to think about you. I draw curlimacews until I think again that I have got to think about an idea for a play. Then I think that it is utterly impossible to *think* of an idea for a play. The darned thing must come of its own accord. One has nothing to start from—one hasn't the faintest idea where one wants to go. I draw a lot more curlimacews. Then I think that I have *got* to think of an idea for a play—that I must start earning some money straight away, and that, whether it is impossible or not, I must think of an idea for a play before I leave that room. I immediately stop thinking about anything. Then I begin to think about you and draw curlimacews until I think again that I have got to think of an idea for a play. It goes on like that until you open the door and tell me that it's teatime. It's exactly like trying to make a blind mule drink out of a bucket that isn't there. There's no use worrying about it. The darn thing must come of its own accord . . . Oh, I wanted to oil the lock of the garage.'

Returning from a call one afternoon towards the end of February, Elsa found him standing in the garden regarding the cottage with a curious frowning intentness. A drizzling rain was falling. She reproached him for standing in it without a raincoat.

'The little shanty got on my nerves suddenly,' he explained, rather shamefacedly. 'I felt I had to get outside. It's such a little box of a place. The ceilings are so low. I've felt all along, somehow . . . stifled . . . cramped . . .'

Her voice trembled a little.

'But I thought you were quite happy here, dear.'

'Happy? Yes, yes, dear, absolutely happy—you know that, don't you. It isn't that. But . . . It's so difficult to explain—so perfectly idiotic. It's all right so long as I am with you, but when I'm alone . . . That little den of mine gives me the horrors now. When I go into it, all I want to do is to get out of it again as quickly as possible . . . Oh, there's that washer for the scullery tap. I shall have time to fix that before tea.'

He abandoned the sanctum altogether. Spring came and was gone. Summer came. Surrey was a garden of drowsy enchantment. The cheery, decorative young people at Myrtle Cottage had made themselves very popular. They played a lot of golf and tennis—had nearly always some engagement for their afternoons. They worked in the garden. Whalley had always some small job to do about the house. Elsa's eyes lost the watchfulness that had grown in them for a little while following that incident in February. He appeared absolutely happy. Nothing else really mattered.

At the beginning of September, however, his interest in the links and the garden declined noticeably. 'We've got to get out of this place, Elsa,' he said abruptly as they drank their early tea one morning. 'Puttiford, I mean, for a bit, anyhow. It's no use to us. It's a backwater—a blind alley for us. These people who live here in those houses in among the trees—well, they're very nice and kind, and so forth—but, you know, they're dead. Stuffed. Nothing ever happens to them. Nothing *could* ever happen to them. They're determined that nothing will ever happen to them. That's why they live at Puttiford. We've got to get away from them . . . get round . . . see people who are alive and do things. Anyhow, for a bit.'

They left the cottage in Mrs Higson's care and took the car up one side of England to Scotland, and down again along the other side, travelling by short stages, and staying at a number of alarmingly expensive hotels. If the people whom they encountered along the way were not dramatically inspiring, most of them were at all events alive and amusing. The two months' holiday was a gratifying success and had a gratifying sequel. Within a month from their return to Puttiford, Whalley wrote a play.

True—it was not a comedy, but a historical play—and a historical play whose theme and characters had been used before by many other dramatists. Nor had any original idea been born to Elsa's fountain-pen. Whalley had merely been strongly impressed by that tragic little room at Holyrood and had decided to write a play about Mary, Queen of Scots. However, it was a play, and, he thought, quite a good one. Elsa considered it perfectly wonderful. They celebrated its departure to Whalley's old agent by a weekend at Brighton.

4

The ice was broken. Before the time came to leave their little cottage two more plays had been written—one a rather gloomy War drama, the other a four-period comedy with a first act set in the 'sixties.

The parting from Myrtle Cottage was, at the last moment, a severe wrench. Some encouraging news from the agent, however, consoled them. His New York office had succeeded in interesting a well-known manager in the comedy. After some weeks in rooms in Guildford, they found a tiny flat in Chelsea to let furnished for three months, and installed themselves there. Whalley wrote another comedy, but soon found London distracting. They returned to Surrey in the spring and spent the remainder of that year at a very comfortable little inn at Albury. Another comedy was written there.

For another year they moved on from one small hotel to another, then settled, successively, in a furnished bungalow near Gillingham, lodgings at Bournemouth, and a boarding-house at Folkestone. Nine plays of various sorts had now been sent off to the agent. From time to time he wrote regretting his failure to place any of them. The New York manager had paid a thousand dollars for an option, but had then faded out. Serious encroachments had been made upon Whalley's six thousand pounds. Those curious spasmodic attacks of dizziness and depressed exhaustion to which he had now grown accustomed, became more frequent and of longer duration. He began to lose appetite and weight and to suffer a good deal from sleeplessness and a chronic soreness of his tongue which robbed smoking of all pleasure. Two doctors failed to alleviate this trouble, which remained with him for the next seven years.

In the spring of 1922—they were living in rooms at Guildford then—he became definitely anxious, and decided to write a novel. Working at feverish speed, he succeeded, without difficulty of any sort, in carrying out this project within the space of three months. The English publishers who accepted the book paid a hundred pounds in advance royalties and its 'fresh and delicate humour' received an unhoped-for number of kindly notices from the press. It fared still more fortunately, for a first novel, in America, where the sales amounted to nearly 5,000 copies. Altogether it brought to Whalley royalties amounting to about £400.

He put aside those golden visions which he had seen so clearly on that September afternoon on which Elsa and he had watched the deer in the park at Ducey Court. £400 a year was not to be sneezed at. His sales would increase as his name became known. In a few years he might hope to be earning a steady £700 or £800 a year. And one could write two novels a year—easily.

He wrote a second—a third—in all, nine. They were all alike. His agent assured him that his publishers and his public expected them to be so. They all achieved the same limited success. Between the years 1922 and 1927, they furnished him with an average income of £550.

In the summer of 1927—they were back at Puttiford, staying at the inn—he had a severe attack of neuritis, brought on, he

then believed, by over-violent tennis and subsequent careless-
ness in sitting under an open window. Three weeks of agonising
pain and sleepless nights left behind a sudden swift wasting of
the muscles of his shoulders and his arms, and for a couple of
months he was unable to brush his hair or put on his clothes
without great difficulty and fatigue. Radiant heat and ionisation
proved ineffectual. Gradually, however, if very slowly, he recovered a restricted use of his arms, though his shoulder muscles
remained wasted. The Guildford doctor who attended him
affixed the label: 'peripheral neuritis' to the attack, was interested in his tongue trouble, and a little vague in his acceptance
of the tennis-and-draught theory. Finally he advised a nerve
specialist.

Whalley went up to London and paid five guineas to a nerve
specialist who told him that there was nothing whatever wrong,
organically, but that rest and change were necessary. The book
for the following spring had been begun and Whalley was
unwilling to move until it was at all events well on towards
completion. They remained on at Puttiford. One day, while he
was writing in the hotel garden, he became aware of a point of
sharp pain at the tip of his right thumb. Next day the tips of
the fingers of both hands were numb. In a week the numbness
had spread to his feet, which felt as if jagged sprigs were
stretched along their soles, inside the skin. He had grown so
used to partial disablement now that these new symptoms did
not perturb him greatly. But he decided that it was time to look
for some air more bracing than that of Surrey, and they set off,
rather hurriedly, for the little inn on the Quantocks, at which
they had engaged rooms by wire.

Stealthily, yet with incredible swiftness, his body began to
wither. At the end of a month he was unable to ascend a short
flight of stairs without utter exhaustion. His ribs became
compressed as if by an iron corset, and he crawled about, bent
like a man of eighty. Chronic indigestion and nausea, accompanied usually by violent palpitation, assailed him. His sunburn

faded to a yellow pallor. From his waist to his toes he was numb, yet always sensible of incessant jarring, aching discomforts. Despite a ravenous appetite, his flesh wasted until it seemed that his bones must burst through the tautly-strained skin. Sitting was an intolerable agony; he could lie in no position for longer than a few minutes at a time; when he stood upright the weight of his pelvis and his legs exhausted him. Elsa, in consternation, at last summoned two doctors from Bridgwater. They were obviously completely perplexed, advised absolute rest, and prescribed a nerve tonic. Whalley, however, went on with his book, Elsa typing from his dictation. He had lost all interest in everything—his own symptoms included—save the necessity of finishing the novel. Within a cloud of sick impotence, his brain still continued to perform one function with extraordinary accuracy and swiftness. Sometimes he dictated five thousand words in a day.

One afternoon, while they were working, he collapsed like a punctured tyre. Elsa telephoned to Dunpool for an ambulance and carried him off to a nursing-home in Rockwood, where a blood-test revealed that he had pernicious anæmia. He had probably had it for a number of years back, they told her; his supply of red corpuscles was down below two million. Yes—he might die, but they hoped not. The new Minot-Murphy treatment had proved very successful in America, even in bad cases. Liver . . . and hydrochloric acid . . . he began to eat liver—eight ounces of it a day—two platefuls of grey, greasy, rank-smelling little lumps of offal which froze to the plate before a quarter of them had been forced, one by one, down his gulping throat. Each gorge was followed by the pungent horror of the hydrochloric acid and violent cramps in which he lay sweating, sometimes for an hour, unable to move a muscle. At the end of a week the mere sight of the loathed stuff made him retch. He chewed away grimly, however—there was no other salvation. After thirteen weeks of the nursing-home—at seven guineas a week—he was able to walk, very slowly, across his room and insisted upon leaving. Half an hour after arriving at the near-at-hand lodgings in which Elsa had been living, he asked for the typescript of the unfinished novel and for a while turned over its pages desultorily and with increasing speed.

'My God,' he said listlessly, 'what tripe. Well, I suppose it's got to be finished.'

Three chapters, only, remained to write. Less than ten thousand words more would secure four or five hundred pounds, defray the expenses of the nursing-home and of the long breathing-space which, he had been warned, would be absolutely essential. Twenty times a day he settled himself on the sofa with a writing-block. But words had ceased to be significances that flowed from the point of his pen in formed phrases and sentences. They had become little, detached, unmeaning weights which had to be lifted on to the paper one by one—odd, useless pieces of some immense, futile old puzzle the rest of which had been lost. He became doubtful about their spelling—perplexed by their sound and meaning. 'When,' for instance. W-h-e-n. An extraordinary-looking word, when one really looked at it. An extraordinary sound, when one really listened to it. 'When.' What *did* one mean when one said 'when?' He could never arrange the little weights in sentences. When he had lifted eight or nine of them on to the paper he always saw that it would take at least thirty or forty more of them to bring the sentence to an end—crossed out what he had written, and cast about for another beginning. But a new little weight at the beginning completely obliterated the vague thought with which he had started and replaced it with another equally vague. Another sentence entangled itself hopelessly. An immense, yawning fatigue overpowered him. He dropped the block to the floor, picked it up again, began again to lift the little weights one by one. He could see them as he lifted them—little visible blocks of letters, very heavy for their size.

He chewed away at his liver doggedly—six ounces a day now. Elsa cooked it herself, on an oil-stove in their sitting-room and the sickly smell hung about the room all day. He made steady progress, however, though he knew now that for the rest of his life he could hope for no more than a thirty-per cent bodily efficiency. The damage to nerves and muscles was irreparable, they told him. His hands and legs and feet and spine would remain numb and partially crippled, and, of course, he would have to eat liver until he died. But the summer had come. Elsa drove him all over the West Country; it was good to be alive. Gradually a placid, cheerful calmness replaced the dejected anxiety of his early days of convalescence. In the autumn he would rattle off those last few chapters; his publishers had written sympathetically. They still had over two thousand pounds. Once more for a little while they were perfectly happy. Except, perhaps, about Mr Loxton.

Mr Loxton had called at the nursing-home once or twice to make enquiries. His sympathy with Elsa in her trouble had, however, been almost at once clouded over by a chilly offence, whose cause, she had divined, had been resentment of the fact that a niece of his should live in lodgings in Rockwood. For a long time the Whalleys had heard and seen nothing of him. Later he had expressed a wish that they should dine at his house on Sundays—a command with which prudence had advised compliance. But, while ostentatiously avoiding any slightest reference to their affairs, past, present or future, he had remained solemnly disapproving. Occasionally, in place of his usual curt, 'Whalley,' he elected to employ a 'Mr Whalley' of icy remoteness. When he looked directly at him—he rarely did so—he pursed his lips and looked at him exactly as if he were a doubtful egg. His conversation during dinner was addressed almost exclusively to Mrs Canynge and her husband who, exhaling wealth and success, usually attended those weekly functions. Whalley and Elsa, with their two thousand pounds and their dog-eared typescript, sat listening to easy, intimate talk of a South American contract for a hundred thousand—a deer-forest for which Canynge and a friend had paid twenty thousand—a new Rolls that had cost £2500—extensions of premises and plant at the firm's Cardiff branch. 'It will run us in, I reckon, just a quarter of a million,' Canynge estimated, while he selected a cigar from the box which Mr Loxton always offered him first. Mrs Canynge, always in the very latest of frocks and hats, had a trick of regarding her sister's modest toilettes through half-closed eyes. The Canynge's chauffeur watched the departure of the shabby little old two-seater with a contemptuous leer. It took a lot of starting now. Sunday was rather a trial.

In July they decided, somewhat hastily, to get a dog, and paid four guineas for a very handsome, well-bred cocker pup, then aged ten months. Because of his blackness, his erect top-knot and his trick of gazing ferociously at imaginary enemies, they called him Bogey-Bogey. He was an affectionate, immaculately clean little creature, and in twenty-four hours became the engrossing interest of their lives. After three days, however, he discovered that he disliked aprons and, whenever the maid entered, rushed at her, barking furiously. At the end of a week their landlady asked them to find rooms elsewhere.

This was a serious upset. Their lodgings had been comfortable; the cooking had been good; Whalley's books had arrived from Ireland in thirteen large packing-cases and been arranged in book-cases. They would have to be repacked—and unpacked again. It was difficult to find good rooms where a dog was permissible, and, within a few days of their installation in fresh quarters, their new landlady gave them notice. She couldn't have cooking done in her best sitting-room, and she couldn't have a dog with paws the size of a young elephant's trespassing all over her house. The books were repacked—unpacked in another sitting-room. Bogey-Bogey upset Elsa's pan of boiling lard during her absence from the room. He escaped scatheless, but Whalley paid fifteen pounds for a new carpet, and had to pack his books again. Another sitting-room—another unpacking. Their fourth Rockwood landlady, they discovered too late, kept two dogs and Bogey-Bogey hated other dogs even more than he hated aprons. All day long he barked and growled at his enemies in the basement. A fifth flitting seemed inevitable. Whalley began to talk of looking for a small flat.

Autumn came and went. One morning at the end of October a bulky packet arrived from the agent. It contained all the type-script copies of the nine plays, for none of which, it was regretted, an opening seemed now probable. Although Whalley had long abandoned all hope of them, this formal final damna-tion of the plays dejected him a good deal. He became silent and restless—got out the battered typescript of the unfinished novel and brooded over it—wrote some pages of a new chapter and tore them up.

'You know, old thing,' he said one night in the darkness, just as Elsa was falling asleep, 'these books that I've been writing have been the most fearful rot. They're all about nothing—just odd people and things we've come across faked up into a weak, would-be-funny little story. I can't go on writing that sort of stuff. I'm sick of it. I've got to make a fresh start—get in touch with actual life—write about people who live and suffer—write books with some meaning and purpose in them . . . something to say . . .'

'Well, but, dear,' urged the practical Elsa, 'all the stories are silly old stories. They're all faked—all as old as the hills. Life itself is a silly, faked-up old story. What does it matter so long as you give pleasure for a little while to a few other people? The great thing for us is that they bring us in enough money to live on, isn't it?'

'No. I can't go on with it. I know now that the reason I can't write is that I know the stuff I've been writing is rot—weak, silly, dishonest piffle. Death . . . I can't go on with it.'

For three or four weeks he wandered about the east end of Dunpool, exploring its grim, dingy squalor, getting into talk with dock-labourers and factory-hands, bribing foremen to smuggle him into deafening workshops, straying through

festering courts and alleys and still more heartrending warrens
of little houses, all the same, where thousands of people, all the
same, lived the same, drab, ugly, hopeless lives. He was shown
over a gigantic workhouse reeking with disinfectant—waylaid
some of the inmates of its casual ward—caught glimpses of a
degradation beyond the belief of sanity. After a fortnight of
these investigations the world became a hive of mean, dirty
streets, half-smothered in the smoke and stench of huge, threatening factories, peopled by burly, sullen-eyed, foul-tongued men,
slatternly, shrill-voiced women, swarms of screaming children—
all clothed in the same shapeless, sour-smelling shabbiness.
Beauty, grace—all those useless illusions of the spirit—all those
artificial decencies . . . of what account were they? *This* was
life—its business. Dismay fell upon him. For the first time he
realised how slight a barrier stood between him and Elsa—and
a destitution of appalling horrors. Two thousand pounds—a
sick brain—a body that could not earn even the wages of a
common navvy. He turned his back upon the gloomy, menacing
landscape of realism. There was nothing for him in that wilderness of grime and noise and stench and bitter, merciless struggle.
Nothing at all—except amazement that human beings endured
living in it. To Elsa's great relief, he abandoned his slumming.

'After all,' he said, 'it *is* something to amuse a few other
people.'

And he got out the unfinished typescript once more, asked
Elsa to retype the tattered first pages, and made several attempts
to begin a new chapter. Elsa caught a bad cold, however, just
before Christmas and Bogey-Bogey for some weeks fell to
Whalley's sole charge. It was always time to take Bogey-Bogey
out—to prepare Bogey-Bogey's dinner (it was cooked in the
sitting-room) or supper—to comb him and brush him—to make
up his bed. December's ending was very wet. After every outing
(he had five a day, regularly, beginning at 7.30 a.m. and ending
at 10.30 p.m.) Bogey-Bogey's paws had to be washed and his
coat dried with a towel. The towel had to be dried. The type-

script of the novel was thrown one day, somewhat irritably, into the sideboard and remained there until, in February, the Whalleys again changed their lodgings.

Once more Bogey-Bogey had done the wrong thing—he had found in the hall a large meat-pie belonging to one of the other lodgers and, in a few miraculous seconds, had eaten all of it save one very small piece of gristle. Another sitting-room—another unpacking of the books. Meeting Mr Knayle one afternoon at a friend's house, Elsa happened to mention to him that her husband and she were looking out for a small flat—preferably, for the sake of Bogey-Bogey's exercisings, close to the Downs. Mr Knayle happened to know of quite a nice little flat above his own, which, he believed, would become vacant at the end of March. He undertook to make more exact enquiry.

On the last day of March, 1929, the Whalleys moved once more. By that time their new quarters had been furnished and looked very gay and fresh and homelike, though some re-papering and repainting would be necessary presently. This the landlord had promised to do in the following spring. Mr Knayle came up the steep outside staircase and had tea with them one day shortly after their arrival. For some reason on the occasion of this visit he substituted 'Mrs Whalley' for 'Elsa' and adhered to this form of address ever afterwards.

Their rent was £100 a year, and their lease was for three years. It would be necessary to get in a woman for some hours each day, at an estimated £1 a week. Their weekly housekeeping account could not be expected to amount to less than £3 a week. They had spent nearly £200 of their capital upon furniture and equipment and they had committed themselves, for three years, to an annual expenditure of over £300, which did not cover clothes, amusements, or possible doctor's bills. There would be the garaging of the little old car—its licence—running costs—repairs. And their income at the moment was Elsa's £50—and save for some small driblets of royalties from past books—nothing at all.

But Whalley had decided that they must gamble—must have a place of their own—space, quiet—their own things around them. He had been all eagerness. He had bought a roll-top desk. It had always been such an infernal nuisance, in lodgings, having to put away one's papers and things. You just slammed down the cover of a roll-top desk, leaving everything as it was— out of sight. Then, when you wanted to go on again, there was everything just as you had left it.

For a little while, at the last moment, he had hesitated over the prospect of spending three more years in Rockwood. Rockwood was dull—dowdy—suburban—a long way from London. Two important considerations, however, had prevailed— Mr Loxton and liver, Elsa must keep in touch with Mr Loxton; and it might be difficult, he had discovered, to find elsewhere a butcher who would supply liver with the daily regularity of the shop at which they dealt in Rockwood. Rockwood decided upon, he was as enchanted with the flat as was Elsa. No more landladies—no more pilfering, perspiring sluts of maids—no more complaining fellow-lodgers. For their £100 a year they had now at their disposal a large sitting-room, a good sized dining-room, a large bedroom, a bathroom, and a delightful little kitchen. Bogey-Bogey, despairing of occupying all these possessions simultaneously, retired, on the day of their home-coming, to one of the gay eider-downs of the bedroom. Whalley dislodged him rather peremptorily and smoothed out the eider-down carefully.

'We can't have him messing up everything, dear. He mustn't be allowed to get up on the beds or the chairs. He has marked this quilt already.'

The roll-top desk arrived just then. When the men had gone away and Elsa had admired and returned to her kitchen, he seated himself at it with her pen and a writing-block and the typescript of the unfinished novel. The part of it on which one wrote was a little higher than he had expected. And one couldn't cross one's legs comfortably in the narrow recess into which they had to fit. He always liked to cross his legs when he was working. But he would get used to it.

He lighted a fresh cigarette from the old one and wrote, very carefully and largely, the heading:

CHAPTER XXI.

He looked round the room. How delightful it all was—gay and fresh—and their own. How extraordinarily sure and shrewd Elsa had been about everything—measurements and materials and colours. How quiet the room was—one heard only the pleasant hum of the passing traffic. Above them, they had discovered, lived a quiet, elderly couple named Hobson; below them lived the quiet Mr Knayle; below Mr Knayle lived a very quiet Mr Ridgeway. It was delightful to raise one's eyes and look out on the sunlit Downs. The trees were dusted with green already. Just the sort of room he had always wanted.

Then he remembered that Elsa wanted some hooks put in along the edges of the kitchen dresser's shelves, to hang cups and jugs on.

Mr Loxton—he was surprisingly vigorous and young-looking for seventy-three—came to lunch at the flat one day—thought everything very nice indeed, praised Elsa's cookery, and was, generally, quite affable.

'Writing away, I suppose, Simon,' he said just before he went away. 'Reeling it off . . .'

'Yes, yes.' Whalley smiled brightly. 'No rest for the wicked.'

5

They became the prisoners of an unavoidable routine.

Justice required that Bogey-Bogey should be taken out not later than 7.30 a.m. At 7 Whalley rose, made tea, shaved and bathed hurriedly and took Bogey-Bogey for his promenade on the Downs, returning at 8 to breakfast, which Elsa had prepared meanwhile. After breakfast she departed to market for an hour. Mrs Grant, the daily help, was busy already with her brushes and dusters, scurrying and blowing and sighing. The sitting-room was topsy-turvy. Any attempt to work was out of the question until her departure at 1 o'clock. Whalley read the *Morning Post*, did some odd jobs, and went out with Bogey-Bogey for a constitutional on the Downs. Two slow miles were the limit of his walking powers. Bogey-Bogey's murderous hatred of the countless other promenading dogs was an incessant anxiety; he returned fatigued and white to the flat to find Elsa busy with the lunch which was actually dinner, and rested or did other odd jobs until it was ready at 1. When they had washed up, Elsa retired to the bedroom to darn and sew and, having taken Bogey-Bogey for another short walk, Whalley shut himself up in the sitting-room until teatime. After tea they went out together with Bogey-Bogey for another walk on the Downs. Their evening meal was at 7; Elsa had to get back to the flat to prepare it. At 8 Bogey-Bogey had another run out of doors and they settled down in the sitting-room until 10.30, when he was taken out for his final outing. By 11 he had been combed and brushed; by 11.30 they were asleep.

It took Whalley some little time to realise that this tranquil programme was practically incapable of variation. Bogey-Bogey had to be taken out—Elsa's cooking had to be done—he had to try to do his own work. These necessities compelled an unalterable time-table which took complete control of life. Save for the Sabbath dinner at Mr Loxton's, occasional visits to or from Elsa's friends, and a still more occasional cinema or concert, each day was an exact replica of the other, lived within the same narrow boundaries. The earth contracted to the Downs and the flat. Its entire population, for all practical purposes, consisted of Elsa, Whalley himself, Mrs Grant, and Bogey-Bogey.

Presently, of course, Whalley became aware of this imprisonment and of its inevitable results. In three months his brain, still anæmic and fatigued by months of failure and growing anxiety, became a mere stagnant morass haunted by a few weary, stale old thoughts always the same. He sickened of them—of his failure—of himself—of that always-happening moment when, after lunch, he entered the sitting-room and shut its door behind him.

Time flew. Towards the end of the summer he abandoned the unfinished novel definitely and, to Elsa's dismay, destroyed the typescript. Another novel was begun in September and came to a standstill at its third chapter. At the end of 1929 his two thousand odd pounds had dwindled to sixteen hundred and forty, and he and Elsa decided that the daily woman must be dispensed with. She had cost a good deal more than they had anticipated. Whalley saw no reason why he shouldn't be able to do the housemaiding of the flat in the mornings—do it just as well and with much less fuss and noise than Mrs Grant. As a matter of fact, he had noticed that she had scamped a good deal. For instance, she had never once moved the roll-top desk so as to get at the dust in the angle behind it.

Elsa undertook to reduce the weekly bills a little. No other economy in their housekeeping appeared feasible. However, a little light work in the mornings, Whalley thought, was probably just what he wanted—exercise—distraction—something to take his mind off things for a while.

On New Year's Day, after breakfast, he changed into his oldest clothes and began his new duties by taking the Hoover into the sitting-room. Mrs Grant had always done the carpets with the Hoover, rapidly and, it had appeared, satisfactorily. But after a very little while he discovered that it failed to pick up some shreds of tobacco near the roll-top desk and, arming himself with dustpan and brush, went down on his knees to collect them. He saw then that the carpet was still thickly covered with Bogey-Bogey's hair, and attacked it vigorously with the brush. A little cloud of dust rose from it. Why, the darned thing was filthy . . .

Inch by inch he went over the carpet with the brush, pausing
from time to time to glance upwards uneasily at the dense mist
of dust which filled the room. All that dust would settle on
the ceiling, the walls, the book-cases, the curtains. But the
carpet *must* be done thoroughly. He found a number of small
stains on it, and spent a lot of time removing them with soap
and hot water. Returning from her marketing about eleven
o'clock, Elsa found him on a step-ladder, dusting the ceiling
with a feather-brush.

'Don't overdo it, dear . . . What about Bogey? It's time for
your walk, isn't it?'

'I shan't be able to get out this morning. I must get this room
done before lunch . . . Oh, very well, dear. I'll take him out.
Rather a nuisance, though. I shall have to change . . .'

The sitting-room was finished by midday next day. It looked
almost exactly as it had always looked. And of course there had
been no time to do anything to the other rooms. Whalley began
to see why Mrs Grant had rushed about and scamped corners.
But, then, on the other hand, one knew now that the sitting-
room had been thoroughly done.

Two days later he thought it advisable to run over its carpet
lightly with the dustpan and brush. It was thickly covered with
Bogey-Bogey's hairs, and at the first touch of the brush, a little
cloud of dust sprang out of it.

He remained on his knees for some time looking at it. It
ought to be brushed, but the dust would settle on everything.
The whole room would have to be gone round with a duster—
every photograph and flower-bowl moved—a couple of hours'
work. There were still the dining-room, the bathroom, the hall,
the kitchen to do. The sitting-room must be left. Reluctantly
he transferred his paraphernalia to the dining-room, but the
dust which he had left in the sitting-room carpet worried him
until, three days later, all the other rooms had been done and
he was able to attack the sitting-room again.

Dust became an active, mocking, invincible enemy. Soon,

when he looked at a chair in passing, he saw only the dust in the angles and small interstices of its back. When he switched on a light he saw the dust on its shade and made a note to clean it next morning. Greatly as he came to hate it, the collection of dust afforded him a curious satisfaction. He even preferred that the dust should be thick. It was a pleasure to watch the dust-pan filling—to watch its contents fall into the dust-bin when he emptied it. There was one variety of it which he hated, however. It was found in the bedroom only, under the beds—long woolly wisps which flew before the brush like thistledown and were difficult to capture. They stuck to the brush when one did capture them and had to be picked off and dropped into the dustpan, from which they kept escaping.

He was always looking at a clock or his wrist-watch. There was never time to do things properly and thoroughly. Yet if one didn't do them thoroughly it was hardly worth doing them at all. He had believed that if all the rooms were once thoroughly done to start with it would be a simple matter to run over them all in the morning. But he found that, really, every room required a thorough doing-out every day. He could never catch up with this ideal. He was always looking at his watch—always in a flurry. The brass plate on the front door had taken him twenty minutes, because the Brasso had caked in the ornamentation of the letter-box's flap and had refused to be dislodged. In the end he always had to scamp—just do what showed.

Of course he saw the absurdity of his over-scrupulousness and joked about it with Elsa. Five minutes later she would find him 'making a thorough job' of the bathroom linoleum.

For a couple of weeks he made no effort to write. Then alarm seized him. For three days he did no housework, and shut himself up in the sitting-room morning and afternoon. Then he discovered that every room in the flat was filthy—everything covered with dust . . .

Time flew. He was always looking at his watch. When he sat staring at his writing-block he thought of dust under the beds or finger-marks on the doorplates. While he polished the lino-leum in the hall he thought of the time which he was wasting—time which should have been spent in there in the sitting-room—doing the one thing that mattered . . . that could avert disaster . . . extinction.

Time flew. It was always hustling him and bustling him. And it was always time to take Bogey out. One had stop in the middle of something and change one's old clothes.

Clothes had become a serious problem. Everything he had was wearing out. The laundry frayed collars—tore shirts and handkerchiefs and vests and drawers. Only one of his suits was now really presentable, only one hat. His shoes had been resoled to the limits of their endurance. His older hats and suit would be soon too disreputable even for the Downs. The lining of his overcoat was torn beyond Elsa's powers of repair. Simultaneously everything had fallen into shabbiness and decay. Nothing could be replaced—every shilling had to be thought of. As soon as he returned to the flat he changed back into his oldest things—put on the collar of the day before to save the clean one put on before going out. All this changing took an immense amount of time.

He had always been particular about his clothes—abhorred trifling defects in his underwear. Shabbiness and dinginess depressed him; he came to loathe the old things which he wore about the flat. Before shutting himself up in the sitting-room he changed into his second best suit, which was reserved strictly for this purpose. His best suit was worn only on Sunday, when they dined at Mr Loxton's. It was three years old now and Canynge always looked it over while he nodded his casual 'how-d'you-do'.

Soon even it would become too shabby to wear out-of-doors, despite every care to husband it. And it could not be replaced.

Fear began to whisper to him as he swept and dusted and polished.

*

The curtains began to fade—the chintzes soiled—the cushions lost their trim, firm shape—the corners of mats became permanently crumpled-up, their fringes began to come off. Bogey-Bogey's big, tumultuous paws had left their marks everywhere. Everything in the flat retreated into a haze of dinginess. Cups and plates had been broken; the sets were incomplete. The landlord had failed to keep his promise. A lot of the paint was in a really shocking condition, and in places the wall-paper had actually peeled off.

Everything was fading—decaying. And nothing could be replaced . . .

He had long ago admitted the truth to himself: he had nothing to write about, no real talent for writing, no real desire to write save in order to make money. The material which he strove to work into trivial, artificial incident and laboured dialogue was all old stuff—the stale thoughts of ten years back—largely, he suspected, reminiscence of novels read before the War. His invincible desire for exactness tortured him. Sometimes he spent a couple of hours over the construction of a sentence of ten words. What he had written with laboured anxiety appeared to him ten minutes later flat, childish, utterly amateurish. He writhed and grew cold when he read it, laid down the writing-block and stared at it in a consternation which was all but panic.

Two more novels were begun during that year. The first was abandoned definitely, the second temporarily in September. On the last day of 1930 Whalley went through his bank-book and found that he had thirteen hundred and sixty pounds. However, he had begun to write again now fairly steadily, and hoped to finish the novel on which he was working early in February.

On the afternoon of that New Year's Eve the Hobsons—the quiet elderly couple in the top flat—moved out of it, and on the following day some new tenants named Prossip (Mr and Mrs Prossip, their daughter and their rather too smartly-dressed maid) moved into it.

6

From Mr Knayle, whom they encountered frequently in the front garden and who sometimes came to tea with them, the Whalleys learned something of their new neighbours.

Mr Prossip, it appeared, was one of three brothers who had inherited an old and very select and prosperous tailoring business in Rockwood. After a very short time, however, he had sold out his interest (there had been difficulties, Mr Knayle believed, with his brothers owing to his uncertain temper and his partiality for whiskies-and-sodas) and had now been for many years a gentleman at large, and a well-known figure in Rockwood. He had married money—the daughter of Dunpool's best-known fish-merchant—and owing to the habitual richness of his attire, his monocle, and his distinguished walk, was known, generally, as 'The Duke'. Mr Knayle rather thought that the Prossips had—like many other people—lost some of their money lately, since they had sold a very large house to move into a small top-floor flat.

The Whalleys' own observations informed them that Mr Prossip was a large, heavily-built man of incipient elderliness, always clothed in apparently brand-new suits of ultra-fashionable cut and material. He walked with a little troubled strut, sticking out his posterior, and looking straight ahead of him through his monocle with a fixed and rather truculent scowl. His voice— the Whalleys soon became familiar with it—was a booming drawl prone to sudden quickenings into irritability. Almost every day, after breakfast, he went off in a new suit of plus-fours, carrying an enormous bag of golf-clubs, and was not seen or heard again until lunch-time.

Both Mrs Prossip and her daughter, too, were also large, heavily-built, and always superbly dressed. Mrs Prossip walked very slowly and ascended the outside staircase with frequent pauses. Subsequently the Whalleys learned that she had heart trouble of some sort which perhaps accounted for the fact that her thin, peevish face wore always a bluish flush. She was evidently nervous about dogs. Meeting Whalley in the front garden on the day following her arrival, she waved him away with her umbrella and stopped.

'I hope you and your wife will keep that dog of yours under control when he meets me or Miss Prossip in this garden.'

Unable to resist temptation, Whalley replied, a little tartly, 'Me and my wife will do our best.'

After that first meeting Mrs Prossip always passed him without looking at him.

Miss Prossip—a sallow, sullen young woman of thirty or so—played the violin. For the first week or so, while the new tenants were settling in, she played it spasmodically and for very brief periods. At the beginning of the second week, however, it became clear that what the Whalleys had hoped an occasional dilatory amusement was a serious study. Twice a day for two hours at a time, the violin squeaked scales and arpeggios, wailed passionate double-stoppings, always slightly out of tune—squeaked and grunted in the effort to play an accompaniment and a melody simultaneously. Sometimes a passage of a few notes was repeated thirty or forty times. Whalley began to cluck when he heard the sound of its long-drawn preparatory tuning.

Other noises overhead, too, made him cluck. The Hobsons had been inaudible; the Prossips were heard all day long. They were all large, heavy, apparently flat-footed, and apparently incapable of remaining still. From morning to night they thudded to and fro—it was impossible to conjecture for what purpose—shouting to one another from different rooms, slamming doors, pushing furniture about with furious energy, opening windows and shutting them again immediately, switching on a wireless set and, after a space of aimless howlings, switching it off again. They all hummed; their maid whistled; in his bath Mr Prossip bellowed like a bull. At night their voices rose—violent quarrels broke out—they all shouted together—doors banged. It was evident that Mr Prossip absorbed too many whiskies and sodas of evenings. His booming rose above Mrs Prossip's nagging hum. 'Oh, shurrup, will you. I'm shick of it.' At half-past eleven Mr and Mrs Prossip thudded into the bedroom over the Whalleys' and resumed their argument. It went on interminably, sometimes until two o'clock in the morning, with incessant trampling of feet and slamming of drawers. One night there was a scuffle. 'Shurrup, damn you,' roared Mr Prossip. Someone fell. Mrs Prossip sobbed loudly.

Twice a week the Whalleys' sleep was further curtailed. Mrs Prossip was an ardent church-worker and church-goer. On Tuesdays and Fridays she got up at 6 am. and, before departing to early service at a neighbouring church, charged about for half an hour, slamming drawers and doors and windows. Mr Prossip's boom protested vainly. 'Oh, do shurrup that damn row, Emma, will you.'

From the landing outside the Prossips' hall-door their pert, whistling maid emptied ash-trays and shook mats on to the Whalleys' landing, filled their dustbin with her garbage, and one day tossed the still lighted end of a cigarette on to Elsa's fur coat as she passed beneath. The cigarette-end stuck and burned a small hole before Elsa discovered it. Meeting Mr Prossip one day in the garden—they had passed with guarded 'good-days' until then—Whalley ventured upon mild remonstrance.

'I should be awfully obliged, Mr Prossip, if your maid wouldn't throw cigarettes and dust her mats on to our landing. And, as regards the dustbins, perhaps you will kindly ask her not to put her stuff into our bin. Yesterday she filled it with cardboard boxes—'

Mr Prossip scowled.

'May I ask, sir, are you instructing me what orders I am to give my servant?'

Whalley stiffened. 'Not at all. But I should be greatly obliged it you would ask her to take a little more care.'

'And I should be greatly obliged if you would mind your own business,' said Mr Prossip, 'and leave me to mind mine.'

Whalley smiled, and the interview ended there. From that forward the Prossips scowled and glared. Their maid continued to empty ash-trays and shake mats on to the Whalleys' landing. They moved their bin up from the front garden, however, and kept it outside their hall-door. It smelt a good deal, and the Corporation men made some difficulty about coming up the staircase for it. But at all events it was now available for their own use again.

Probably, Elsa surmised, because he was not getting enough sleep, this slight friction worried Whalley a good deal. Hitherto relations with the tenants of the other flats had been of the most placid and tranquil kind. Mr Knayle was friendliness itself. The Hobsons had never been heard, rarely seen—had always stopped to exchange agreeably the usual remarks about the weather. The solitary Mr Ridgeway in the basement flat, too, was practically invisible; occasionally during the past two years Elsa had thought it kind to linger, when she met him in the garden, for a brief, hurried little chat. But he was shy, and clearly afraid that he was detaining her, and kept edging away while they talked. Sometimes he was not seen for weeks. The Prossips were always going in or coming out; it was impossible to dodge their ostentatious hostility always. And even when they were not seen, Whalley thought of them above his head, scowling and glaring. He kept watch so that Elsa could slip out without meeting them on the staircase or in the garden.

For some weeks he toyed with the idea of trying to obtain some sort of clerical employment. But he knew that the project was a futile one. In Dunpool, as elsewhere, staffs were being cut down. He was a stranger—without introductions and recommendations—over forty—in bad health. He refused to consider Elsa's suggestion that her sister's husband might perhaps find some place for him at the foundries. It was bad enough to have to put up with Canynge's supercilious smile as an equal. He resumed his efforts to write, feverishly.

*

Time flew. It was always seven o'clock—the factory sirens were screaming down in the city. He dreaded awakening . . . Another day . . . Today the bedroom and the bathroom must be done. Elsa's weekly cheque must be written—two pounds five. The electric-light bill *must* be settled—three pounds five . . . The same old round . . . Bogey-Bogey and the same old walks . . . The same old Downs . . . The same old clothes . . . The same old liver . . . The same old noises overhead . . . Everything fading—decaying—going. His pyjamas had slit down the back again. He sprang out of bed and saw the long, still drowsy eyes that smiled up at him. Her hands came out from beneath the bedclothes and drew him once more into the warm fragrance of her arms. He bent and kissed her eyes and remained for a little space in that world of sunlit courage in which her spirit lived and laughed. But then his head twisted to see the little clock on the table between the beds. Five past seven. Bogey-Bogey was whimpering and scratching at the door, impatient for his walk, damaging the paint. There was no time—even for *her*. He picked up his ragged old dressing-gown. The sunlight faded. Overhead Mr and Mrs Prossip had begun an angry argument in bed . . .

The novel, after many falterings, came again to a standstill at the end of April. Whalley spent a long time over the *Morning Post* now and sometimes brought home other papers over which he brooded in the afternoons. The housework fell into arrears and was completely neglected sometimes for days on end. Elsa found him one afternoon standing in the passage looking about him vaguely.

'Don't tell me that you're thinking of repapering the passage, Si?' she smiled.

He shook his head, still looking about him. 'No. I wasn't thinking of that.'

'Of what, then?'

'I don't know really. I've had a funny feeling lately about this flat somehow—a feeling that there's something hidden in it somewhere—waiting for some frightful disaster that is going to happen to us. I can't shake it off. Oh! *damn* that fiddle . . .'

'Sh. They can hear, you know . . .'

The noises overhead began to worry him acutely. Miss Prossip had gradually extended her hours of practice, and when, at the beginning of June, he resumed the novel with renewed hope, he decided to offer a protest. To avoid personal collision with Mr Prossip's truculence, he put his remonstrance in writing.

'DEAR MR PROSSIP.—Would it be possible for Miss Prossip to shorten her violin-practice somewhat for at all events some weeks to come? I am endeavouring to complete some literary work, and you will understand, I feel sure, that the practically continuous sound of a violin overhead renders concentration upon mental work of any sort very difficult. I think it possible that you are not aware that sounds from your flat are very clearly audible in ours, and trust that you will not consider my request unreasonable.

'Yrs. sincerely,
'S. WHALLEY.'

He went up one Saturday morning and dropped this missive into the Prossips' letter box. A couple of hours later he found it in his own box, enclosed in a crested envelope addressed 'Whalley', and torn into small pieces. While he and Elsa were still standing in the dark little passage, discussing this discovery in undertones, a gramophone began to play in the Prossips' flat, just above their heads. It was a raucous, powerful instrument, and the sudden outbreak of its blaring startled Bogey-Bogey into a yelp of alarm. The Whalleys had not known that the Prossips possessed a gramophone. Their eyes rose towards the sound sharply and remained fixed on a small square of white-painted boarding which in one place broke the plaster of the passage's ceiling. The gramophone, they divined, stood on the upper surface of this boarding.

They recognised the tune which it was playing, an air popular with messenger-boys a couple of years back. A nasal baritone sang the refrain, 'I can't give you anything but love, Baby.' The banal melody was repeated and came to a blaring close. Instantly the same tune was begun again. When again it ended, it began again. Again it ended—began again . . . ended, began again. The Whalleys retreated to the kitchen and listened. At the end of the tenth repetition there was a brief silence. But footsteps hurried from the Prossips' kitchen along their passage. The dismaying blare burst out again.

Elsa laughed, not very successfully. 'Well, I must get on with my lunch. Don't get worried, dear. They'll soon tire of it. Take Bogey-Bogey for his walk.'

She busied herself with her pots and pans. Whalley went out into the passage again and listened.

The gramophone did not tire. It played that day from eleven o'clock until lunch-time—from two o'clock until half-past four—and from five until half-past six. It played always the same record and each performance was continuous. Whenever its blaring ceased for a moment or two, footsteps hurried along the Prossips' passage, usually from their kitchen, but sometimes from their sitting-room. Long after it had ceased to play, the Whalleys heard it still playing.

During the following day—a Sunday—nothing was heard of it. But on Monday morning it began at eight o'clock and played until ten. It began again shortly after one o'clock and played until four. At ten o'clock it began again and played until eleven. It played always the same record, and when it stopped Miss Prossip's violin began.

On Tuesday, with slight variations of hour, this programme was repeated—on Wednesday—on Thursday. On Friday Whalley wrote a letter of complaint to Mr Penfold, the landlord. But there had been trouble with Mr Penfold over his failure to keep his promises as to repainting and repapering. There was little hope of help from him. He tore his letter up. Besides, the Whalleys agreed, the wisest and most effective course was to avoid letting the Prossips see that the gramophone annoyed or disturbed them in the least. The Prossips had to pay pretty dearly for their amusements. They would tire of it. They must tire of it soon. The mere labour of keeping the gramophone going was enormous. It was incredible that at all events the elder Prossips could stand its noise much longer. And the performance of the gramophone had necessarily cut down the performance of Miss Prossip's fiddle. She, too, would tire of it very soon. Much the best plan was to grin and bear it.

So the Whalleys argued. The incredible went on happening however. The gramophone continued to play. When it had played for eleven days Whalley forgot his counsels of prudence and consulted a solicitor. The solicitor was doubtful, but wrote a guarded letter of complaint to Mr Prossip, to which Mr Prossip's solicitors replied in a letter of guarded defiance. Further letters were exchanged, the solicitors held conferences; Whalley had to attend one of them. It was a day of heavy rain, and his raincoat and umbrella were too shabby to face the solicitor's office; his best suit suffered considerable damage. Growing alarmed at the prospect of a large bill, he paid five guineas and withdrew his complaint. The only result of this serious expenditure was a further addition to the disturbances overhead.

Not a word had been written since the gramophone had declared war. His mind was a mere prickling, impotent irritation, incapable of any coherent thought that did not lead to the gramophone. He knew that it was entirely useless to attempt to work. None the less, every day after lunch he put on a clean collar, changed into his second-best suit, and shut himself up in the sitting-room, to sit there until tea-time in vacant torpor, scribbling on his writing-block.

He was sitting there on the afternoon following his final

interview with his solicitor when a violent thump shook the ceiling of the room and set its windows a-rattle. Someone had jumped violently on the floor of the room overhead.

Thump. Thump. Thump. Thump.

He half rose from his chair, but sat down again, looking upwards, waiting.

Thump. Thump. Thump . . .

CHAPTER III

1

Mr Knayle heard a good deal of Rockwood gossip at the Edwarde-Lewins' that thundery afternoon. One piece of news which concerned Mr Loxton interested him particularly and made him rather thoughtful during the remainder of his stay. Before he left he took his hostess into the garden and induced her to cut off a large number of her cherished roses.

As he drove homewards his blue eyes remained fixed upon the big posy whose fragrance filled the coupé. Their habitual slight surprise was more marked than usual and tinged with doubt. For he was both surprised and doubtful—surprised that he intended to present Mrs Whalley with a large bunch of roses, and doubtful that, in the end, he would do anything of the kind. His whole state of mind had suddenly—within the last couple of hours—become surprised and doubtful—restless—fluid—unsteady—utterly different from the calm, stable, reliable equilibrium in which his standards of judgment had balanced themselves for half a century. He seemed to have no standards. He couldn't judge things. He didn't want to judge them, really. He wanted to do things without thinking whether it was prudent or becoming to do them. He wanted to do things without thinking of what other people would think of them—of what their consequences might be. He didn't know what things—just things generally. He felt at once uneasy and extraordinarily gay and happy and a little silly. From time to time he smiled at the roses somewhat fatuously, then became dubious and perplexed again.

There they were in his hand, and he was bringing them to her. He had no clear idea now why. After tea, while he had been chatting with Vera Edwarde-Lewin as they strolled round the garden, a sudden warm, tender eagerness had flooded him—a delightful, even thrilling, sensation—and he had asked her to give him some roses for his sitting-room. He had encouraged her to make the bunch larger and larger—pointed out the finest roses. At the time it had seemed to him perfectly clear why he was doing this, but now, though he was striving to do so, he could recover nothing of that tender, eager warmth—no explanation that satisfied common sense. He had no clear idea at all why he had done it.

There had been that piece of news which he had heard concerning old Loxton. That had come into it. It had seemed to him that it would be a kind, sympathetic, consoling thing to bring her some roses. An absurd idea. As if the gift of a few roses from a friend could in any way soften a blow like that when it fell. Perhaps it had fallen already. Perhaps she had heard the news about old Loxton. He had not spoken to her for some days. Though, from behind the curtains of his sitting-room he had seen her twice that morning in the garden, going to and returning from her shopping. She had appeared, as always, bright and smiling and happy. No. Probably the blow was still to fall. Old Loxton, it seemed, had kept the whole thing very dark . . .

A serious blow for her and her husband—a very serious blow, he was afraid. Things were going badly with them. Apparently Whalley was never going to recover anything like decent health. He looked badly, poor devil—white and strained and haggard. No wonder, leading the life he did, shut up there all day long except when he went out to prowl about for a bit on the Downs. Knew no one, apparently. Finding difficulty, too, with his writing, he said—especially since this business of the gramophone had started. Not much money in writing—except for a few lucky ones—at the best of times. And now, of course, with this depression in every business . . . Whalley appeared to have 'world-depression' on the brain—always brought it up when one stopped to chat to him for a minute—seemed possessed by the idea that a general crash was coming. Quite strung up about it. Partially Irish, of course . . . and the artistic temperament. He must be pretty hard-up to wear those shabby clothes, and not to be able to afford a servant of some sort. Jolly hard on her. Possibly no private means . . . constant anxiety . . . probably no provision for her if anything happened him. No doubt he had built all along on old Loxton. It would be a very serious blow indeed . . . Not much use in bringing her a bunch of roses . . .

Well, well—these things happened. What was it to *him* if things were going badly for her.

Yes. That was the point. He was coming to it now.

What was she to *him?* Why had he begun to think of her so often of late? Why had he begun to watch her from behind his curtains as she went in or out—to contrive meetings with her in the garden? Why had he been so concerned, on her account, by the spiteful hostility of the Prossips? Why, on her account, was he concerned about her husband's ill-health and inability to earn money . . . about this business of Mr Loxton? What had been the real truth and essence of that warm, delicious, urging, reckless impulse that had suddenly moved him to bring her a bunch of roses? Had he . . . there it was; it must be answered . . . had he, after over thirty-five years of entirely platonic friendship, suddenly fallen in love with her?

Naturally, Mr Knayle did not speak his thoughts aloud, but he heard the words 'in love with her' distinctly, and their sound was like the pealing of triumphant clarions. He saw them distinctly, too, written across the cream and crimson splendour of the roses. The perfume of the roses became intoxicating. His eyes closed for a moment. A dancing rapture surged upwards within him. He wanted to dance and snap his fingers and sing: 'I am in love with her.' His body had no age—no weight—no substance. His mind was a marvelling exultation in the thing that had happened to him. Actually, he hummed a little, lest his chauffeur, Chidgey, should detect some outward symptom of his agitation. He ceased to look at the roses, for it was decided now—he knew. He was bringing them to her because he was in love with her. Impatiently he watched the well-known houses and lamp-posts and side-streets go by. In a few minutes he would be giving them to her . . . close to her . . . touching her little cool hand with his . . .

It was marvellous. For—yes she must be thirty-eight now— and he had known her since she could walk. Longer than that—he must have seen her often in her perambulator down at Whanton, though he had no recollection of it. For that matter all his recollections of her were rather indistinct, until the period during which she had lived in Rockwood. Even then, for a long time, he had merely been aware of her as one of the daughters of an old friend of his own parents—a flapper, like other flappers. Then had come a period when he had met her at dances and other functions of the sort—grown-up—grown slight and very pretty and gay . . . But no. He had admired her, certainly—thought her a charming girl and all that, but no, he couldn't recall having taken any but the most ordinary of friendly interests in her. During the War he had met her much less frequently. He could not recall that her marriage had had any but the most ordinary of friendly interests for him either. After that she had disappeared from Rockwood for ten years. He could not remember having even thought about her during all those years. Certainly he had been sorry, a couple of years ago, to discover that her husband was seriously ill. Certainly he had been very glad to assist her in finding a flat. And certainly, during the past two years, he had enjoyed casual meetings with her, and occasional visits to her flat. But no . . . there had been no change in his views of her during those two years . . . until . . .

Until when?

Mr Knayle's memory travelled back, eager to discover the first moment of enchantment. It came to a pause, provisionally, at a morning, about three weeks back, on which he had found himself standing by one of the windows of his sitting-room, concealed behind one of its curtains, and keeping watch on the front garden. Never before in his life had he kept watch from behind a curtain. And his breakfast had been cooling in his dining-room. But he had continued to stand there until a trim, slim little figure in jade had flitted down the garden and out through its gate. He had had then, he realised now, no idea at all why he had allowed his breakfast to become uneatable that morning in order to see her depart to her marketing. He had simply found himself watching. None the less it was almost certainly the marvellous truth that he had turned away to his congealed bacon and eggs a lover.

For three weeks, then, this stupendous secret had been locked away within him, and he had guessed nothing of it. When he had started for the Edwarde-Lewins' that afternoon he had guessed nothing of it. He remembered that he had looked up to her windows as he drove away from his flat and thought merely that it was a pity that Whalley was taking the feud with the Prossips so seriously. The first premonition of the astounding truth had come, he saw now, when, to his surprise, he had told Edwarde-Lewin that he would remain on at 47 Downview Road. How utterly inconceivable it was now that he could have even contemplated separating himself from her . . .

It was marvellous—a revolution—the birth of a new Harvey Knayle—a whole new world. He was neither unmanly nor selfish nor cynical, and he had known thousands of charming women, many of them intimately. He had liked them, admired them, respected them, sympathised with them, found in them all the virtues, but no magic. None of them had been able to make this marvellous, delicious, painful thing happen to him. He had believed that it couldn't happen to him—to regard it as a thing that happened to other people and led, generally, to unprofitable and troublesome consequences. And now it had happened to him, and he didn't care a jack straw what the consequences might be—so long as he could serve her. That was it—he wanted to serve her—to help her—to shield her.

Chidgey slowed up behind a 'bus, approaching a dangerous corner. 'Get on, get on,' commanded Mr Knayle impatiently.

Chidgey opened his throttle, passed out, and rushed round the corner at thirty miles an hour, narrowly escaping a cataclysmic collision. But he didn't care if he did have a jolly good old smash-up. When he had left Mr Knayle at the Edwarde-Lewins' he had returned to the garage with the car, resolved to do the gear-box and the back-axle. But in the end he hadn't done them. He never would do them again. 'Get on, get on'—as if he couldn't be left to drive the car as he thought right. Suddenly he decided that he would give Mr Knayle notice. Yes—and give it to him straight away. What the blinking hell did it matter if he did give up a good job? What did anything matter so long as one dropped all the old stuff and got on to something new . . .?

2

'Very well, Chidgey,' said Mr Knayle. 'I shall be very sorry to lose you. But, of course, you know your own business best. I shan't want you again this evening.'

He went up the outside staircase, subduing his ascent to sedateness. Rather annoying about Chidgey. Very annoying in fact. Chidgey appeared to have no reason for wishing to leave. Really, it *was* rather extraordinary the way people did things now without having the slightest reason to do them. They had been talking about it at the Edwarde-Lewins'. Idiotic things—and perfectly sensible people did them.

As he ascended, a confused medley of sounds became audible. The gramophone was blaring away, there was a violent hammering and smashing, a whistle was blowing, a tin can or something was being beaten.

'Tsch,' Mr Knayle exclaimed indignantly. 'Well, really, what a damned shame.'

Then he saw her. She was standing with Whalley on the landing of the staircase outside their hall-door, holding on with both hands to the arm which he was trying to free from her grasp. Her eyes were fixed imploringly on his face—a set white mask whose frozen desperateness was turned upwards towards the Prossips' door. All her slight strength was strained in the effort to keep her hold. Neither of them saw Mr Knayle, who stopped, dismayed.

'Darling, don't—please. What's the good? Simon—look at me. Don't look like that. We'll go away—right away from Rockwood. We'll go back to Surrey. You were happy there. We can sublet the flat. Don't look like that, dear . . .'

Mr Knayle retreated down the steps with his posy stealthily. Arriving at the recess beneath the steps in which the rubbish-bins were kept, he paused and lifted the lid of his own bin. He felt very elderly and futile and out of everything. After some meditation, however, he replaced the lid, and went on into his flat, still carrying his roses. She would go away . . . he would see no trim little figure flitting through the front garden. Of course, now, he wouldn't stay on when his lease terminated. He couldn't now. Still, the wonder remained—he loved her. His heart had leaped at the sight of her. His secret would remain to him—for a few days the roses would share it with him.

Chidgey was waiting in the hall, eager to withdraw his resig-nation. 'Very sorry I made such a fool of myself, sir,' he concluded.

'That's all right, Chidgey,' said Mr Knayle kindly. 'We all do foolish things occasionally. It makes a bit of a change. Have a bottle of beer with Hopgood and forget it.'

3

Mr Knayle could not get to sleep that night. Towards two o'clock he was lying in the darkness of his bedroom, still wide awake, revolving vaguely an idea which had occurred to him. Whalley could probably not afford to take any legal steps to obtain redress. But why should not he himself do so? Why shouldn't he instruct his solicitors to write to Prossip, threatening application for an injunction if the nuisance of the gramophone was not abated. Prossip would probably get frightened—he was a mere blusterer. The noise in the top flat would stop. The whole thing would blow over—and the Whalleys would not go away.

And, of course, he *did* hear the gramophone in his own flat. No matter if he only heard it partly—no matter what Edwarde-Lewin said.

At this point he became aware that he heard at that moment a sound which had no business to be heard in his flat at that hour of the morning—the sound of water splashing. He listened for a little space, then rose, slipped into his dressing-gown and went out into his hall. A considerable portion of the hall was awash, and from one point in its ceiling—the boarding covering in the old staircase well—a small but steady trickle of water was falling into it. He routed Hopgood out of his bed, and they held counsel for a little space. Obviously the water came from the flat above. They listened—no sound was audible overhead. Ultimately Mr Knayle brushed his hair, put in his two false teeth, lighted a cigarette, ascended the outside staircase and rang the Whalleys' bell. After some delay Whalley opened it.

'Awfully sorry to disturb you, my dear chap,' began Mr Knayle, 'but have you had an—?' His eyes took in the little lighted interior, and his unnecessary question died away. The hall and the passage were two glistening ponds connected by a miniature waterfall which was descending the little flight of stairs. From the ceiling three small cascades were falling as if from three open taps. In the background Elsa was hurriedly removing saturated coats from a hanging cupboard. Carpet, rugs, mats, furniture, walls, everything was sodden—splashing. Bogey-Bogey splashed as he gambolled excitedly. One cascade rebounded from the balusters of the stairs and splashed Mr Knayle's face. Elsa's slippers splashed as they moved hurriedly.

(How adorable she was in her dressing-gown and pyjamas and the little net cap which, evidently she wore at night to keep her hair from tossing). 'Hullo, Harvey,' she said vaguely. 'I suppose it has gone through into your flat.'

'Dear, dear,' Mr Knayle exclaimed in consternation. Then the light fell on Whalley's face and his tone changed sharply. 'Now, now, my dear fellow. Take it quietly. They can't possibly have done this on purpose. I'll go and knock them up.'

He slipped past Whalley adroitly and went up and rang the Prossips' bell several times, without success. Descending, he met Whalley hurrying up the steps and urged him downwards again.

'No, no—it's no good. I've tried. They're either asleep or they don't want to hear. There's a tap running up there. Somewhere near their front door. In their bathroom, I rather fancy. Take it quietly, old chap. It must be an accident. Their hall must be in a flood, too. We must turn the water off at the main, that's all. The tap of the main is in Ridgeway's flat. I'll go down . . .'

He descended and returned a few minutes later with Mr Ridgeway and Hopgood. Elsa and Bogey-Bogey had disappeared. Whalley was standing looking up at the ceiling stonily. 'We'll mop this up in no time,' said Mr Knayle cheerily, 'when the water has stopped coming through. I wonder if they *are* upstairs. Funny they didn't hear the bell. I rang about twenty times.'

He prattled on cheerily. No one else said anything, however, and gradually he too subsided into silence. The four men stood clustered at the hall-door, looking at the swimming desolation within, listening to the tinkling, dreary splash of the water as it fell into the two buckets which Hopgood had carried up. For a long time it continued to fall steadily. When at last the three cascades had dwindled to three drips, they set to work, and by four o'clock had restored some semblance of dryness. Dawn had come. Elsa reappeared and gave them coffee gaily in the kitchen. Mr Knayle began to prattle again. Mr Ridgeway, in a dingy old dressing-gown and looking very blowsy in the early light, smiled at Elsa with his fine, tired eyes and suddenly told two very funny stories. Bogey-Bogey performed his three tricks. Hopgood, standing respectfully at the door while he drank his coffee, made a pretty speech. 'Well, I must say, madam, you do keep your kitchen a treat.' Whalley, however, remained outside this concluding cheerfulness and sat staring at his cup as if, Mr Knayle thought, he was alone. Mr Ridgeway's attention was also attracted by his absorbed silence. He reached out a hand suddenly and laid it on Whalley's wrist, feeling with the other hand for a watch which was not in a waistcoat which he was not wearing. His bristled, sagging face became confused and alarmed, and his hands retreated hurriedly to his cup. But no one, to his relief, had noticed their abrupt movements. Whalley continued to stare at his cup, unaware that a hand had caught his wrist.

Hopgood went off with his buckets to mop up Mr Knayle's hall and shortly afterwards, disclaiming gratitude, Mr Knayle and Mr Ridgeway went down the outside staircase, whose railing was festooned with sodden mats and strips of carpet. Though they had been neighbours now for over four years, their only contacts hitherto had been the occasional exchange of salutes in the front garden. But the adventure of the night had made them for the moment intimate.

'They're leaving, I understand?' said Mr Ridgeway, looking back over a shoulder in the direction of the hall-door which had just shut behind them.

'So I understand,' said Mr Knayle. 'I think they're wise.'

'Yes, yes,' agreed Mr Ridgeway. 'I suppose so.' They went on a few steps. 'A sweet little creature, Mrs Whalley, I always think. One will miss her going in and out with that little cocker of hers.'

'Yes, yes,' agreed Mr Knayle.

They reached the front garden, paused at the head of the

short flight of steps leading down to Mr Ridgeway's hall-door, looked at one another, and then decided, quite unnecessarily, to shake hands. Then, as if the handshake had had no signifi-cance whatever and as if important business awaited them within, they hurried into their respective flats.

3

The inundation, it may be said here, remained for Mr Knayle a mystery. He had a talk with Mr Prossip about it a couple of days later, but Mr Prossip (he was nervous and shaky, Mr Knayle noticed—the strain of the vendetta had evidently begun to tell on his bluster) could or would throw no light upon it. He and Mrs Prossip had been in London that night. His daughter Mawjery had given Agatha, the maid, permission to spend that night at her own home. Mawjery herself had spent it at her Aunt Maggie's, having felt nervous about sleeping in the flat without male protec-tion. There had been no one in his flat that night. Mawjery hadn't left the bath-room tap running—the maid hadn't left it running. Mawjery had found no water about the flat when she had returned to it on the following morning. Mr Prossip couldn't understand the damned thing. When Mr Knayle suggested, urbanely, that a few words of polite regret might ease matters a little, Mr Prossip said he was damned if he would apologise to any b—y penny-a-liner. Mr Knayle decided to drop the matter.

The Whalleys had apparently arrived at the same decision. They were out a great deal in their shabby little two-seater. The gramophone—which played only when they were in their flat—was sometimes silent until evening. Mr Knayle went off to fish in Wales for a fortnight with the confident hope that the whole ridiculous business was going to blow over.

On the evening on which he and Hopgood returned, he went up to deliver a twenty-pounder which he had brought back for the Whalleys. The Prossips' saucy maid met him on the outside stairs and flashed a bold smile at him.

'If you're going up to the Whalleys, they're left.'

'Left?' repeated Mr Knayle vaguely.

'Yes. They cleared out last week. Their flat's to let—by what I hear Missus say.'

'Oh,' said Mr Knayle. 'I see. Thank you.'

He sent the salmon to a hospital. One can't share a secret with a fish.

CHAPTER IV

1

THERE were no further demonstrations in the coal cellar and the thumpings overhead, though always expected, became dilatory and less violent. The gramophone, however, continued to play. It played while they dressed, while they ate, while they sat talking, despite themselves, in daunted undertones. Its blare pervaded their lives; they heard it in their sleep and awoke, to lie awake thinking about it.

The landlord's solicitors wrote demanding that they should immediately get rid of 'your savage and noisy dog.'

And then the blow over which Mr Knayle had meditated fell like a thunderbolt. On the Sunday following the flooding of their flat they learned that Mr Loxton was to be married, very shortly, to a Mrs Gaythorne, of whose existence they had been until then unaware.

They were introduced to Mrs Gaythorne in the garden before dinner—a good-looking, hard-eyed, smart woman of forty-five or so, whose presence remained unexplained for a moment or two of silence, while Mr Loxton smiled with mysterious archness. Then, dismayingly, he slid his arm into Mrs Gaythorne's and she patted his wrinkled hand. All the dignity, the acute intelligence, the masterful self-sufficiency of this man who had transformed a small local firm into an immense business with ramifications all over the world disappeared; he grinned foolishly, a senile dotard.

'I don't know whether you have heard the glad tidings already, Elsa?' he enquired jocularly.

There was another little silence. 'No, Uncle Richard,' Elsa said at last.

He wagged a finger. 'Guess, then. Guess.'

'I'm afraid I can't.'

'You can't? You can't see that you are looking at the happiest and luckiest man in the world? You don't hear joy-bells ringing? You don't see favours fluttering in the wind? Well, well, well. Look at us again. Don't we look like two people who are going to do the most wonderful thing that has ever been done? Now?'

Over Mrs Gaythorne's plump shoulder Elsa's eyes met her sister's.

'Oh?' She smiled valiantly. 'Uncle—you sly old thing—'

Mrs Gaythorne detached herself from Mr Loxton and took Elsa's hands in hers. 'My dear,' she said with careful intensity. 'Tell me that you and I are going to be very, very great friends.'

The gong rang and the party moved towards the house. From Mrs Canynge Elsa received some hurried enlightenment as to Uncle Richard's love-idyll. Mrs Gaythorne was the widow of a naval commander. She lived at Bath. Uncle Richard had met her at a garden-party there only three weeks before. She had no money. And she had three children—a daughter of twenty and two sons in their teens.

'Silly old creature,' said Mrs Canynge. 'That little cat will lead him a dance. Harold and I are perfectly furious about it. I expect you and Simon are too. We have to run away as soon as this ghastly meal is over. But do come over and have a talk about it. It's too devastating . . . Any time.'

2

The Whalleys were silent as they drove home. There was nothing to say. They had left Mrs Gaythorne behind them in the garden, already its mistress, planning a new herbaceous border. This clever, determined woman with no money and three children held Uncle Richard and his million, they had seen, in a grip of steel. Her hard, vigilant eyes had scarcely troubled to conceal their cool triumph; she had captured this foolish, amorous old creature of seventy-five and no niece or niece's husband (she had snubbed Canynge during dinner so adroitly that he had become quite friendly with Whalley) was going to dispute her prize with her. Uncle Richard had already ceased to be. That ultimate dependence which, in spite of recurring doubts and distrusts, had remained a background of reassurance had been swept away. When Uncle Richard went there would be—for Elsa—Aunt Gladys, with her alien interests, her hard smile and her three children, to deal with. There was nothing to say.

When they reached the flat Whalley looked about him vaguely, heedless of Bogey-Bogey's rapturous welcome.

'We must get out of this, Elsa,' he said abstractedly. 'This book simply must be finished. It's no good—but it must be finished. We must get out of this at once. I hate asking you to leave the flat. But it's our only chance. I can't work here. We must sub-let the flat and go somewhere.'

She bit her lip to stop its trembling. The flat had been her little kingdom—despite all troubles, her little paradise. She had made it. Every chair and mat and cup and saucepan (she had chosen them all so carefully) had shared all sorts of thoughts with her.

'Where, dear? To Surrey?'

'No. I've thought it over, coming back. We'll buy a piece of land out there at Camphill—where we sat yesterday—on that slope. We'll buy a piece of land there. There was a board saying that it was for sale in lots. Quite a small bit will do—an acre or so. Or two acres. I expect the land out there is cheap. We'll put up a hut and some sort of garage for the car. We can get water from that cottage down the hill. We shall be right away from everything out there. It's not twenty minutes walk down the hill to that village—Clapenham. There's a sort of general store there and a butcher's shop. We can run into Rockwood for other things—it's only half an hour—barely ten miles . . .'

He developed his idea, pacing up and down the little passage, looking at his watch, seeming not to hear her when she suggested some obvious difficulty. For him his plan had no difficulties; he saw it already accomplished. With a simplicity which hardly hesitated, he arranged a complete uprooting of their lives. She was familiar with this curious, primitive naïveté which contemplated difficult and complicated undertakings as if they were already performed. Sometimes it took him a whole week to decide to write a letter of a few lines. But she had known him jump up in the middle of breakfast and begin the writing of a novel of 90,000 words, whose plot had occurred to him while he buttered his toast. So, she divined, he had decided to write plays. So he had decided to live by writing novels. So, perhaps, he had decided to marry her. But she would not have it otherwise—it was Simon; and he was right. His voice and his eyes always made her feel that he was right in spite of everything. They must leave the flat. The novel must be finished; it was three years since a book of his had been published—authors' names were soon forgotten. There would be difficulties, but they must be faced. How was liver to be got every day? But it must be managed. It would be lovely out there in the early mornings . . . And perhaps if the novel was sold, they might be able to come back—

'Very well, dear, let us just think it over for a day or two.'

But he was looking at his watch again.

'We shall have time to run out there before tea. The agents' name was on that notice-board. I'll show you the bit I think we ought to try for—from the edge of the wood up to the gap where we went in through the hedge. We'll have our gate at the gap. We shall have only three sides to fence. The hedge will fence the other side . . .'

Within a week his vision was accomplished fact. No conveyance had yet been signed, but Whalley had agreed to pay ninety-six pounds for two acres of land, paid a deposit of fifty pounds, and obtained immediate possession. The living-hut and the garage and the fencing had been erected by a Dunpool firm. A gate had replaced the gap in the hedge. Arrangements had been made as to water-supply, delivery of letters, and meat and groceries from the village shops. A hundred and twenty-five pounds had been spent—the chestnut fencing had proved an expensive item—and a further liability of forty-six pounds—not including lawyers' fees—contracted. But everything had gone smoothly; everyone had been obliging and helpful—there had been every encouragement to spend money.

The piece of land which they had bought lay some ten miles south of Rockwood, on one slope of a high, densely-wooded ridge, which had once formed part of the Ducey estate but had been sold towards the end of the war to various small specu-lators hopeful of large profits from the sale of the timber. The war had ended unexpectedly—the woods had remained, save for some small gashes, uncut. Through them wound, for two miles, along the ridge's crest, a narrow deeply-rutted track, formerly used by the wood-cutters' carts. One end of this debouched into a secluded by-road; the other came to an abrupt stop at the little cottage from which the Whalleys had arranged to procure water, a quarter of a mile beyond their new gate. For centuries the ridge had been a mere preserve of game, aloof from the fertile valleys which it divided, and this silent remote-ness still made of it a wilderness. A bare inch of soil covered the limestone. Nothing but the pines, the gorse, and the bram-bles had ever found a living there; the fields of the lowland farms had never crept up the steep, stony slopes. Save for the cottage, there was no habitation nearer the Whalleys' huts than the straggling houses of the little village, a mile below them and hidden by the woods from their view.

The sub-letting of the flat had been entrusted to a house-agent. They shut its hall-door silently behind them one afternoon and drove off in the two-seater, followed by a small lorry laden with their personal belongings. Just before they left, Whalley went round the flat, looking into each room from its door. No housework had been done during that hurried week.

Every room was thick with dust, disordered by the hasty packing, stripped of things that had always belonged to it. He shut each door reluctantly; all the rooms ought to have been done thoroughly—left in apple-pie order for the eyes of a possible tenant. But there was no time, and all that was done with. There would be no rooms to do out at Camphill.

Bogey-Bogey made a last trial of the closed doors. They puzzled him. He whimpered and had to be carried out. Elsa kissed her hand, 'Good-bye, little flat. Coming back.' As they went down the outside staircase, the gramophone began to blare exultantly.

But when the last houses of the suburb had fallen behind and they were driving through the undulating, fertile country-side to southward of the city, their spirits rose. The heavy rain of the night and morning had left behind a delicious, soothing freshness. The sun-bathed fields and placid farms seemed set in an everlasting security into which they themselves were being received. The Prossips and their malice faded into childish absurdity. They were able to laugh over Uncle Richard's amorous playfulnesses. All the difficulties and anxieties which had threatened them for the past two years dwindled—receded— were left behind. They were making a new start. They had escaped.

Three miles out from Rockwood one of the aged tyres of the car punctured. Whalley gave the driver of the lorry explicit instructions as to the remainder of his somewhat complicated route and, when he had driven off, began to unfasten the two-seater's spare wheel. The tyre of the spare wheel was deflated. Investigation revealed that the rubber of its valve had perished. There was no valve-rubber in the dilapidated repair-outfit. The two-seater bumped forward slowly until, two miles further on, it reached a little roadside garage whose proprietor appeared to have never seen a punctured tyre before. Whalley kept looking at his watch. When at length they started off again in pursuit of the lorry, they were an hour and a half behind it.

Two miles further on they left the main road, twisted for another mile along deserted by-roads, and turned then into the narrow, darkling track which was their avenue. The by-road had not dried. The track was a bog. The two-seater crawled on, skidding perilously, until, at length, it reached the new gate. No lorry was in view, but a small car stood near the gate, over which a burly, unshaven elderly man was leaning, rubbing his nose with the bowl of his pipe contemplatively. When he turned, the Whalleys recognised him as Mr Denman, the Dunpool builder from whom they had bought their two acres.

'Afternoon,' he said curtly, when Whalley had alighted. 'I see you've put up a gate here, and put up two huts as well, eh? And fencing.'

His air, unexpectedly, was hostile. Whalley's reply was guarded.

'Yes, Mr Denman. You have no objection, I hope? It was agreed that I should have immediate possession.'

'Possession?' smiled Mr Denman. 'Possession, yes. But it wasn't agreed that any structure should be erected on this land, was it, until I conveyed the land to you and it was yours?'

'Well, I took it for granted—'

'Took it for granted? You've been taking a lot for granted, Mr Whalley, what I can see of it.' Mr Denman turned to the gate and pointed. 'Look here. Look at that fencing you've put up there. Who gave you permission to put that fencing up on my property? Possession or no possession, you have no right to put up anything on my property until the land has been marked off by a surveyor and the conveyance has been signed. That fencing and them huts and this gate's got to come down— that's what it comes to. And the sooner they come down the better.'

It was impossible to mollify him or to elicit the real reason of this change of front. During the negotiations of the week he had been civil and friendly, had seemed even anxious to sell the piece of land, and had raised no difficulty whatever regarding its immediate occupation. Now he was an enemy, bitterly suspicious, surly to the verge of abusiveness. He didn't want to sell the land, although, Whalley divined, he was getting an exorbitant price for it. He was sorry that he had agreed to immediate possession. He had thought he was dealing with a gentleman. The best thing would be for him to return the deposit and call the deal off.

He pointed again to the line of chestnut fencing which had offended him.

'Look at that fence,' he said. 'Where does it start from? Where does it go to? That's what I want to know.'

Vainly Whalley explained that he had, personally, measured his plot off with a chain and that, in actual fact, his fencing contained something less than the agreed-upon two acres. Mr Denman scoffed. '*You* measured it—?' He went off saying that he would see his solicitors about it, and left the Whalleys to look at one another ruefully.

They opened the gate and drove the car on to the scrubby grass inside. After a few yards it slewed violently and came to a standstill. Whalley opened the throttle until the engine roared menacingly. The back wheels spun round. He got out—got in—the engine roared—the back wheels buried themselves to their hubs. After a quarter of an hour of vain pushing and heaving, the Whalleys took two battered suitcases from the dickey and carried them up to the living-hut. The door of the hut refused for a long time to open; the rain had swollen the badly-seasoned wood. Inside there was a smell of damp earth and cresote. A snail was climbing one wall. The flooring was still muddy with the boot-marks of the workmen. They set down their suitcases and went out into the sunshine again. Whalley examined the door of the hut.

'I must get that right. And we shall have to make some sort of drive for the car. Stone it. We shall want a wheelbarrow and a sledge.'

There was no alternative but to await the now doubtful arrival of the lorry, and they made a tour of their little demesne, Whalley planning improvements as they went. At the top of the steep slope, by the huts, some young beeches and ashes and pines had survived Mr Denman's clearing operations of fourteen years before. But the greater part of their two acres was bare, burnt scrub, pocked with pine-stumps and strewn with loose stone. At the end remote from the huts was a jungle of gigantic thorn-bushes. All this would have to be tidied up, the stumps taken out, the loose stone collected and broken down for the construction of the drive, the thorn-bushes cut down. They found a large number of bottles, broken thermos flasks, fragments of crockery, and rusty tins. Evidently the place had been extensively used by picnickers; it would be necessary to put up notice boards. They came on a headless rabbit. 'Stoat,' said Whalley, and they turned and went back toward the huts.

But the view out over the valley to the silver river and the mountains beyond was even lovelier than they had believed it. They sat in the car and smoked cigarettes and looked at it until, at seven o'clock, hunger drove them down to the cottage in search of tea and eggs. But there was no one at the cottage. They returned to the car and sat there until the woods disappeared and the stars grew chilly. Then they wrapped themselves in rugs and lay down on the floor of the hut. Before they fell asleep they heard a rabbit squealing lamentably.

However, the lorry arrived early next morning and by midday the hut had been transformed to cheerful, if somewhat crowded, comfort, its door eased, the car safely garaged, and the course of the projected drive marked out. The Clapenham butcher had undertaken to supply liver, but not to deliver it. Whalley descended to the village by a sheer, tortuous path through the woods. The return journey took him half an hour. At half-past two he began to collect loose stones and carry them up the slope.

The day was sultry, perspiration streamed from his face. Elsa remonstrated, but nothing would induce him to stop. The drive must be made at once—if it rained, the car would be unusable. Each time that he went back down the slope empty-handed he looked at his watch.

After tea he hurried off down the slope again.

It rained that night. No gutters had been fitted to the huts; no one had thought of gutters. They lay awake listening to the never-ending patter and splash. 'We must get gutters,' Whalley said. 'And butts to catch the rain-water in.' Next morning he went down to the village and telephoned for their immediate delivery.

They arrived on the following day. The men were in a hurry to get off—paid, they said, only to deliver the stuff. When they had gone Whalley discovered that both butts, owing to their height, would have to be sunk some four feet, and set to work upon this task at once. It was a tremendous business. An inch below the turf was solid rock, which had to be broken out, piece by piece, with a pick and a crowbar. As the narrow hole deepened the movements of the tools became more and more circumscribed. It took him five days to get the two butts into position.

The butts and the gutters had cost him another eight pounds. But when they got things into some sort of order, he would set to work on the novel. Money did not seem to matter at all out there, under the sky all day long, with the wind blowing one's thoughts away . . .

The days flew by. There was always something to do—he was always rushed for time. There was the water to get from the cottage—two trips of half a mile each. Three times a week he went into Rockwood for supplies; that took up the whole morning. There were interviews with his solicitor about Mr Denman, who still refused to sign the conveyance and insisted that that fence began nowhere and went nowhere. It took a whole day to stone three yards of the drive thoroughly—lay the stones—break them down—pound them in—level them neatly.

Of course he had to take a breather every few minutes. And the sledge was a bit too heavy for him. Still, it took a deuce of a time . . .

It was a long hot walk to the village and back. The Clapenham butcher, finding that his new customer did not call for liver regularly, ceased to keep it for him regularly. Elsa grew uneasy and bribed an elderly drunkard from the village to bring it up each morning. Invariably he arrived an hour late and disorganised the remainder of Whalley's day.

She, too, was busy all day long, and, on the whole, happy, except when she thought of the flat and its deserted rooms. No prospective tenant had yet applied for an order to view, the house-agent reported. She could not always help hoping that none would. No one else would understand her things . . .

By-and-by she would make a little garden—wire it in, on account of the rabbits—grow roses for the hut. And by-and-by they must have daffodils in the grass—perhaps by the spring after next.

Bogey-Bogey, too, was happy, though, because of the adders, he was not permitted to escape from sight. However, there were always the rabbits that were not there, and the dog that had passed the gate three weeks ago . . .

The days flew. Whalley began work at five o'clock. They had been out there a whole month and practically nothing had been done. The thorns had still to be cut down, the pine-stumps uprooted, the ashes thinned. The drive had to have a second coating of stone—the first had sunk in. Paths would have to be stoned round the huts; in wet weather the place was a quagmire. The huts would want another coat of creosote. Elsa's garden must be fenced and dug. Those gaps in the hedge must be wired. But by the middle of August everything ought to be pretty shipshape. Two months would finish the novel, once one could settle down to it, knowing there was no job to be done.

They never saw a newspaper. At first, friends of Elsa's drove out to inspect the encampment; but Whalley disliked being caught in his old working-clothes, and Elsa ceased to encourage visitors. They heard no news. The world trembled around them. Elsa went on cooking liver, and Whalley went on breaking stones.

Mr Denman had been worried about things for a long time back. The caving-in of the building boom had left him with a lot of land and empty houses on his hands. There was a lump in his throat which his doctor thought ought to come out. His wife had been nagging at him to buy a new car. And he had had a good deal of trouble with his men since the Labour Government had come into office. One day, towards the end of August, after eating a hearty dinner, he went up on to the roof of his own house and jumped off it, head first. Curiously enough, the last thing he did before eating his last dinner was to sign the conveyance of the Whalleys' piece of land. Whalley paid the balance of forty-six pounds to the executors. He had now a little over nine hundred pounds.

CHAPTER V

1

TOWARDS the end of August Mr Knayle began to sing in his bath and hum as he moved about his flat. He had no voice and no ear and he had never learnt the whole of any one tune in his life. His humming began to get on Hopgood's nerves. In the morning Hopgood sometimes glanced at the bathroom door with one eyebrow cocked, as he passed, and muttered, 'My God . . .'

Mr Knayle had begun to find it quite difficult not to worry about things. He continued to scoff amiably at the gloomy predictions of his friends and had cultivated for their benefit a brisk brightness of air and voice which was at times a little aggressive. But things certainly did look queer. Snowden's speech about the Budget—the May Report—Germany on the verge of another crash—France crowing, America draining our gold away—the Socialists threatening all sorts of insanities—three million unemployed—trade at a standstill—a nigger in a loin-cloth kicking us out of India. The *Morning Post* was no longer a pleasant, comfortable accompaniment to eggs and bacon. Mr Knayle read it with puckered brow and sometimes forgot about his eggs and bacon altogether. There was no doubt about it, everything was in an appalling mess. No one seemed to be able to do anything about it; everyone seemed to be trying their hardest to make the mess worse. Mr Knayle gulped down his chilled coffee and hummed a little tune of his own, took the *Morning Post* into the sitting-room to re-read the money article. He sat now with his back to the sitting-room windows; he had not looked out through them for weeks.

Then there was the noise of the traffic. All day long the cars and the 'buses and the char-a-bancs and the motor-cycles swished and banged and hooted past the front-garden gates. Mr Knayle grew very tired of them. The traffic in Downview Road increased every summer. He regretted acutely that he had agreed to renew the tenancy of his flat, although the reason why he had done so remained part of that moment of rapturous wonder. Next year the noise would be perfectly unbearable. He would have to leave.

He had grown very tired of the Downs, too. All day long they were covered with family parties from the east end of the city, who littered them with papers, bottles, abandoned food, orange peel, and empty cigarette-packets. Swarms of children shrieked and shouted. Bands of young hooligans slogged cricket-balls and threw stones, bawling indecencies, easing themselves publicly. After dusk every bush and every dip in the ground held a prostrate couple; the Downs became a brothel. Sinister, mad-eyed creatures prowled, watching. Save in the early morning, Mr Knayle never walked on the Downs now. Even then they were strewn with paper and haunted by prowlers questing in the hollows and under the bushes. This year no attempt had been made to collect the litter. The mounted police, who had formerly patrolled with vigilant regularity, were now seldom seen and, when seen, saw nothing. Seats were smashed, branches of trees broken off. Mr Knayle had seen one day a respectable elderly man tear a whole newspaper into flitters and scatter the pieces deliberately along one of the paths. No one had seemed surprised. He was concerned by all this; things had got curiously lax. Formerly the Downs had been a peaceful, orderly pleasaunce; their complete surrender to the proletariat perturbed him. The proletariat were, in the main, quite good, decent people, but he preferred them in their own place. Lately, it seemed to him, they had been allowed to get out of it. And, unfortunately, it looked now as if they were never going to be put back into it. There were too many of them. In twenty—perhaps ten—years there would be only one place, and they would have it. They knew it. Mr Knayle had seen the eyes of the picnickers on the Downs looking at him curiously—expectantly—with amusement. And one afternoon four young louts, walking abreast along one of the paths, had elbowed him off it, and, when he had looked at them in reproof, had made obscene noises at him. This had upset him a good deal.

Then there was Chidgey. It had been necessary to speak sharply to Chidgey about the Prossips' maid. Mr Knayle had happened to require his car late one night and, when he had gone round to his garage, had come on Chidgey and the Prossips' maid sitting in the car, smoking cigarettes. The car had not been running at all well lately, and sometimes had not been cleaned. Chidgey had been rather impertinent when spoken to, and would probably have to be dismissed.

A number of his friends had died during the past twelve months—one of them had shot himself in a public lavatory in Dunpool at the beginning of August. Also, some of his July dividends had been seriously reduced this year; three of them had been passed. He had sold his two hunters and had decided not to go abroad. Although he had felt no least inclination to go abroad this year, this departure from the habit of twenty-five summers had been upsetting. For the first time in his life he had had to consider seriously the spending of money and refrain from doing something which he considered himself entitled to do. This year many of his friends had not gone away for the summer. But he found people of his own age preoccupied now and, somehow, flattened—their young folk inanely boisterous. An afternoon party at the Edwarde-Lewins' had developed suddenly into a pillow-fight, in the course of which Edwarde-Lewin's youngest girl had assaulted him with maniacal violence and broken his dental plate. Everyone—Edwarde-Lewin and his wife included—had screamed with delight as he had extracted the broken pieces of the plate. Since this episode he had spent most of his time in his flat, reading desultorily and thinking about things. The club was deserted. The men who dropped in to see him all said the same old gloomy things; he did not press them to stay.

He read a number of depressing books about Russia, and, in an omnibus volume dealing with recent movements in scientific thought, he came on things called hormones and four-dimensional continuums which somehow made it seem quite an unimportant thing to be a Knayle.

After some weeks of this seclusion he made three discoveries. He was getting old. He didn't matter in the least to anyone. And there was nothing whatever he wanted to go on living for. It was about this time that he began to sing in his bath and hum as he moved from room to room. And for some little time he took a vegetable laxative every second night.

Despite the noise of the traffic the house was extraordinarily quiet. Since the departure of the Whalleys the gramophone had not played; Miss Prossip's violin practice had dwindled to an odd half-hour. No sound whatever rose from Mr Ridgeway's flat. Mr Knayle was undisturbed—save by the silence over his head.

Sometimes he thought he heard footsteps moving about up there, and listened. The silence became very loud then, until, gradually, the noise of the traffic blotted it out and, gradually, Mr Knayle's eyes returned to his book.

Oddly, he always pictured her up there—never in her new surroundings, though with these he was in some measure familiar.

Shortly after his return from Wales he had met Mrs Canynge and had learned that the Whalleys were living in a hut out at Camphill. He had shot over Camphill many times before the war, and had often lunched, he believed, on the very slope on which their piece of land lay. Sometimes he was tempted to run out there. But the distance was just too great—the place itself just too isolated; an uninvited visit would seem, not a casual friendliness, but a deliberate intrusion. After all, his acquaintance with Whalley was very slight. And, after all, what was the use? They wanted to be alone. They were probably quite happy out there, with one another. Probably she had never even thought of him since she had left Downview Road. The temptation always faded into the most depressing of his three discoveries. He didn't matter in the least to anyone.

He joined a flying-club and in a fortnight became an expert if somewhat reckless pilot. One of his first solo flights took him over the little enclosure at Camphill, and he saw the Whalleys erecting a fence of wire netting round a patch of freshly-dug ground. They were absorbed in their work and did not raise their eyes towards the plane, though it was flying so low that Mr Knayle could see a bundle of small shrubs lying on the ground close to them.

He met Mr Prossip in the garden on the last day of August and learned that Mrs Prossip had had a rather bad heart-attack on the preceding afternoon while ascending the outside staircase.

'We shall have to leave that damned flat,' said Mr Prossip. 'Those cursed steps are too much for her. I told her all along that they would be. But you can't argue with my wife. She's as obstinate as a mule. She's got angina, you know. Not the ordinary angina, but something—I forget the damn name. *I* shan't be sorry to get out of that rabbit-hutch up there. I've lived in dignified houses all my life. I can't stand these pokey little flats. Fact is, that flat up there's got on my nerves since this infernal row with the Whalleys. This whole place has got on my nerves. Why, my God, you never see a man in Rockwood dressed like a gentleman now. Present company excepted, of course. But you know what I mean. I want to get somewhere near London— not in London—but somewhere you can run up from in half an hour when you feel like it. What I have in my mind is one of those good-class residential hotels—sort of place where you'll come across decent people and see a bit of stir and life. You know the sort of thing I mean . . .'

Mr Knayle disliked Mr Prossip—had disliked all the Prossips so acutely since the flight of the Whalleys that he had taken pains to avoid meeting them. But, as he looked at Mr Prossip's twitching lips and glaring eyes (the beggar reeked of it—at ten o'clock in the morning) an idea occurred to him, and he became brightly helpful. He knew exactly the sort of thing Mr Prossip wanted and thought that he knew where Mr Prossip could find it. Some friends of his had spent part of the preceding winter at a delightful residential hotel outside Guildford, run by an aged naval officer and his wife, and had found it very gay and smart and comfortable. At the moment Mr Knayle could not recall the exact name of the place, but, at Mr Prossip's request, undertook to procure it without delay.

'Reason I'm in such a hurry, ole chap,' explained Mr Prossip, patting him on the shoulder, 'is that I'm afraid the Missus'll try to rush me into another flat here in Rockwood. I've had enough of Rockwood, and enough of flats. Lucky I only took this one for a year. I'll have it on my hands for the balance of the term, of course; but I'd pay twice the money to get out of it. You'll let me have that address, then, Knayle? Right. I'll run up and take a squint at the place.'

2

About a fortnight later Mr Knayle went down the little flight of steps leading to Mr Ridgeway's hall-door, one afternoon after lunch, and rang the bell. Since that early morning handshake of two months back, they had not met half a dozen times and had never stopped to speak. But Mr Knayle had news which, as he ate his cutlets, he had decided Mr Ridgeway should share.

After a prolonged delay Mr Ridgeway, collarless and wearing his seedy old dressing-gown, opened the door, yawning.

'Oh,' he said. 'I thought it was the laundry. Hope you haven't been ringing long. My char goes at one. I was asleep. Come in.'

Mr Knayle followed him into a dark, untidy sitting-room, apologising for his intrusion.

'I thought it might interest you to hear that the Prossips are leaving,' he explained. 'They're going to Guildford, I believe, in a very few weeks.'

Mr Ridgeway yawned.

'Oh yes,' he said. 'Sit down.'

'No, no, thank you,' said Mr Knayle. 'As a matter of fact I'm going out to Camphill—the Whalleys are living out there, you know—to tell them about it. I don't know what their plans are, of course, but I don't suppose they contemplate spending the winter out there. It's a bleak place, and they've only got a wooden hut. I should think they'll be very glad to come back to a comfortable flat in October.'

'Oh, yes,' yawned Mr Ridgeway again. 'Do sit down.'

Mr Knayle sat down. 'I wondered if you'd care to run out there with me this afternoon and see them. It's quite a pretty run. We can get back easily before five.'

A little flush spread over Mr Ridgeway's sagging cheeks. His tired eyes brightened. He made an effort to subdue the excited eagerness of his voice.

'That's very kind of you, Knayle. Very kind of you indeed to have thought of it. When do you want to start? Now? I shall have to change. I shall have to shave. Can you wait?' He hurried out of the room, peeling off his dressing-gown as he went.

Mr Knayle lighted a cigarette and waited for half an hour, smiling sometimes as he looked round the comfortless, shabbily-furnished room. On a dusty table lay some dusty newspapers and after some time he strayed over and, picking one up, saw that it was an old number of the *British Medical Journal.* A cutting had been made from one of the pages which lay open. A little surprised by Mr Ridgeway's taste in literature, he returned to his chair and continued to wait until Mr Ridgeway reappeared, freshly shaven, resplendent in a light-grey suit smelling strongly of naphthalene, and ten years younger.

Curiously, as he re-entered the room, his eyes went first to the table on which the newspapers lay—a little uneasily, Mr Knayle fancied. But he hurried on to an aged escritoire and picked up a small brown-paper parcel which lay on it, then put it down again.

'No,' he said. 'I won't bother about that. Some books which Mrs Whalley lent me. I had thought of taking them out to her. But if they're coming back to their flat . . . I shan't want gloves, shall I? Perhaps I had better take them. I must say, Knayle, it's extremely kind of you to have thought of it. No. I won't take gloves. Does this suit look very creased? I haven't worn it for eleven—for some years.'

They were very gay as they drove along in the sunshine. They had bought a large box of chocolates and some illustrated newspapers in Rockwood and Mr Ridgeway held these tightly in his gloved hands—he had decided, after all, to bring his gloves—while his eyes remained fixed on the furthest visible point of the road. Mr Knayle began several little things of his own but was too happy to finish any of them.

Half-way along the track through the woods, they met a rough-looking fellow with a couple of terriers, and stopped to enquire the exact position of the Whalleys' huts.

''Bout a mile on, sir—right at the end of this track. I just been down there now, helping Mr Whalley to look for his dog. It got lost last night. So when I heard about it this morning I thought I'd go down and give them a hand to look for it with these two dogs of mine.'

'You found it, I hope?' Mr Knayle asked. 'I know that Mrs Whalley sets great store by that little cocker of hers.'

'Yes, we found it all right,' said the man. 'The dogs found it in the wood. It was dead, though. Must have gone for a stoat, I reckon. Its head was et off. The gen'lman and me just buried it near their huts—where it used to sit, the lady said. She's in a bad way about it.'

With considerable difficulty, Mr Knayle turned the car round and drove back to Rockwood. He took Mr Ridgeway into his flat and there, over a whisky and soda, they composed a telegram to a well-known dog-breeder at Whanton.

'Wanted immediately, handsome thorough-bred male black cocker dog, 10 mos. over distemper; write tonight sending photos if possible, go to twenty guineas.—Knayle, 47 Downview Road, Rockwood.'

Mr Knayle perused his draft. 'I wonder,' he mused. 'Perhaps we had better wait a little.'

'They won't stay out there now,' said Mr Ridgeway.

'I don't know about that. Perhaps they will stay out there—now.'

They discussed the matter for a little while over another whisky and soda and finally the draft was torn up. When Mr Ridgeway went away, Mr Knayle opened the windows of the sitting-room to let out the smell of naphthalene and his eyes fell on the garden path. To his horror, he had a vision of a little black satin-coated thing. He turned away from the windows, humming and poured himself out another little whisky.

No. She wouldn't come back now—she'd stay out there. Of course old Ridgeway couldn't understand that. Funny old beggar, Ridgeway. Quite badly cut up about the dog. Must be five or six and fifty. Rather amusing, this subterranean tendresse of his. She had been lending him books, then. What on earth did he do down there all day? Funny to think of him sitting down there, in that filthy old dressing-gown of his—thinking about her. Thinking what about her? For that matter, what did one think, oneself, about her? Anyhow, what did anything matter? She would stay out there, now.

Mr Knayle finished his drink and went off to the ærodrome.

Mr Ridgeway let himself into his flat and, without stopping to take off his hat, entered his sitting-room and went straight to the table on which the newspapers lay. He stood looking down at them, frowning; he was almost certain that there was some slight change in the position of the *BMJ*, although the two *Lancet*s appeared not to have been disturbed. Every day for two months now, he had intended to get rid of them; but they had continued to lie there, so long that now the slightest alteration in their appearance would, of course, catch his eyes at once. Some slight alteration had caught his eye, when he had returned to Knayle, after changing, he had noticed it immediately he had entered the room. Knayle must have moved the *BMJ*. Probably he had looked about for something to read while he waited, and had seen the newspapers.

But, after all, Knayle would think nothing about it. He was not that sort. He might have been a little surprised to find medical journals lying about; but he would think nothing about it—forget it at once. A curious, jumpy little chap. Never spoke two sentences about the same thing—kept changing the subject. Not a bad sort of little chap in his way. Cut up about the dog. Rather annoying, that way he had of smiling when he spoke about her, as if he knew something about her that no one else knew. No. He would think nothing about the papers. There was nothing to be uneasy about. They must be got rid of, though—taken out and put in the rubbish-bin. It was only a few yards away. But not now. Presently. There was plenty of time.

A filthy business about the dog. Everything ended that way. In the end the stoat pulled you down . . .

She'd never stay out there now. Of course, Knayle couldn't understand. A funny, insensitive little chap—limited—probably had never suffered anything worse than a toothache in his life. Two false teeth; his plate wobbled sometimes. But she'd never stay out there now; she'd come back. And when she did, it must be done. It must be got over. She must be told.

Presently Mr Ridgeway took off his grey suit and put it away in a travelling trunk, packing its folds with naphthalene balls. Then he went back to his sitting-room and lay down on the sofa in his old dressing-gown, covering his face with his handkerchief.

3

He had left them. They had been working in the dusk, finishing the fencing round Elsa's garden, and had not seen him go. Something had called him—perhaps that enemy which his liquid eyes had watched so long. He had been found quite a long way off in the woods. He had left them—that was the worst bitterness of it.

He was gone; no trace of him was left. Everything that had belonged to him—his basket, his pillows and cushions, his collar and lead, his two dishes, his brush and comb, his ball—had been buried with him. He might never have been.

And yet they had never been so aware of him, never seen him so vividly. He was always lying there, near the door of the hut, watching, listening, sometimes scratching his ear, wagging his tail when one or other of them passed near and chirruped to him or said, 'Hullo, old chap,'—too busy to stop. It would have been so easy to stop and pat his little satiny head, throw his ball for him, make a fuss of him for a moment or two. But there had been so many other things to do.

It would pass. They decided not to speak of him and found that there was nothing else to speak about. The little enclosure had become intolerably desolate. There was no spot in it, however bare, from which something had not gone for ever— save the jungle of thorn-bushes at its further end. This had always been forbidden territory for Bogey-Bogey, and after supper, now, they took two camp-chairs up there and sat, waiting until it was time to go to bed.

One evening in the second week of September Whalley decided to cut down the thorns and, having procured a bill-hook from the garage, set about this formidable task forthwith, Elsa aiding him to withdraw the severed tendrils after each sweep of the hook. Considerable force was necessary to free them and their hands suffered severely. Ultimately they decided to postpone the work until hedging-gloves had been procured from the village stores.

Two days later Elsa complained of slight pain in the centre of her right hand. They examined the hand, somewhat perfunctorily, extracted several thorns with a needle, but could find none at the painful spot, which, however, looked a little angry. She washed the floor of the hut that day and, growing accustomed to the slight discomfort, thought no more of the matter until the following morning when, on awakening, she saw that the hand had swollen noticeably. They painted it with iodine, but by evening it had swollen so much that it seemed incredible that so ungainly and shapeless a thing should belong to her fine slenderness. They walked down to the village and interviewed a harassed elderly doctor whose telephone bell rang three times while he examined the hand with grubby fingers, recommended hot fomentations, made up a little package of boracic powder, and got rid of them with the assurance that there was nothing whatever to worry about. Elsa passed a feverish night and was awakened by shooting pains in her right arm, which had also begun to swell.

Whalley grew a little uneasy. The village doctor had assured them that, at that time of the year, swollen hands were as common in the neighbourhood as blackberries. It seemed, however, prudent to have the hand inspected by less cursory eyes and, after lunch they drove into Rockwood and had a suddenly disquieting talk with the kindly practitioner who had attended Whalley during his own illness. Mrs Whalley would have to go into a nursing-home at once. A small operation—probably with a local anæsthetic, merely would be necessary. There was no need to be unduly alarmed. But the matter was serious; the hand ought to have been attended to at the first symptom of trouble.

Over his telephone the doctor arranged with a nursing-home, while the Whalleys, in a hurried undertone, strove to adjust their plans to the practical necessities of the moment. He hung up the receiver and turned to them again. 'Yes, Mrs Whalley, Mr Hilton can operate at three o'clock. He is at the home now

and would like to see you.' They embraced in the hall of the
nursing-home under the placid, interested eyes of the matron,
and Whalley scurried back to Camphill to pack the two battered
suitcases. When, towards five o'clock, he reached the home
again, he was shown into the matron's room. The placid, capa-
ble-looking woman looked up from her tea-tray and rose,
brushing a crumb from her lower lip.

'Well?' he asked hurriedly. 'Is the operation over?'

She laid a podgy hand on his sleeve.

'Yes, Mr Whalley. Mr Hilton operated at three. But—you will
be very brave, won't you—Mr Hilton and Mr Carruthers decided
at once that it would be necessary to amputate the arm.'

He stared at her speechlessly. Amputate—cut off Elsa's arm
. . . Elsa without an arm? Christ. What had this woman said?
What had they done to her?

'Sit down for a moment,' the matron advised. 'Perhaps you
would like something? Naturally, it is a great shock for you. But
it was absolutely necessary. The operation has been most satisfactory. Mrs Whalley was very plucky. She's still asleep, of
course. Oh, her things are in that suitcase, I suppose?'

Most satisfactory . . .

'When can I see her?' he asked at length.

'Well, perhaps you will ring up in the morning. We shall be
able to judge better then. Are you on the telephone, in case—?
No? Very well, then, you'll ring up in the morning. Good afternoon, Mr Whalley, I'm so very sorry.'

The matron went back to her tray. She was a kindly woman
and she was sorry for the plucky little thing in No. 14—just as
she was sorry for the cancer case in No. 13 and the tetanus case
in No. 15. But, one way or another—as probationer, nurse,
theatre sister, and matron—she had had thirty years of it now.
And, really, if one allowed oneself to think of patients as anything
else—a little to her annoyance, she discovered that her tea had
grown too strong and that the hot water was tepid.

*

From the little hotel at which he had engaged a bedroom Whalley rang up Mr Loxton's house. Mr Loxton, however, was in Belgium, on business, and was not expected to return for some days. The Canynges were in Scotland; he sent off a wire to Mrs Canynge and then rang up the nursing-home. 'Mrs Whalley is going on quite satisfactorily,' a cheerful voice informed him, and then changed its tone. 'Oh, Nurse White, Matron wants clean sheets in number 4.'

At ten o'clock he rang up again and received the same reply. The dreary smoke-room of the hotel was lighted by a single whistling gas-jet and reeked with the cigars of two commercial travellers who eyed his restless silence with suspicion as they talked knowingly. A little after eleven he went out, and after some aimless wandering made his way to the nursing-home.

It was past midnight. The quiet street was already asleep, save for the lighted windows of the home. Outside it waited half a dozen big cars, whose chauffeurs dozed in their seats or read their evening newspapers by the light of a headlamp. 'Say, Bill—what's this yere gold standard they're makin' such a fuss about?' one asked. Whalley stood, looking up at the windows, for a little time, wondering which was hers. Was she awake? Was she in pain? Was she safe? Had they finished with her? Her arm—Good God, what had become of it—her arm that had strained him to her—he caught at the railings to steady himself. The chauffeurs looked at him with a grin.

Two doctors came down the steps, laughing. '"Oh, no," she said. "But it's the first by my second husband."' Whalley went back to his hotel to lie awake all night, listening to the gurgling of the cistern in the lavatory next door.

The matron was grave next morning. Another operation had been necessary. Mrs Whalley was unconscious; but Mr Hilton hoped that everything would be all right. No. It was out of the question that he should see her. But would he leave the telephone number of the hotel?

He was lying on the still unmade bed towards midday when

the boots came to summon him to the telephone. The matron's placid, capable voice answered his curt 'Whalley speaking.'

'I'm afraid I have very terrible news for you, Mr Whalley. Your wife died a few minutes ago. She never recovered consciousness. She had no pain. I'm very sorry. Will you come?'

He heard someone's voice say, 'Yes. I'll go.'

CHAPTER VI

1

Mr Knayle heard the news that afternoon on his way to play bridge at the Grevilles'. As he passed the Canynges' house, Mrs Canynge, emerging from them in a sporting two-seater, all but ran him down. She pulled up with screaming brakes and leaned out to him as he approached the car.

'Have you heard, Harvey? Elsa is dead.'

'Dead?' he repeated, watching her dab her eyes with her handkerchief.

She blubbered for a little space while he patted her hand vaguely. There was no trace of sisterhood with Elsa in her full, rather heavy face; she was a Loxton. He had never liked her very much, and he knew that she and her husband had been jealous of Elsa before her marriage, frigid towards her after it. She looked very plain when she blubbered, he reflected. Blubbering was the only word for it. He could think of nothing to say, could feel nothing but impatience for further information. How long would she consider it necessary to go on blubbering? He wouldn't say, 'Good God,' or 'My God,' or repeat 'Dead?' He mustn't think of the shock to himself—of what he himself was thinking. He must think that *she* was dead and feel terribly sorry for her—because she was dead. 'Good God!' he said at length. 'Dead?'

'She died this morning in St Margaret's nursing-home,' sobbed Mrs Canynge. 'I—I haven't been kind to her—since her marriage, Harvey. I shall never forgive myself.'

Thinking of herself. 'But what happened? A motoring accident?'

'No. She got a thorn in her hand—out at that dreadful place.

118

She must have neglected it. They took off her arm—but it was too late. Oh—'

'Good God.'

Another 'Good God.' She was dead and he could only say 'Good God.' And now he was thinking about himself again and what he could say and couldn't say.

Mrs Canynge blew her nose and dropped her handkerchief to the level of her nose, holding it ready, and looking at him over it. 'Harold and I were in Scotland. We only got back an hour ago—we've heard practically nothing yet. I'm so stunned that I don't know what I'm saying or doing. Poor darling. Unlucky thing. What an ending—no one with her—no one she loved—no one who loved her. They've taken her to the mortuary chapel at St Jude's. Oh, it's too perfectly ghastly. Well—now I have to go and get things—'

'Where is Whalley? In Rockwood?'

'Yes. I haven't seen him. I don't want to see him. He's staying at an appalling little hotel—the something-or-other Arms, in one of those little side-streets off the Mall. Can you believe it, Harvey—he refused to see us when we went there. Refused point-blank to see us. When we sent up a message to ask when the funeral would be, he sent down a note saying that there would be no funeral—that she would be cremated and her ashes scattered out at that awful place he took her to at Camphill. Uncle Richard is perfectly furious. Harold got him on the 'phone. He's coming back at once from Brussels by air. I needn't tell you that we won't hear of any ghastly mummery of that sort. I must go now. Good-bye, Harvey. You've been just sweet to me.'

Mr Knayle went on slowly towards the Grevilles' house. The road was a very quiet one; the few big houses whose grounds bordered it were concealed from view by tall trees, already turning to gold and russet. There was no one in sight. He stopped, bowed his head, and covered his eyes with his hands.

'My dear. My poor, lovely little dear—'

His hand dropped and he raised his eyes. It was a mild, yet crisp, afternoon, the shrubberies had a pungent, faintly musty smell; the first gentle melancholy of autumn was in the air. She had always been fond of trees, and she would never see the autumn tints again. No funeral. He was glad of that. She had been light as air. The air would bear her up for ever.

He went on to the Grevilles' and won thirty shillings—he was very punctilious regarding the keeping of engagements. On his homeward journey he called at Whalley's hotel to leave a card of sympathy. A portly, melancholy man, whom he recognised as Rockwood's most select undertaker, saluted him in the fusty little hall. From him he learned that the ceremony at the crematorium would take place on the following morning. Then he went to a florist's.

'I want,' he said, 'all the jolliest, gayest, brightest flowers you have in the shop.'

He was on foot that afternoon, because his car had developed gear-box trouble and had gone into a garage for repair that morning. On his way to Downview Road he met a number of people to whom he told his news. They were horrified, shocked, grieved or interested for a moment or two and then, in most cases, had some other Rockwood calamity to tell him about, connected with themselves or their friends By the time he reached his flat his news was old for him and dulled by other peoples' woes; she had been dead a long time. He didn't want to tell anyone else about it. Chidgey was waiting at the flat with the report that the car would not available for three days; two pinions would have to be replaced. He was short with Chidgey about this.

When Hopgood brought him tea he told him about it. Hopgood said, 'Dead, sir? Good God.' And, after a moment, 'Major Turill rang up to know if you'd play golf with him tomorrow morning at Dobury. Have you everything you require, sir?'

Hopgood told Chidgey, and Chidgey said, 'Dead? Gawd.'

As Chidgey went away he found the Prossips' maid emptying a bucket into one of the rubbish-bins and told her. She said, 'Dead? Go on. You're kiddin'.' The Prossips were packing and Mr Prossip was busy nailing down a packing-case when she told him. He said, 'Dead? Well, I'm damned.' And sucked one of his thumbs which a nail had torn slightly a few minutes before. 'Better put some iodine on that,' he decided, frowning uneasily. 'Bring me the bottle from my wash-stand, will you.'

After tea Mr Knayle went down and told Mr Ridgeway about it. Mr Ridgeway threw back his head and laughed with savage sharpness, and then sat down on his old sofa and said nothing for a long time.

'I took the liberty of putting your name with mine on the card which will go with some flowers to the mortuary-chapel,' Mr Knayle said at last. 'I thought that perhaps you'd like to send some flowers.'

'I'm sorry you did that, Knayle,' said Mr Ridgeway unexpectedly. 'It was kind of you to think of doing it. But I'm sorry you did it.'

'Why?' asked Mr Knayle reasonably.

'Well—simply because my name isn't Ridgeway.'

He pointed to the little table on which the dusty newspapers lay.

'When you were alone here—that afternoon we went out to Camphill—you picked up one of those newspapers, didn't you?'

'I believe I did,' Mr Knayle admitted, rather taken aback.

'Perhaps you were a little surprised to find that it was a medical journal?'

'I believe I was. Though—forgive me—are you a medical man?'

Mr Ridgeway nodded, then looked straight before him, producing phrases in little harsh, staccato chunks. 'My real name is Winsley. I had a very large practice in Manchester. I don't know why I'm telling you this. Or, yes—I do know— though you wouldn't understand in the least. You see—I always intended to tell her. I got into trouble—oh, it's a long time ago now. Eleven years ago. A woman, of course—a woman I cared nothing about—a good, stupid poor creature. I lost my head—performed an operation—and she died. They struck me off the register, of course, and I went to gaol for two years. No. It was simply a rotten, silly, ugly business. All my own fault. You needn't try to say anything polite. But I always meant to tell her. The first day I saw her—the day she and her husband came with you to look at the flat upstairs. I met you in the garden—but you don't remember. She smiled at me—and I knew then that there was someone in the world I could tell about it and who could wipe it away—clean me of it—forgive me for it. I see you don't understand. But I see you're trying to understand. You were fond of her, weren't you?'

'Yes,' said Mr Knayle. 'I was very fond of her.'

'I always meant to tell her. I hated that she should speak to me and smile at me and not know. Well—that's why I wish you hadn't put Ridgeway on that card. However, it was very kind of you to think of it. There is to be no funeral, you say? Hell! I'm thinking that I should have had to buy a silk hat. Are you going away now?'

Mr Knayle was not even faintly surprised to find that he was not in the least shocked. He simply noted the fact: illegal operation—prison. Two months ago he would have been horrified to have found himself in the sitting-room of a man who had performed an illegal operation, talking to him intimately. But in that short space of time his whole outlook had altered—humbled itself. He was no longer a spectator, aloof and safe. Life had tapped him on the shoulder and told him that all kinds of queer things might, and probably would, happen to him. He had pictured himself scrambling for a place in a food-queue, for example—fighting for it with athletic young louts like those who had pushed him off the path that day. The things that happened in life had become imminent and acutely interesting. He was acutely interested in the fact that Mr Ridgeway's hands had performed an illegal operation. He found himself looking at Mr Ridgeway with something that was almost respect, as a man who had passed through dangerous and desperate experiences. And this strange desire to confess to her—that was very interesting. So that was what he had been thinking about her, down there . . .

'No, no,' he said. 'I'll stay and smoke one of your cigarettes, if I may. Yes. I was very fond of her. I knew her when she was so high. Better still—let's go along and change that card.'

2

The news had spread quickly through Rockwood and next morning the little mortuary chapel was smothered in flowers. A theatrical young curate declaimed some prayers; the undertaker's men shouldered their burden. Whalley watched them put it into the motor-hearse and deck it carefully with the largest and most ornate wreaths and crosses. He got into the car which waited behind the hearse and, to the horror of the undertaker and his aides, lighted a cigarette. The two vehicles drove off into the morning mist, followed by the disapproving eyes of the curate, whose attempts at fraternal consolation had been received with a blank stare. Mr Knayle and Mr Ridgeway, too, lighted cigarettes and went home to breakfast.

The crematorium lay four miles away, at the further side of the city. As the little cortège descended from Rockwood it was swallowed up in a dense fog. The houses and streets disappeared; it moved on slowly, interminably, noiselessly, through a world of dirty cotton-wool. Glaring eyes appeared—hooted or clanged, angrily disappeared. The air in the big limousine smelt of countless deaths. Would it never end? Would she never have done with it?

They were stopping at last. A pillared façade looked out of the fog. The undertaker opened the door of the car commandingly and he got out, followed up the steps. The undertaker's men had her—she was their business, their property. He followed, an unimportant detail of their solemn, high-class interment ritual. If he rushed at them and tried to wrest their burden from them, they would push him off for a madman—never dreaming that they were mad.

What was this cold, ugly, pitiless place? Half an imitation temple, half a Turkish bath, with a few shrubs in pots. They were putting her on a kind of little altar now, shaped like one of those high tombs one saw in old country graveyards. Now they were covering her with a purple cloth with a white cross—arranging it very carefully. They were going away from her now—they had finished their business with her.

The purple cloth was moving—it was going down, very slowly—terribly slowly—terribly silently. It had stopped now—it lay flat. But she had gone on. Where? To what?

He sprang up from his knees with a strangled cry. They took him out into the fog and put him into the limousine and waited at its door until he lighted another cigarette. They left him then, silently.

The undertaker was at the door again, carrying something—exhibiting it. 'The casket, sir. Where shall I say?'

'To Camphill.'

'Camphill? Very well, sir. I trust that everything has been to your satisfaction? Good morning.'

The fog had thickened and settled down for the day. Out at Camphill everything was lost in muffled blindness. He opened the gate and went in, undecided still, strayed forward, lost his bearings and stumbled into the incinerator. He strayed on, still undecided. Her garden? But no. The wire netting would shut her in. What did it matter where, so long as she was free?

The undertaker's car had set him down at the head of the track and returned to Rockwood. When he had burnt the casket, he made his way to the hut, which his hasty packing of the suit-cases had left in disorder. The clock had stopped; he wound it up and then attempted to sweep some clothes from a deck-chair. A gigantic hammer fell very softly upon his head and he pitched forward, pulling down the chair with him.

3

Next morning Mr Knayle called at the little hotel behind the Mall and, having learned that Whalley had not returned there since the preceding morning, decided to hire a taxi and drive out to Camphill. He found Whalley lying where he had fallen and brought him back to his flat.

For two days he lay in Mr Knayle's bed, in a suit of Mr Knayle's pyjamas, sometimes rambling, sometimes groping to the edge of consciousness, but slipping back always into a motionless stupor. There was not a great deal to be done. But Mr Knayle was curiously happy sitting hour after hour by his bed, interrupting his reading now and then to rearrange the bed-clothes or stir the fire very softly. Sometimes, when the doctor had gone away, Mr Ridgeway came up, lifted one of the patient's eyelids and felt his pulse, and then sat down by the fire with a newspaper for a little while.

They were sitting there together on the third morning when the gramophone began to play. The sound was very faint, barely audible above the rustle of the newspaper and the gentle crackle of the fire, and they went on reading until an abrupt movement behind them turned their heads towards the bed. Whalley had raised himself on an elbow and was listening.

The two men glanced at one another and then rose hurriedly.

'It's all right, old chap,' said Mr Knayle. 'They're leaving today, damn them. Don't trouble about it. Come on—lie down. That's it—that's it.'

Agatha Judd, very smart in a bowler and a long black coat which accentuated the curves of her now, she feared, not so slim figure, stood in the passage of the top flat, waiting for the taxi which was to carry her and her trunk to her new situation. Her face was flushed beneath its powder, her breathing was quick, and one toe tapped the passage-carpet. She had just told Ma Prossip what she thought about her bed. But she had forgotten a lot of things.

Her eyes fell upon the gramophone. It had not been played for several weeks and Mr Prossip had strictly forbidden that it should be played. Well, just to annoy the old rotter, she would play it before she went.

Mr Prossip heard the gramophone while he was taking off his plus-fours and, as soon as he could button up his trousers— his hands were always slippery and fumbling now—he came to the bedroom door and scowled out into the passage:

'Oh, it's you, is it? Now then—stop that damn thing.'

Agatha stuck her arms akimbo.

'Stop it yourself, you old blighter. Don't give me any more orders. I'm not your servant any longer. And look here—don't you forget what I said to you last night on the steps. Don't think, because you're going to Guildford, that you're going to wriggle out of it. If you don't—'

'Sh, damn you,' hissed Mr Prossip, advancing in his socks along the passage, his face turned towards the door of the sitting-room. 'She's in there. I told you I'd send you the money.'

The hall-door bell rang and Agatha picked up her bag and her umbrella.

'All right, old cock. The sooner the better. You have my address. Ta-ta. Be good.'

When her trunk had been carried out, she followed it, slamming the hall-door. Well—that was *that*. No more Prossips. She was fed up with them—fed up with their barging and their nagging and their tinned food and their ugly faces and that rotten old fiddle and their rotten little flat, stuck up there, away from everything. She had had two and a half years of them and she was sick of them. No matter what happened, she was going to have a change—change—have a bit of fun—anyhow, for a while. Perhaps, after all, she was mistaken—just had the wind up. She had often missed a month before—though never two running. Anyhow, what did it matter? It happened to other girls—let it happen to her. It was worth trying it on with the old blighter, at all events. Other girls she knew had pulled it off all right—why shouldn't she? He was properly frightened, the old sneak, with his bad breath—he'd pay something, anyhow. But, anyhow, she was done with the Prossips and that rotten little bed you could never turn over in without all the clothes slipping off. There were three man-servants at this new place . . .

She whistled blithely as she went down the outside steps and caught sight of Chidgey, who had just brought back the car from the repair-garage and had come to report the fact to his employer. Since the guv'nor had caught him canoodling with her in the car that night, Chidgey had avoided her, and now he feigned solicitousness as to the condition of one of his tyres, bending down so as to avoid seeing her. It occurred to her suddenly that it would be a bit of a lark to give Bert a jolt-up too, just to see what he would say.

She stopped beside him.

'Hullo, my pet. Very rude to turn your back on a lady. Got a puncture or something?'

'A bit soft, that's all.'

She prodded his bent back with the handle of her umbrella.

'Look here, Bert. I can't talk to you here, with that old Hopgood watching us from behind the curtains. But there's something I want to tell you about. You know the place I'm going to—the Grevilles'. Old Knayle goes there often, you told me. You'd better come over there some night soon and we'll have a talk about it. I'll send you a p.c. to say what night, when I know.'

He raised a gloomy, uneasy face to her, still stooping over the tyre.

'What do you want to talk about?'

She lowered her tone, and cast down her eyes. 'Well—you

remember that day you took me the sharrybang trip to Cleeveham?'

'Yes. Well?'

'Well—I'm afraid there's going to be consequences.'

'Consequences?'

It had given Bert a proper old jolt-up, she saw. He had gone white, and his mouth was open like a fish's.

'Yes. Anyhow, we've got to have a talk about it. I'll send you a postcard. And, look here, Bert—can you lend me ten bob? I'm stony till I get my wages. I owe every red the Prossips gave me.'

He laughed, half in fear, half in anger.

'Ten bob? Like that? What do you take me for, my girl? You go and ask old Prossip for ten bob—and talk to him about consequences.'

His anger angered her. He got good wages, Bert—three pounds a week. She wouldn't just give him a jolt-up for a joke—she'd try it on with him, too, the mean little skunk. Her eyes darted venomous hate at him, while her scarlet lips smiled contemptuously. She made every curve of her body a threat—cunning, vicious, and experienced.

'You come over, Bert. You and me's got to talk business, see? Ta, now.'

Chidgey stood kicking the tyre gloomily until two taxis drove up and came to a halt behind the car. In these the Prossips departed presently with their luggage. Before he went, Mr Prossip ran in to say farewell to Mr Knayle.

'Well, we're off, old chap—and jolly glad I am of it. Many thanks for kind assistance and so forth. Oh, look here—I wonder if I might leave one of the latch-keys with your chap, so that he could round up occasionally and see that everything's going on all right, I mean, until the flat's let. There's been a lot of breaking into flats in Rockwood lately.'

'Certainly,' said Mr Knayle, stiffly, accepting the key. 'You're letting your flat furnished, then?'

'Going to try to, anyhow. I hear you've got Whalley staying with you. A bit knocked out by his missus's death, I suppose.' Mr Prossip smiled. 'We're not taking our gramophone with us. Any time he wants to cheer himself up with a little tune, you can lend him the key. All the best, old sport.'

He held out his hand; but Mr Knayle was busy opening the door and did not see it.

4

Two days later Whalley was up and able to discuss his plans for the immediate future with a calm matter-of-factness which at once relieved Mr Knayle and made him a little uneasy. One expected self-control—manful acceptance—the stoicism due to oneself and to others. But one hardly expected a man who had just lost—well, even the most ordinary of wives—to sit down and make out a neat list of things to be done—to haggle over the telephone as to the charge to be made for the lorry which was to bring in a load from Camphill—to remember that chimneys wanted to be swept and windows cleaned—to think of giving Hopgood sixpence for the messenger who would bring up a suit-case from the nursing-home. Whalley's calmness struck Mr Knayle as being too calm, somehow—his matter-of-factness too deliberate. Whalley knew that he had known her all her life. He might have made some little reference to her—not tried to keep all the sorrow to himself—as if he was the only person in the world who had any right to be sorry. But when one tried to lead the conversation towards her, he began immediately to talk about something else—the General Election, or the Prossips, or so on. Oddly enough, he seemed to have no feeling at all about the Prossips now—had been quite interested to hear how it was that they had decided to move to Guildford. 'We lived at Guildford,' he had begun. But, because the 'we' had included her, he had stopped there, and gone off to ring up the house-agents' and ask them to send up the key of his flat.

Mr Knayle was hurt by his exclusion. It had seemed that so tremendous an event should have produced some tremendous sequel. But there was no sequel. The stone which had fallen with such tragic violence into the placid pool of his life had sunk. The ripples that had been stormy waves for a moment were slowing into sluggishness. The whole dreadful, poignant thing was ending in flat dullness. Already she was being forgotten. Whalley had begun to eat heartily; Mr Knayle's own appetite had been unusually good during the past few days. There was no help for it—one just went on living and forgetting until one forgot.

On the third morning after the Prossips' departure he accompanied Whalley to the foot of the outside staircase and stood there until he heard the door of the first-floor flat shut. Then he went back into his flat and looked into his bedroom, which Hopgood had already re-arranged for his own use. The smaller bedroom in which he had been sleeping was rather draughty and dark in the morning; it would be pleasant to get back to his own bedroom again, with the compactum, and the dressing-table in a good light, and the new reading-lamp over the bed. But the obliteration of Whalley's tenancy of the room seemed to him the end of his brief and, after all, futile romance. Some friends of his were to start a few days later upon a month's pleasure-cruise to the Mediterranean; he went to the telephone and arranged to join the party, taking Hopgood with him. Hopgood looked as if he wanted a change too. During the last few days he had developed a rather trying habit of sighing as he moved about.

5

The letter-box had overflowed. When Whalley opened the hall-door, it pushed back a little mound of envelopes addressed to him in unfamiliar handwritings. He stared at them in surprise for a moment, then, realising that they were letters of condolence from Elsa's friends, stooped and picked them up. They would all have to be answered—fifty or sixty of them. But there was plenty of time. He stacked them neatly on the landing and then went up the little flight of stairs, set down the two suit-cases which he had carried up with him, and stood looking at the closed doors of the rooms. The last time he had looked at them had been when Bogey-Bogey was running from door to door, whimpering. He hadn't wanted to leave. They had had to carry him out, struggling and whimpering.

What had she said—there, at the hall-door—'Good-bye, little flat. Coming back.'

Well . . . now . . .

Now he was shut in there in the stillness—alone again. He could sit down and plan it out, without Knayle's silly babbling and curious smile to disturb him.

He opened the door of the sitting-room and looked across at the small oval table by the windows. There—he would sit there and plan it all out and pat it into shape. No more weary, useless strugglings. No more tricking with words—no more faking and padding. That was all done with. No plot to invent. This plot was ready-made, with only its four chapters to arrange. He moved towards the table, but turned back. There was plenty of time. No hurry. He must guard against hurry.

And, first of all, everything must look as she had always seen it—everything must be done as if she was in there in the kitchen, busy with her pots and pans, moving about swiftly in her gay overall. He moved from room to room, opening the windows and then, having unpacked some old clothes from his suit-case, changed into them and set to work upon the tidying of the flat.

In a week everything was spick-and-span. Everything had been brushed and dusted and washed and polished, the sitting-room chimney had been swept, all the windows cleaned, all the curtains taken down and shaken, every corner visited. The brasses shone like gold, the linoleum was perilous to walk on. The lorry had brought in its load from Camphill; Camphill, locked up and sodden with the October rain, was finished with. Every item on that neat list of which Mr Knayle had disapproved a little unreasonably, had been ticked off.

All the letters of condolence had been answered save one. Mr Loxton, who had interrupted the negotiations for an important contract to return for his niece's funeral, had returned, a day too late, to discover to his horror and indignation that there had been no funeral. He would refrain now from useless protests. But it must be understood that he could never forget or forgive the deplorable—he might say, the outrageous—slight which had been offered to his niece, himself, his family, and every person of decent and religious feeling in Rockwood. There would be certain matters to be discussed with his solicitors in reference to his niece's estate. Whalley would please communicate with them at his convenience; but any personal meeting with Mr Loxton himself, he must please understand, was and would remain out of the question. Whalley threw the letter into the rubbish-bin. Mr Loxton, too, was done with. And the Canynges, and the Sunday dinners. There would be all Sunday to think and plan—pat it into shape . . .

At seven the scream of the factory-sirens down in the city awoke him. For a moment he lay, paralysed by the horror that surged back into his brain. It was not an evil dream—he was awake, back in it. He sprang up and bent down over the pillows of the other bed. 'Good-morning, dear.' There must be no moment of the day in which she was not remembered.

In the mornings he worked about the flat. The bedroom was done every day—both beds aired and re-made—all the little trifles on her dressing-table dusted and replaced exactly. The other rooms were done in rotation. He worked calmly and methodically, scarcely ever looking at his watch or a clock. The days seemed endless.

From Elsa he had picked up sufficient skill in cookery to prepare the simple food which supplemented his daily ration of liver. He cooked and ate the liver now without any repugnance;

it was part of his rite of remembrance—part of his plan. The click of the switches when he turned on the electric-cooker always vividly evoked her gay overall. Though it hung behind him from a hook on the kitchen door, he saw it there by the cooker, bent a little forward.

One day he saw her. He was busy in the kitchen when he heard her voice call 'Si.' He hurried to the door and saw her in the darkness of the passage, close to the balusters enclosing the little landing, looking, not towards him, but towards the bathroom. The illusion was so vivid that he went along the passage and touched the balusters. He went back to the kitchen, looking over his shoulder. She had stood just there, he remembered, that afternoon of the thunderstorm in June. There had been something that had attracted his attention, so that he remembered her standing there that afternoon. Something about the light. But he couldn't remember.

Some trick of his nerves. He must be careful about his nerves—there would be strains for them to meet; they mustn't be allowed to play tricks—cause any oddnesses of look or manner or movement that might attract attention. He must try to make his body as efficient as it could be made now—eat more—take exercise—get out into the open air—learn to move about amongst people without looking as if he was alone. That attracted attention.

Unconsciously, however, whenever he passed along the narrow passage, he left a space between him and the balusters, as if someone stood there.

Mr Loxton's solicitors wrote to him in reference to his wife's will. He wrote back saying that she had made none and formally renouncing inheritance of the fifty pounds a year which had been paid to her in quarterly cheques signed by Mr Loxton, her trustee. He received an acknowledgment and heard no more of the matter.

Mr Ridgeway came up one afternoon to see how he was getting on. It was a raw afternoon and, before he rang the bell, the caller blew his nose. As he did so his attention was attracted by some sounds within the flat—the same sound repeated several times rapidly, as if a cushion or a pillow, he thought, were being beaten with great energy. When Whalley opened the hall-door he appeared somewhat out of breath.

'Hope I haven't disturbed you,' said Mr Ridgeway, in his gruff, abstracted way. 'You seem to have been indulging in rather violent exercise. Not overdoing things yet, I hope. By the way— while I think of it—I wonder if you've seen anything about this new method of absorbing liver? Intravenous—injections of liver extract. Saves having to eat the beastly stuff. You find it rather an ordeal, don't you?'

They went into the sitting-room and talked about pernicious anæmia for a little while, and then Mr Ridgeway held out the small brown-paper parcel which he had brought up. He had debated anxiously as to how he should speak of her, and for a moment or two he resumed the debate. Finally he said, very gently:

'I brought back some books which your wife lent me.'

But Whalley merely thanked him and put the brown-paper parcel aside. They went for a walk on the Downs, now deserted and melancholy in the October twilight. Mr Ridgeway found it difficut to keep up with his companion's stride and, observing that Whalley's wind appeared to be perfectly normal, surmised that he was keeping himself fit by using a punching-ball.

CHAPTER VII

1

His determination had been formed in the flash of a thought. It had been an inspiration—a revelation; he had not considered it or reasoned about it. It had stated to him, once and for all, an unchangeable sequence. They had killed her—he would kill them. They had driven her out of the flat—driven her out to Camphill—driven her to her death. They were for him now the incarnation of the malign spirit which, blow by blow, had beaten down her happiness and crushed her laughing spirit to dust. They had killed her—he would kill them. She had died in pain and fear; her lips had been twisted in bitter agony; they would die in pain and fear. All four. One by one they would pay their debt to her. His momentary vision had seen four figures standing in space waiting to be struck down—then three—then two— one—none. The thing had been already accomplished.

In the afternoons, as he sat by the windows of the sitting-room, he saw his project almost as one of those skeleton schemes which he had been accustomed to construct before beginning the writing of a play—a brief jotted note of the central action of each act. As yet there were no details, but the outline was definite. He might have scribbled on his writing-block:

Act I.	Agatha Judd.	Rockwood (Abbey Rd.)
Act II.	Margery P.	Guildford (Deepford R. Hotel.)
Act III.	Mrs P.	"	"
Act IV.	P.	"	"

And then turned over and written on the next page:

SCENARIO
Act 1. Sc. 1.

Already his imagination was busy with details, but it weighed them and pondered over them with almost complete detachment from reality. Already it was foreseeing difficulties; but they were the difficulties of a play which would be adjusted within the enclosure of the sitting-room walls, just as so many difficulties in the plots or characterisation of his novels had been adjusted. There was hardly any thought of possible interference from outside agencies in the long, motionless reveries of his afternoons. His plot was framed by the four walls that had shut in all his creative thoughts for two years. The world with its suspicion and its vigilance lay outside, an irrevelance.

Even when he went out into it, his plan, always in his thoughts, remained apart from it. He had begun to walk regularly, selecting usually the most frequented streets and roads of the neighbourhood. The faces that passed him, depressed, anxious, or merely blank, betrayed no awareness of him; the eyes that rested on him for a moment glanced on to a shop-window or a passing car. He was surprised when, one evening, a glove which he had dropped that afternoon when alighting from a 'bus at a crowded corner nearly a mile distant from Downview Road was returned to him at his flat by an elderly man whom, to his knowledge, he had never seen before.

'I was in the 'bus,' the visitor explained, 'and saw you drop the glove as you got out. As I happened to know where you lived, I thought I'd take charge of it and bring it along to you the first time I was coming this way.'

'How did you know that I lived here?' Whalley asked.

'Well, I saw you one day a couple of weeks ago, coming into this house. And so, of course, I recognised you in the 'bus. I'm like that. I never forget a face once I've seen it. Mother was the same . . .'

The 'of course' arrested Whalley's interest for a moment;

this man took it for granted that he should remember every
face he had seen once. But the incident was soon forgotten as
the merest of accidents. There would be no accidents—
everything would be foreseen—patted into perfect shape—made
accident-proof. It was simply a matter of adjustment while one
sat at the little oval table and drew curlimacews.

Sometimes, when he had sat for an hour without any movement save the lighting of a new cigarette from an old one, he
got up and went into the bedroom. It was the place in which
most of her survived for him. He opened the door of her wardrobe and touched a frock or a jumper, trying to conjure up
places in which she had worn it, pressing the material to his
nostrils to assure himself that her perfume still clung to it. Or
he picked up some knick-knack from her dressing-table and
tried to see her fingers using it. For some reason unknown to
him, she had always kept her best pair of shoes at the foot of
her bed instead of in the boot-press in the passage. They still
stood there and there was always a little dust to flick from their
toes before he went back to his chair in the sitting-room.

2

Knayle had prattled away. There had been no difficulty in
finding out where the Prossips had gone; he had volunteered
the information that their maid, according to Hopgood's
account, had found a new place as housemaid with his friends,
the Grevilles. Whalley had known that her name was Agatha;
Knayle had supplied the surname Judd. The Grevilles, he had
added, kept a large staff of servants; Miss Agatha Judd's new
situation would be an improvement upon her last.

The Grevilles had been old friends of Elsa's and Whalley
had occasionally accompanied her on her visits to the house,
of which his mind contained a definite picture. He saw it as he
and Elsa had always approached it. One turned right-hand out
of the dullness of Durston Road into Abbey Road—a quiet,

almost rural road whose further end was already in the country. In the whole length of the road there were not more than a dozen houses, all of them large and standing in extensive grounds whose trees concealed them, he fancied, entirely from view. Dense shrubberies bordered the road on both sides, separated from the pathways by low ornamental railings. Little traffic passed along it; it led nowhere in particular and existed almost solely for the purposes of the wealthy residents who lived there in select seclusion. Sometimes one met a large car or a tradesman's van and saw a solitary pedestrian disappear round a bend. Usually the road was deserted—though, doubtless, in the evenings there would be occasional courting couples straying along the footpaths.

One went along for nearly half a mile. The third gate on the left-hand side was the Canynges'. The fourth, two or three hundred yards further on, was the Grevilles'. The gates had always been open when he had seen them, and he saw them open. A narrow drive ran away from them through a shrubbery, overhung by the trees. It curved twice, and then one saw the house some fifty yards ahead—heavy, ugly, pretentious, but saturated with wealth and security. A man-servant out of one of Pinero's plays opened the hall-door . . .

If one went back to the gates and looked up the drive—the shrubbery grew very thick on either side—one could stand upright amongst the shrubs without being seen. What were they? Laurels, some of them; he remembered the smell on hot days. Round the first curve of the drive one was out of sight of both from the road, through the gates, and from the house. There . . .

He must go and look at it—one day soon, now—and verify his picture. Perhaps go up the drive to the curve and make certain that the shrubbery was as dense as he remembered it—perhaps decide which side of the drive he would select. It would be necessary to do that twice—in the daylight and after dark.

The Grevilles kept a lot of servants. No doubt they were

well treated and had afternoons and evenings off, probably twice a week. One would have to be careful. It would be necessary to keep watch in order to discover on what evenings she went out—at what hour she returned. There would be other servants coming down and going up the drive in the evenings—curious, observant girls, suspicious men. One would have to be careful. One would have to wear different clothes.

But all that could be adjusted. And who would—who could—suspect? No one—not even she herself, if by some accident she saw him and recognised him. But there would be no accidents.

Probably on her evenings off she would have to get back to the house by half-past ten at latest. Some night—a Wednesday night or a Friday night—she would come back in the darkness along Abbey Road, (were there lamps along Abbey Road?) hurrying because she was late and the road was lonely. Probably she would have spent the evening at a cinema with some young fellow. But Abbey Road would be too far out for him at that hour; he would almost certainly leave her, at latest, at the 'bus halt in Conyngham Place. She would come hurrying along Abbey Road alone, turn in through the gates, hurry up the drive, turn the first bend, see him step out from the shrubbery—and stop. She must see him and recognise him before he struck—she must know what was going to happen to her—and why. That was a difficulty, because she mustn't be allowed to scream. It would be very quiet out there at that hour. One would have to think over that and adjust it and pat it into shape. It was simply a matter of tiny moments—of position . . .

Then, when it was done and when he had made certain that it was done (one would have to make quite certain) and she was lying in among the shrubs, he would go quietly back along Abbey Road, turn in to Durston Road, and who would—who could—suspect? No one.

He would come back to the flat and sit down there by the sitting-room fire and begin to think about Act II.

*

One afternoon he walked to the further end of Abbey Road and back again. Some fifty or sixty cars and vans passed him before he reached Durston Road again. He met thirty or forty people, including the Edwarde-Lewin girls, who bowed to him, and Mrs Canynge, who cut him dead. The trees had thinned and the upper windows of some of the houses, including the Grevilles', were visible from the road. The shrubberies, he discovered, were not all so dense as he had fancied them. There were lamps along the road. They were widely-spaced, it was true, but one of them stood only a little away from the Grevilles' gates. A patrolling policeman was a rarity anywhere in Rockwood—a phenomenon in its outskirts; but he met a policeman that afternoon as he turned the corner into Durston Road.

On the following afternoon he repeated the same walk. Not a single car passed him in Abbey Road; the only persons he met there on foot were two small boys from the College, who passed him under one of the lamps, absorbed in a discussion concerning reinforced concrete.

He slackened his pace as he approached the Grevilles' gates on his return journey and listened. Excepting for the hooting of a tug down in the river there was no sound. He walked up the drive until he reached its first bend and then made a hurried exploration of the shrubbery. On both sides it ran back for a considerable distance from the drive. There was no necessity to explore it to its further limits; it was sufficient that, near the drive, it formed an entirely satisfactory hiding-place. He decided upon the right-hand side as he faced towards the house. His left hand must be the nearer to her as she came up the drive.

3

From the first he had told himself that he must guard against hurry. There must be an interval, sufficiently long to dissociate the Prossips and Agatha Judd from the top flat. They must be given time to settle down in their new surroundings, to develop new habits and associations, to forget to talk about things that had been of interest and importance to them in June. Nearly four months had already intervened; another two, or, at the outside, three, would, he estimated, completely detach them from all possible connection with himself.

As the interminable, eventless days went by, however, it began to appear to him that this estimate was excessive. In a few days a girl like Agatha Judd—unusually good-looking, pert, assured, and feather-brained—would have established herself as a conspicuous feature of the Grevilles' household, squabbled with her fellow-maids, set up flirtations with the men-servants, and forgotten all about the Prossips and their flat. In a few weeks she would have become a familiar figure in Abbey Road and its immediate neighbourhood—the Grevilles' pretty housemaid. Probably her vanity would restrain her from talking to her fellow-servants about her last place; to do so would involve the admission that she had been a general maid in a small flat.

Though Mrs Greville, of course, would know who her last employers had been and where they had lived. There was that to think over. But why should anyone think of enquiring as to her last situation, when she had been with the Grevilles for two months? Or, for that matter, a month?

A doubt arose in his mind. His plan had supposed Agatha Judd fixed permanently in her new setting. But was she?

She was an impudent, careless, malicious girl. Mrs Greville might decide that she was unsuitable and dismiss her. If that happened, it would be very difficult to trace her to a new place. She might leave Rockwood—go to Bath, or Cleeveham, or even to London. Knayle was a great friend of the Grevilles, but Mrs Greville would be extremely unlikely to discuss the whereabouts of a dismissed housemaid with him. And one would have to be careful with Knayle. That smile of his was curious.

Perhaps Mrs Greville had already dismissed her.

He meditated upon this anxiety for an afternoon and then went out to buy cigarettes. His way to the tobacconist's led him past Knayle's garage and he saw her standing in the doorway, talking to Chidgey. When he passed again on his way back to the flat, Chidgey was still standing in the doorway—alone now— and saluted him gloomily.

In the earlier part of the year Chidgey had lost the effective use of a raincoat under rather unusual circumstances. He had left the raincoat lying over the saddle of his motor-cycle at the side of a country road while he refreshed himself with sandwiches in a near-by field. Returning to the motor-cycle he had found a cow eating his raincoat. He had interviewed the owner of the cow without any satisfactory result and had subsequently consulted Mr Knayle as to his chances of obtaining compensation. Mr Knayle had laughed and said, 'Better ask Mr Whalley, Chidgey. I understand that he's a person learned in the law.' Recalling this remark of the guv'nor's, Chidgey threw away his cigarette and overtook Whalley with an urgent 'Beg pardon, sir. May I speak to you for a moment?'

'Certainly.'

'You'll excuse me asking you, sir, but are you connected with the law? Mr Knayle happened to mention to me one day that you were.'

'Rather distantly,' Whalley replied in some surprise. 'However— Well?'

'Well, it's like this, sir. That young woman you saw me speaking to—you know who she is, sir, of course—she's been threatening me—charging me with being responsible for her being in a certain condition—which I know for a fact I'm not responsible for it and couldn't have been responsible for it. And I know who is responsible for it, what's more—that old swine with the eyeglass—Prossip. She as good as told me so herself a while back, before she started this game with me, though she won't admit it now. Well, what I wanted to ask you, sir, and how you may be kind enough to help me is—can I go into a police-station and lay a charge against her of trying to extort money from me by threats which I can prove on oath are false? For it's blackmail she's after, sir, that's what her game is. You'd never think she was the dangerous little—I'll show you a letter I got from her yesterday.'

He produced a soiled sheet of paper from his hip-pocket and came round to Whalley's side to exhibit it. Whalley glanced at it and, when he had seen the address at the top, shook his head.

'If you mean to do anything, Chidgey,' he said, turning away, 'see a solicitor. Take my advice, however, and do nothing.'

'It's killing me, sir,' said Chidgey. 'My life isn't worth living. I can't eat and I can't sleep and I can't read. I can't do anything without thinking about it. Sometimes I feel like going down and chucking myself into the river. Well, thank you, sir. You'll excuse me for troubling you, I hope.'

But Chidgey was relieved. For a moment he had made up his mind to take even the most desperate of steps to rid himself of the fear that had made his life a poisoned hell for the past three weeks. But the moment he had begun to tell his story aloud and put it into words he had realised that he couldn't face it—that he couldn't walk into a police-station and say, 'I want to charge a girl with accusing me falsely of having got her in the family way'—that he didn't want to do anything. And now he had been advised, by a lawyer, to do nothing. To do nothing was no longer funk; it was the right thing to do—advised by a lawyer. He had always liked the look of Mr Whalley—one of the right sort. He went back to the garage comforted, and a little regretful that he hadn't thought to say a word about poor little Mrs Whalley.

She was still there, then . . .

But the anxiety remained. At any moment she might leave Abbey Road and disappear completely. To find her again, even if she remained in Rockwood, might easily prove an impossibility; one would have to depend almost entirely upon chance. The search for her would involve delay. The Prossips, too,

might leave their present quarters—perhaps leave Guildford.
They, too, would have to be found again.

She had been a month with the Grevilles now. Why wait?
What was there to wait for?

He strove with his impatience. But his days were weeks—the
month had been a year. For ages and ages he had spoken to no
one, except to Ridgeway and the assistants and messengers of
the shops at which he dealt. No one had spoken to him. No
one was aware of him. He was forgotten.

4

On the whole Mr Prossip was pleased with Guildford and the
Deepford Residential Hotel. He liked the High Street and
walked up one side of it and down the other twice every fine
morning before he went to play his nine holes and twice every
fine afternoon before he went back to the Deepford's lounge
to play bridge until dinner-time. He liked the people you saw
shopping in the High Street—smart live women and men who,
though they dressed a bit carelessly, were unmistakably sahibs.
He liked to turn into the Angel for a sherry and bitters on his
way back from the links. And he had already had some very
pleasant little trips to London—very pleasant indeed. Though
London wasn't what it had been.

The Deepford was very gay and comfortable and the cooking
not at all bad, though his table in the dining-room was just
beside a door and always in a draught. The guests came and
went, but there were always a number of bright young things
and always some unmistakable sahibs of his own age to play
bridge with and hob-nob with in the bar. To these he had
conveyed that he was feeling a draught of another sort and had
decided to shut up his place down in Westshire until things
cheered up—if they ever did. It was damn pleasant to sit in the
bright little bar and talk to unmistakable sahibs about the Land
Tax and his bit of shooting and what the Duke had said to him

one day out with the Beauforts. Damn pleasant, too (though, of course, that five-point-nine had ended *his* dancing days), to watch the bright young things dancing—glued together—not caring a damn who saw them. Gave you something to think about in bed, instead of worrying about things. The bright young things liked his little jokes and his paternal winks. On the whole, he thought, he was about the most popular person in the hotel.

Mawjery, as usual, was making herself a bit of a nuisance. She was sulky because she was plain and a rotten dancer and because the management had objected to her violin. However, fortunately she had raked out some school-friends in Farnham who went in for music and all that, and spent most of her time with them. He had bought her a second-hand Baby to encourage her to go to Farnham as often as possible. The more she was away from the Deepford the better. He didn't want more rows about her violin-playing; he had had enough of that sort of thing.

He supposed he'd never get rid of Mawjery now. Thirty—and plainer every time he looked at her. None of the young chaps at the hotel took the slightest notice of her. As long as he lived he would be saddled with her sulks and her scraping. Christ— what a prospect for a chap . . .

However—one good job—he had a bedroom to himself again now. When Emma got up at six o'clock in the morning, now, he didn't hear her banging and thumping about the room like a hippopotamus. She had started that business up here, now, found out some oily-voiced canoodler or other, he supposed, like that beggar in Rockwood she used to go to confession to. Damn keen about him, too, evidently. No joke riding a bicycle on these dark, cold mornings.

He thought a good deal about Emma's bicycle. She had bought it without saying anything to him about it—solely, it seemed, for the purpose of her early church-goings—the church to which she went being some distance outside the town, along the Leatherhead Road. He had made no reference to it—though perhaps he should have said something about its being unwise for her to ride a bicycle with her heart. But, anyhow, it would have been quite useless to have said anything—only have led to a row. It was her own look-out.

There was no doubt that riding a bicycle on a cold morning might very easily bring on one of those attacks of hers. It was all very well to say to yourself that you oughtn't to think of such a thing—but one morning Emma *might* fall off her bicycle and die on the London road. Funny to think about that—Emma being dead. What would one do—?

Sometimes Mr Prossip's meditations upon his wife's bicycle caused him regret, and one day he surprised her by entering her room—she had spent most of her time in her bedroom since her arrival at the Deepford—and embracing her with tears in his eyes. She concluded, however, that he had had too much whisky and, disengaging herself from his hold frigidly, went on burnishing her nails. After that he thought about her bicycle as entirely her own look-out.

One day towards the end of October he received a disagreeable reminder of a matter which had begun to fade into the somewhat musty twilight in which he kept the things that were a damn nuisance to remember. A threatening scrawl arrived from Agatha Judd.

Ivanhoe,
Abbey Road
Rockwood, Dunpool.

Mr Prossip—As you havint kept your promise im writing to say that if you dont let me have a hundered pounds by return ill go to Guilford and inform your wife of your conduc to me mind i mean what I say dont think im a fool or because im a poor servant girl you can put it across me and throw me to one side after runing me for life i have friens who will see that im treated fair and square and unless you want to see me landing into your hotel and exposing you to your wife and everyone you better come down here and bring the money with you in cash mind as I want no cheques or any more trouble about it having trouble enough god knows which you are the cause of so youd better come to Rockwood and meet me somewhere if not ill go up to Guilford this day week as certain as im writing these words so now no more for the present but behave like a gentleman and there will be no more about it you can rely on it.—Agatha.

Mr Prossip drank a great many whiskies and sodas and found courage to do nothing until, two days later, he received a telegram:

NOT HAVING HEARD FROM
YOU GOING GUILFORD SATURDAY.

His nerve went and he wired a reply arranging a meeting at half-past seven on the evening of that day—a Thursday—at the junction of Abbey and Durston Roads. He reached Dunpool a little before seven and arrived at the place of rendezvous in a taxi a minute before the arranged time.

The interview which followed was brief and, for Mr Prossip, extremely unpleasant. He had gulped down two large whiskies in the restaurant at the terminus and when Agatha, having greeted him with an amicable 'Hullo,' turned and went back along Abbey Road, he followed her unsuspectingly, trying to recall the little oration which he had composed in the train. But he could only think of bits of it, here and there.

'Now, my girl,' he began, when she had slackened pace a little and he was level with her again, 'this is a very serious business, you know. Very serious.'

What came after that?

'Very serious. I don't know whether you are aware that when

you wrote me that letter you were committing a very serious criminal offence. In fact, a crime. Perhaps you are not aware that the punishment for—'

'Oh, come off it,' snapped Agatha contemptuously. 'Have you brought the money? That's what I want to know.'

'Now, my good girl, don't speak to me like that. And I may as well tell you that the first thing you've got to do is to get it out of your head that because, for your own sake, I've come all the way down here from Guildford to have a talk with you—'

Agatha turned towards the road and called, 'Jim. I want you.' A figure emerged from the gates of a house at the opposite side and, moving obliquely and very rapidly, cut off Mr Prossip's retreat to Durston Road. The newcomer, a husky young man in a tight-fitting jacket which he buttoned with leisurely menace, spat preparatorily.

'Well,' he asked, 'what about it, cocky? Brought that stuff along all right, eh?'

Mr Prossip decided to make a bolt for it and received a blow on his jaw which sent him reeling against the low railing which separated the footpath from the bordering shrubbery. He was jerked into erectness again and held by one of Jim's hands while the other punched his face and his body several times. While a car passed his throat was imprisoned in a grip of steel. He was whimpering a little when he produced a little wad of notes from his breast-pocket and handed them over to Agatha in dizzy silence. She counted them, puffing with anger.

'Ten quid? What's this for, you dirty dog?'

She slapped his face. He was punched again and kicked excruciatingly as he tried to rise to his feet. When they were satisfied that nothing more was to be got from him, they left him with the warning that they had only begun with him, and went off laughing, towards Durston Road. Mr Prossip, leaning against the railings, saw them turn the corner, two bobbing, derisive silhouettes, and then, while he endeavoured to climb the railings in search of his hat, was violently sick.

He found his hat at length and tried to decide what he would do. In the expectation that he would catch the 8.40 back to Reading, he had brought nothing with him for the night; but he couldn't face the train and the Deepford and Emma with his face in the state which he felt it was in. It felt like a huge, bursting bruise; his nose was still bleeding, and at least one of his eyes, he was sure, was already black. Of course, he could go to the flat in Downview Road; but he had left the key with old Knayle's man, and he didn't want old Knayle to see him in that state. There was still some loose silver in his trousers pockets. He would find some small hotel.

In a public-house in Rockwood he had two more large whiskies and then remembered a girl who had had a room over a small shop in Gorrall Road. A quiet girl with a cough. Perhaps she would be able to do something for his face.

CHAPTER VIII

1

AT first Whalley kept watch from the road, crossing from side to side whenever he heard anyone approaching and avoiding the light of the lamp near the gates. At the hour upon which he had decided—from half-past six to half-past seven—Abbey Road was almost completely deserted. But, since his movements were necessarily limited and retraced always the same short stretches of footpath, they began very quickly to seem to him conspicuous, even when there was no one to observe them. The figures which emerged from the gates (he had been right, he found, in surmising that the servants went out about seven o'clock on their evenings of liberty) emerged at a smart pace and went off towards Durston Road rapidly, looking neither to right nor left. The interests of an evening off lay ahead of them, down in the city. Which of them, as it came down the drive, had turned towards the laurels? It would be much easier and simpler to wait in there—wait where he would wait.

On the third evening of his vigil—a Thursday evening—as he sat on a little heap of twigs in the pungent darkness of the shrubbery, Agatha Judd came down the drive with one of the men-servants. He recognised her voice; she was talking about a dog which had been run over. He looked at his watch. Twenty-five past seven.

He waited in his hiding-place until her shrill chatter died away, tempted to follow. The important thing was to discover at what hour she returned to the house. If, as was probable, she was bound for one of the cinemas, the intervening time could be spent there, near her, keeping her in sight. But, on the other hand, perhaps she was going to her home or to some other house—or going to meet someone. It would be necessary to keep watch on the house or loiter behind her along brightly-lighted roads—perhaps only to see her carried off by a 'bus. It was far simpler and far easier to wait there, at the point to which she must return.

He waited for nearly four hours, lighting one cigarette from another to avoid the striking of a match. Few people passed along the road; sometimes for half an hour no one passed. He listened to the footsteps as they approached and receded, picturing their owners vaguely. Every pair of feet made a different noise. It was chill and damp under the laurels. In collecting the twigs for his seat his hands had become smeared with cold, clammy earth, and their palms and fingers stiffened after a little while. Occasionally he sat up a little and drew his overcoat closer to his body, then bent forward again, his elbows resting on his knees.

At eight o'clock a car came down the drive and, as it turned the curve, the beam of its lamps found its way into his hiding-place and, for an instant, flooded it with daylight. From his ankles upward he remained in darkness, but the ends of his trousers and his boots were brightly illuminated. For an instant he saw the boots with satisfaction. They looked immense—utterly unlike any other boots he had ever worn. He had bought them some days before in a little second-hand shop in east Dunpool, kept by an old Jew with a large wen on his neck over which a few straggling grey hairs crawled. Immense—gigantic. He had had to put on a second pair of socks to prevent them from slopping as he walked. The heel of one of them rested, he had time to see, on a large stone half buried in the clay and twigs. Then was back in a darkness darker and chillier than before. The car passed on, sounding its deep Klaxon warningly as it passed out through the gates. The Grevilles going to dine somewhere.

A long time after, someone came down the drive, smoking a cigar. Its fragrance came in under the laurels after he had passed, soured a little by their pungency, but still a fragrance.

A good cigar. The smoker walked slowly—stood awhile at the gate, cleared his throat, and then went back slowly.

A dog came up the drive, questing—growled, went out through the gates again growling. It was high tide down in the river; the sirens and whistles blew continuously.

A quarter-past nine—

A little after ten someone came up the drive, hiccoughed, threw a cigarette end in among the bushes and went on towards the house, muttering to himself. The man-servant who had gone out with her, probably.

A quarter past—twenty past—not half-past yet.

He laughed savagely. If Elsa who had known him as he had always been for her, saw him now—sitting there on a heap of twigs, hiding under the shrubs.

Her feet had passed up and down the drive many times. Many times she had passed the place where he sat now, hiding under the bushes. The annihilation of everything that he had seemed to her filled him with a murderous fury, and his clenched hands rose above his head as it dropped to his raised knees. He sat motionless, his heart beat thundering in his ears, a mere desire to kill.

Why wait?

In a few minutes, now, she must come. Why not now, in a few minutes, and finish with her?

Was it certain that she would go out always on Thursday evenings just because she had gone out this Thursday evening? If she came back at eleven tonight, she might come back at ten next Thursday night. There would be more long hours of waiting there—never any greater certainty than that of now.

Why not now?

But he sat up again and tightened his overcoat about him once more. He wasn't ready—he hadn't come prepared. His plan must be carried out exactly as he had conceived it. The first blow must silence that shrill voice of hers for ever.

Why hadn't he brought it? He had thought of bringing it,

so as to grow accustomed to the feel of it in the sleeve of his overcoat—

That stone—where had he seen it? Under the heel of one boot.

As he bent forward, groping over the wet clay with numb fingers, he heard her coming—hard, hurrying little heels that were already at the gates—through the gates—in the drive. She was whistling, the little evil devil, with those mocking lips of hers . . .

2

He turned into Durston Road and stopped to light a cigarette. It was a quiet suburban road, whose lamps were separated by a distance of over fifty yards, but by comparison with Abbey Road it was brilliantly lighted. He was in the open now. He must accustom himself again to being seen.

Along Abbey Road all his faculties had been occupied in watchful scrutiny of the darkness ahead of him and behind him, and in struggling with the impulse to run. But now thought began to emerge through thoughtless instinct. As he lighted his cigarette he noted that the hand which held the match was perfectly steady and that, though it was vaguely painful, it had not been cut in any way. As he had come along Abbey Road he had brushed his overcoat with his gloves and scraped the clay from his boots against the kerb of the footpath. There must be no trace of that clay left. The coat must be thoroughly brushed and the boots thoroughly cleaned when he got back to the flat. The day after tomorrow, as he had decided, he would take the boots out to Camphill and burn them in the incinerator. His hat must be brushed, too, and the ends of his trousers, as he had decided. He must get back to his plan again, and do things exactly as he had arranged to do them—not get hurried and carried away. He had waited too long in there, listening to her whistling, and had had to hurry as he moved towards her whistling through the laurels. She had heard him and begun to run towards the house . . . There must be no more hurrying.

But it was done—very simply, and, in the end, very nearly as he had imagined it. He went on, concealing his soiled hands in the pockets of his overcoat and trying to subdue the clumping of his feet. When he had cleaned the boots and brushed his clothes, he would go into the sitting-room and sit down before the fire. The fire would probably be out, but he would relight it. He would get back to his plan—begin to think of Marjory Prossip's ugly, sullen, white face.

In fear and pain . . .

CHAPTER IX

1

MR KNAYLE returned to his flat on the afternoon of the first Friday in November. The Mediterranean cruise had not been a great success so far as he had been concerned; his new plate had been exceedingly troublesome and there had been a number of noisy young people on board who had talked an exasperating jargon of their own, danced every night until four o'clock in the morning, and nicknamed him K'tack. He had left the ship at Marseilles—heard in Paris that a revolution had broken out in the north of England—experienced some rather humiliating difficulty in settling his hotel bill—found London in the throes of the General Election—and sighed with relief when, at last, he found himself driving in his own car through the drab streets of Dunpool. It was pleasant to be back.

Hopgood had left London two days before him; everything at the flat was prepared for his reception. While he sipped his tea before a blazing fire his eyes strayed round his sitting-room resuming possession of it. It was deucedly pleasant to be back in one's own place, amongst one's own things and one's own memories. The past month had been all noise and fidgety restlessness. For four weeks he hadn't had a moment to himself. And his bed was in there next door—the bed of good, long sleeps. No saxophones tonight.

The morning papers lay neatly folded in their accustomed place on a small table within reach of his accustomed arm-chair. He had already seen the London papers; he stretched an arm and picked up the Dunpool *Daily Times*. There would be nothing of interest in it which he had not already read in the *Post*. But it would be pleasant to see the familiar old-fashioned type and run an eye over the obituary notices. Some Rockwood landmarks, he had heard in London, had been removed during his absence—old Sir James Filsham and his low-crowned hat— old Miss Bruce— What would become of those three black pugs of hers?

While he was adjusting his glasses, Hopgood came in to remove the tea-tray. Observing the newspaper in Mr Knayle's lap, he lingered to put some coal on the fire.

'You haven't looked at the *Daily Times* yet, sir, have you?'

Mr Knayle looked at him over his glasses. 'No.'

'You remember that girl of the Prossips', sir—their maid, I mean?'

The Prossips and their maid were a long time ago for Mr Knayle. He had begun to wonder whether he wouldn't dine at the Club that evening.

'Yes?'

'Well, she's been murdered, sir. She was murdered last night, over in Abbey Road—in Mr Greville's drive.'

'Oh,' said Mr Knayle. 'Murdered? By the way, Hopgood, I think I'll dine at the Club tonight. Ask Chidgey to bring the car round at half-past seven, will you?'

Hopgood retired with the tray, disappointed, and Mr Knayle settled himself again in his chair and opened the *Daily Times*. Murdered, eh? Very unpleasant for the Grevilles. Oh yes—of course she had gone to the Grevilles from the Prossips. Very unpleasant for the Grevilles.

ROCKWOOD TRAGEDY
HOUSEMAID BATTERED TO DEATH
IN
ABBEY ROAD

Battered to death—h'm.

When had he seen that girl (what was her name?—Agatha something) last? He had seen a lot of things since but after a moment or two he remembered. It was that day the gramophone had begun to play—the day the Prossips had gone away. He had left Ridgeway with Whalley in the bedroom and come into the sitting-room for another book and seen her talking to Chidgey outside the gates, beside the car. Yes. That was the last time he had seen her—talking to Chidgey beside the car. She had looked very smart in a long coat and one of those abominable bowler hats.

He arranged the newspaper conveniently and read the quarter column devoted to the tragedy on the last page. A housemaid named Agatha Judd, in the employment of Mrs Greville at 'Ivanhoe', Abbey Road, had left the house at half-past seven on the preceding evening. Her subsequent movements had not yet been traced. Mr and Mrs Greville and their daughter had dined with some friends and returned in their car shortly after midnight, when their chauffeur had noticed, by the light of his headlamps, a purse lying in the drive close to the gates. When he had put away the car he had gone back along the drive with a pocket-torch and, while picking up the purse, had noticed that the shrubs bordering the drive had been pushed aside at one spot so as to leave a narrow path along which some large heavy object been dragged recently. His curiosity had been aroused and, after a brief search, he had come upon the body of Agatha Judd lying beneath the bushes some ten yards in from the drive. Neither the purse, which had been identified as hers, nor the bag from which it had fallen or been taken, and which had been found close to her, appeared to have been disturbed by the murderer. The hurried report, which was given in the 'Late News' column, concluded with the statement that the police were already in the possession of sensational information.

Very unpleasant indeed for the Grevilles—the police coming to the house, asking questions, people gaping in through the gates—Mrs Greville, a nervous woman, might have to attend the inquest. What a nuisance for them.

There hadn't been a murder in Rockwood for a long time

now. It was rather interesting that, when one did happen, the heroine of it should have lived in the same house with one for quite a considerable time. Hopgood had seemed to think that she had been largely responsible for the performance of the gramophone—an impudent-looking little piece. Battered to death—h'm. But really there was so much of that sort of thing now . . .

Not a murder for robbery, apparently—though the chap who killed her might have got frightened and thrown away the purse. But more probably one of those murders that had been committed all over the country during the last year or so—women attacked in lonely places. Just the sort of girl that sort of thing might happen to—good-looking, ready to pick up with anything in the shape of a man. She had got hold of Chidgey—persuaded a sensible chap like Chidgey to take her into the garage at night.

So that sort of thing had begun to happen in quiet old Rockwood now. Already in possession of sensational informa-tion. But the police always were in those cases—and then nothing happened. There had been a list in the *Post* a couple of days ago—ten or eleven recent murders which had baffled the police completely.

Someone moving about up there—

Mr Knayle dropped his newspaper to his lap and looked up at the ceiling of the sitting-room when he had taken off his glasses. A gentle melancholy mingled with his comfort. How often he had listened, looking up at the ceiling from his armchair. He waited, glasses in hand, half hoping, half fearing that he would feel again the stilling desolation which had descended upon him when he had looked up at it last—on the morning on which he had started on his trip. But he felt only a gentle melancholy which was not altogether disagreeable. He was disappointed. Often, sitting in his deck-chair looking up at the unfamiliar stars, he had thought about what he would feel when he sat in his sitting-room and looked up at its ceiling. He had expected something sharp—a pang. But the ceiling interfered somehow with what he felt and made it dull and soft.

But he had only just got back.

He must run up and see Whalley tomorrow or next day—give him a day's shooting now and then—persuade him to come down for a game of bridge now and then.

And old Ridgeway, too. He must look up old Ridgeway one day. Was he lying down there on his sofa now in his old dressing-gown, thinking that he would never tell her that he had performed an illegal operation and been in prison? Poor old devil—not quite normal, of course.

Well, well, it was very pleasant to be back. Perhaps the wipe-out of the Socialists did mean something more than that the country was panic-stricken. Perhaps old England was going to wake up.

Mr Knayle rose, switched off the lights and then settled himself again comfortably in his chair before the fire. He hadn't slept at all well in London; he never did sleep well there. He dozed off gently.

What had Hopgood's voice said? '. . . see you.'

He opened his eyes, turning his head sharply, and saw Hopgood standing by the switches regarding him doubtfully.

'A police-inspector to see you, sir.'

2

Inspector Bride, a stalwart kindly man in mufti, with completely expressionless grey eyes, came to the point at once when he had seated himself at the other end of the hearthrug. His eyes had taken possession of Mr Knayle the moment they had fallen on him and Mr Knayle was a little annoyed to find that their fixity made him slighty uneasy.

'I've come to make some enquiries, sir, about a man named Albert Chidgey, whom you have in your employment at present as chauffeur.'

Chidgey? Before Mr Knayle's eyes grew a vision of Chidgey's face as he had seen it that afternoon outside the station—white and peaked and pinched.

'Yes. My chauffeur's name is Chidgey.'

'He has been with you for some time as chauffeur, I think?'

'Yes. For over three years.'

'May I ask, Mr Knayle, what sort of character you would give him—generally?'

'Character? Oh, an excellent chap. A good driver—very steady—most satisfactory in every way.'

'Does he drink? I mean, have you ever known him the worse for liquor?'

'Never.'

The inspector rubbed his forehead with two fingers for a moment, and then glanced at the newspaper which lay on the arm of Mr Knayle's chair.

'I believe you have been abroad for the past month or so, sir—so your man told me just now?'

'Yes, I only got back this afternoon.'

'You may have seen that a young woman named Agatha Judd was found murdered in Abbey Road last night.'

Confound those eyes. 'Yes,' Mr Knayle replied stiffly. 'I have just read the account.'

'For some time, I am informed, she lived in the top flat of this house, during the past year, as servant of a Mr and Mrs Prossip who occupied the flat from, I think, January until the end of September. You probably knew her by appearance?'

'I remember that the people in the top flat had a maid, yes.'

'Naturally you wouldn't pay any great attention to servants belonging to the tenants of the other flats. This was a good-looking girl—very smart in her appearance—'

'Yes, yes. I remember.'

The inspector was discouraged. There was nothing in Chidgey. He hadn't thought there was anything in him. His head was aching a good deal. There had been trouble down in

East Dunpool during the elections and he had received a severe blow on the forehead from a stone which had left behind an ugly dull pain behind his eyes. And anyhow the case would be taken out of his hands and passed on to the Detective Division.

'What I wanted to ask you, sir, was, whether you had any reason at any time—say within the past six months—to suppose that there was any sort of intimacy between your chauffeur and this girl?'

'Intimacy?' Mr Knayle's tone sharpened. This was really too much of a good thing—the very afternoon one got back. 'No. I've seen him talking to her occasionally out there in the garden. Nothing more than that. Why do you ask?'

'Well, I may as well be frank with you, sir. One of the maids at the house where this girl was employed has stated that Agatha Judd told her that she was going to be married to Chidgey. This other girl knows Chidgey well, owing to his having been at Mr Greville's house when he drove you there in your car. She states that she saw Chidgey on three occasions lately talking to Judd near the house at night—twice in the road, outside the gates, and once in the drive. Now, the medical report is that Judd was going to have a child. So that you'll understand, sir, that we've found it necessary to make full enquiries about Chidgey and his relations with her.'

'Yes, yes. Of course.'

'I've seen Chidgey, and he denies that he was going to be married to her or that he had anything to do with her being pregnant, though he admits having been with her over in Abbey Road at the times when the other maid says she saw him. According to his statement, from what Judd told him herself, another person—I won't mention his name—was responsible for her condition. Of course, that's only Chidgey's statement—though we have information, I may say, which goes to show that it may be the fact. I'm bound to say that Chidgey strikes me as a respectable, decent fellow. Your man Hopgood, too, gives him a good character, and says he never noticed anything at all special between him and Judd. However, there it is, sir. You understand, of course, that we have to follow up every clue in a case like this. I may take it, then, that so far as you are aware, there was no special intimacy between Chidgey and this girl—say, round May and June last.'

'None whatever, so far as I am aware, Inspector,' said Mr Knayle, pulling down his waistcoat and rising.

He was annoyed by this stupid, large alien force that had taken possession of his sitting-room and his rights interrupted the comfort of his homecoming. He was annoyed by his big stupid, shapeless hands and his fixed, expressionless eyes— annoyed by his dogged questions and his habit of rubbing his forehead with his fingers when one answered them, as if to see that he didn't believe one. Let him get on with his clumsy prying and poking. What was he looking at now? The ceiling? What the deuce was *he* looking at the ceiling for?

'Who lives above you, sir?'

'A Mr Whalley.'

'Does he keep any servants?'

'No.'

'And underneath?'

'A Mr Ridgeway.'

'Does he keep any servants?'

'No.'

'Mr Prossip occupied the top flat. It's to let at present, your man tells me?'

'He would know.'

'Very well, sir, thank you. I needn't trouble you any further. Good afternoon.'

Mr Knayle settled himself again in his chair before the fire. But his comfort had gone. A crumb had lodged between his plate and his gum; the fire had died down, and, when he picked up the *Daily Times*, he saw only Chidgey's face—a close-up of Chidgey's face—dirty-white, set, and shadowed under the eyes. It was absurd to think of Chidgey battering the life out of anything—raining one ferocious blow after another— And yet, without doubt he had been carrying on with her in the car that night—

Curious that the last time he had seen her she had been with Chidgey.

What an infernal nuisance—the very day one got back.

Hopgood came in to ask if Mr Knayle would like the lights off again.

'Did *you* ever notice anything between Chidgey and the Prossips' maid, Hopgood?'

'No sir.' Hopgood permitted himself a faint smile. 'He didn't get anything out of *me*.'

'Quite,' said Mr Knayle. 'Yes. You can switch them off.'

It was quite dark outside, and Inspector Bride stopped at the head of a little flight of steps leading down to the basement flat to light his pipe and think about things for a moment. There was no reason he could think of why, if Mr Knayle and his man had seen anything going on between Chidgey and Judd, they shouldn't have told him so. But they had both choked him off. There had been something—and they both knew that there had been something. Well, he wasn't going to be choked off. He didn't think that Chidgey had the guts for a job of this kind. And it was certain that—quite apart from Prossip—she had had a number of chaps hanging after her—that clerk at the West Counties Bank, a fitter at the Oriel Garage, this chap she used to talk about as 'Jim,' a tram conductor named Allenby, a young fellow with a green and yellow sports car. But, on the other hand, where had Chidgey been last night from half-past seven on? At a picture-house, he said, alone. Of course he *would* say that.

He'd have to go up to Guildford and see Prossip about that wire of his. Prossip looked fishy. The wire hadn't been signed, but it had come from Guildford—and Prossip was living in Guildford now. Nice place Guildford; nice up along the river in a canoe on a summer evening—

Someone coming down the steps—probably the Mr Whalley who lived in the first floor flat. The inspector's pipe had not lighted properly and he struck another match as Whalley passed close to him. No use asking him. He kept no servants—he'd know nothing about Judd's carryings on with Chidgey.

'Good evening, sir.'

Whalley stopped. 'Are you looking for anyone?'

'Well, I am, sir.' Inspector Bride laughed. 'But I don't think you can help me to find him. Turned cold now.'

'Yes. Quite sharp.'

3

A little way down Downview Road Whalley looked back. A large figure stood outside the gates of No. 47, facing towards him. A little way further on he glanced back again. The figure was following slowly. But when he looked back a third time it had turned and was moving away from him.

He had remained indoors all day, waiting until the evening papers would be selling in the streets, working desultorily about the flat, and smoking continuously. The sudden encounter at the foot of the steps had startled him for a moment. Only the striking of the match had averted actual collision with the darkness that had suddenly become a man. What had he been doing there? Why had he laughed that way? Hopgood had come back; perhaps a friend of Hopgood's, waiting for him. His voice and face had belonged to that class—a respectable-looking fellow, like a small shopkeeper. But if he was looking for Hopgood, why hadn't he asked where he would find him? Why had he stood there, waiting? Why had he laughed that way as if it was a joke of some sort that he was looking for someone?

But he hadn't been following. Probably merely trying to make up his mind which way he would go. If he *had* been following, one oughtn't to have looked back. That must be remembered.

Perhaps someone looking for the Prossips. But no one had gone up the steps to their door. Why had he been waiting?

The report in the evening newspaper was merely an elaborated version of the *Daily Times* story. He read it in a little restaurant while he swallowed tea and stale buns, propping the paper against a vase filled with artificial asters and turning it over whenever the waitress approached the table. As she made out his bill her eyes rested on it.

'That's a dreadful business over in Abbey Road, sir, isn't it? Two buns? I was along there myself only two nights ago with my young man and we were only just saying what a lonely road it was at night. Two pats, isn't it? Thank you very much, sir.'

Just what he would have made a waitress say.

Mr Knayle came up to see him next day and thought him looking much fitter. The conversation concerned itself chiefly with Mr Knayle's trip and it was only when he stood outside the hall-door again that he made any allusion to the Abbey Road tragedy in his own thoughts. He had come up resolved to make no reference whatever to the Prossips or anything connected with them. But as he turned away to descend the steps he forgot his resolution for a moment

'By the way, Whalley, did you have a police-inspector up here yesterday afternoon?'

'No. Why?'

'Oh, I had a chap bothering me with enquiries about my shover—you know him—Chidgey. Er—I thought he might have come up to you. Now, look here, I shall be seeing Burdon at the club tonight. Do let me tell him that I'm bringing another gun out on Tuesday. He'll be delighted. Do you no end of good, my dear chap. You'll come? Good. That's a fixture, then.'

Whalley shut the hall-door and stood looking at it as if this sudden danger stood at its other side. At once the connection which had seemed to him impossible had been made. At once they had viewed that thing which they had found under the

Grevilles' laurels not as Grevilles' maid, but as the Prossips'. At once they had begun to search for her killer, not in Abbey Road, but in Downview Road. The first time he had gone out he had found a searcher—outside the door—waiting.

Chidgey—how was it possible that he hadn't thought of Chidgey?

But Chidgey would be able to clear himself. He would be able to account for his movements that night. They would have found plenty of footprints to compare with his; that would clear him—he was a small man. And when they had failed with Chidgey they would turn away from Downview Road. No searcher would come up the steps. If Chidgey talked about Prossip, the Prossips were in Guildford.

For a few days the sharp whirr of the hall-door bell stiffened every muscle of his body. Sometimes he waited until the trades-man's messenger rang a second time before opening the door. When he went out, he went down the outside steps slowly, despite himself, expectant of a burly figure standing waiting at its foot. When he returned, he went up them slowly. The top flight cut off his view of his own hall-door until he was within a few feet from it. There was, however, no personal apprehension in this vigilance; his fear contemplated solely the possible disruption of his plan. He slept well, ate well, felt his body and his mind stronger than he had felt them for several years. To occupy his time, he re-papered the bathroom.

The days passed, and nothing kept happening. The Abbey Road murder disappeared from the *Daily Times*. He had his day's shooting with Knayle and shot well. On the way home Knayle told him that Chidgey's little trouble had passed over, and then began to talk about something else.

'What about another day next week?' he asked as they parted outside his flat. But Whalley said that he would be away for the following week—Mr Knayle understood, at Bournemouth, though he was not quite sure about this because Mr Ridgeway came up his little flight of steps just then and began to tell them about the mice which had suddenly become very troublesome in his kitchen. When Whalley left them and went up the steps, the two elder men looked after him.

'He looks better, don't you think?' said Mr Ridgeway. 'He's able to bang a punching ball about, at all events. Everything passes.'

'Oh no, no, no, no,' laughed Mr Knayle cheerily as he turned towards his own door. 'Everything that has been is for ever.'

He was a little dejected by Mr Ridgeway's platitude, and a little interested to hear that Whalley was using a punching-ball to keep himself fit. He had wondered as to the explanation of some peculiar sounds which he had heard occasionally over his head during the past week or so.

CHAPTER X

1

On the morning on which he went up to Guildford Whalley's preparations for his journey were all completed an hour too soon. His old suit-case stood in the passage; his old overcoat hung over the balusters. He wandered from room to room slowly; but there was nothing to do—everything was spick-and-span. While he was straightening the mat outside the sitting-room door, the hall-door bell rang. He went down the stairs slowly; the whirr of the hall-door bell still tautened his muscles and made the movements of his numb legs and feet stiff and difficult.

But it was only Penfold, endeavouring to look friendly and sympathetic as he held out his hand.

'Good morning, Mr Whalley. I just happened to be up this way and thought I'd drop in and see you for a moment. I'm sorry to hear that you've had a bereavement.'

'Yes.'

'I know what it is. I've been through it myself. I lost my own wife last year, and . . . well, the way it is, it's only when people are gone that you know what they were to you. Yes. Well, what I wanted to see you about, Mr Whalley, was about that bit of papering and painting you wanted done a while back. Perhaps I might have a look round, just to see what's necessary—'

'No. I don't think you need bother about it, Mr Penfold. My tenancy has only a year to run. I'm quite satisfied to let the flat go on as it is.'

Mr Penfold was rather hurt. He was not in the habit of offering people something for nothing and money was precious tight just now. Number 48 would have to be done up in the spring. It had taken him a fortnight to decide that he would offer to do that bit of papering and painting—after all, for no more reason than that this chap Whalley, who had been damned overbearing and cocky with him, had lost his wife too. It would cost a tenner, at least. Not a word of thanks.

'Well, yes, I know,' he said, tilting his bowler to the back of his head. 'But of course there's the question of keeping the property up. I got to consider that. Do I understand that you intend giving up the flat at the end of the year?'

'I don't know at all.'

Mr Penfold tilted his hat forward again. 'Well, but—how it is, you'll have to give me notice in June what you intend to do. I'll be wanting to find a new tenant for it. It'll have to be put in good order before June, you see, so that when people come to look at it— I suppose you wouldn't think of terminating your tenancy now? It can't be very agreeable for you now. I'd agree to that, if you had any idea that you'd like to have it off your hands. In fact, I believe I could find a new tenant for it tomorrow. Anyhow I had better have a look round and see what's to be done.'

He stuck at it, edging his way in, determined now to do that bit of papering and painting, gradually resuming his normal surly truculence. When at last he went away, sniffing and hostile, Whalley went up the stairs and stood looking about him, disquieted. His solitude—the hiding-place in which he had been able to shut himself in with all that was still his— was threatened. Already they were trying to drive him out of it—thinking of a time when he and his thoughts and his secrets and his plans would be gone from it, when the very last trace of her would have been swept away. Already they were preparing for the time when there would be nothing left of her or him and what they had been and loved and suffered and lost. They were trying to drive him out into the open—where he couldn't think and plan—where everyone would see him. Already the bell was whirring, eagerly, peremptorily; but they could do nothing. For a whole year his hiding-place was his.

A year—that was for ever. Long before that it wouldn't matter whether the bell whirred.

He opened the door of the sitting-room, looked in, and shut it again, thinking of the set of Crown Derby on the Welsh dresser. What would become of it when they had forced their way in? What would become of all the things that had been hers and his? There would be no one to claim them—no one with the right to sell them. Perhaps Mrs Canynge would claim the Crown Derby set—it had come to Elsa from her mother. And Elsa's jewellery . . . Some time he must make a will. St Dunstan's . . . The things wouldn't fetch much, but St Dunstan's would be glad to get a few pounds. But even then her things would still go on being—scattering, wandering into all sort of queer alien places—handled by people who did filthy things with their hands—

He strayed into the bathroom and looked round it doubtfully. It had always been the eyesore of the flat, and Elsa and he had discussed many times the advisability of having it repapered and repainted, like the bedroom and dining-room and kitchen, at their own expense. Now, with the new wall-paper, despite the dinginess of the paint and the cracks in the ceiling, it looked bright and cheerful. She would have liked it so. But he regretted now that he had repapered it; it was no longer as she had known it. His eyes fell on the geyser which had dulled a little, and he glanced at his watch desultorily. There was plenty of time to do it.

The polishing of the geyser had always been a troublesome business—one of those small jobs which had taken up a lot of time and whose useless, endless repetition had at times produced in him an actual physical nausea. Now, however, the intricacies of the pilot-jet and the tap, the difficulty of getting at the back of the cylinder owing to its proximity to the wall, and the impossibility of removing altogether the small marks on the lacquer, produced in him no emotion whatever save in so far as the mechanical movements of his hands formed part of the purpose for which his consciousness still continued. He stepped back to look at the results of his polishing critically, tidied away his cleaning things, put on his hat and coat and, picking up his suit-case, let himself out into the tepid colourless morning. Its greyness pleased him a little; his old overcoat had grown so shabby that people looked at it sometimes as they passed. But he had decided that it wasn't worth while buying a new one now.

During the last stage of his journey, from Reading to Guildford, he was alone in his fusty smoker and he resumed his dispassionate musings upon the enterprise which lay before him, peering out occasionally through the fogged windows to discover the train's whereabouts.

There had been no Deepford Residential Hotel, so far as he could recall, when Elsa and he had lived in Guildford, all but ten years before. Knayle's description of it, however, had fixed its position fairly definitely in a limited area of quiet residential roads lying some little distance outside the town, along the rising ground which ran up towards Merrow Down. His recollections of the eastern outskirts of Guildford had grown vague; but he recalled that many of the roads in that particular area had then been newly made and that along some of them building had not yet been begun. He saw a typical quiet, newly-made suburban road, with widely-spaced villas, tree-bordered footpaths, a car standing outside a gate, a straying dog, an elderly man prodding a piece of paper into the gutter with his walking-stick before he strolled slowly on. Somewhere along it was the Deepford, a large, quiet, dull-looking house standing in from the road, beyond a lawn dotted with small trees and shrubs. The quiet road led into other quiet roads; it was all quiet out there. He saw only this limited area of quietness ignoring all the rest of Guildford, its busy streets, its thirty thousand inhabitants, and all the complicated organisation which watched over their safety. Along that quiet road one could pass and repass a dozen times slowly without meeting the same person twice—

loiter—stop to read a newspaper. After dark it would be almost as deserted as Abbey Road. All the difficulties to be contended with, all the advantages that would help, were contained within a patrol as limited as that which he had kept, for two nights only and for an hour only each night, outside the Grevilles' gates. The advantages lay uppermost in his detached calculation of chances; difficulties would be dealt with as they had been, simply and with complete success. It was merely a matter of patience—adjustment of small working details. No hurrying. This time everything would be as sure and sharp and accurate as the snap of a lock.

At Guildford station his confidence received a sudden shock.

His carriage was at the end of the train and, when he rose to leave it, his legs, as always when they had remained for any length of time in one position, were cramped and painful. As he passed along the platform, left behind by the rapidly-moving stream of passengers making for the exit, two men, who had been standing with their backs towards him, laughing as they looked up at a poster representing a bottle of stout, turned, still laughing, and looked at him. There was no resemblance between them either in face or figure, but both pairs of eyes made the same guarded, deliberate scrutiny of him—took in his hat, his face, his overcoat, his suit-case, his trousers, his shoes, his stiffness and slowness of gait, and then left him, as something judged and noted provisionally. At once he had recognised one face vaguely. Someone, he concluded, who belonged to ten years ago—probably one of the tradespeople (he looked like a shopkeeper) with whom Elsa had dealt when they had lived in Guildford. But, as he gave up his ticket, an abrupt realisation turned his head over his shoulder. The face belonged to now. It was the face which he had seen by the light of a match—coming out of the darkness suddenly.

He stiffened as if the hall-door bell had whirred.

The police-inspector who had visited Knayle—who had waited at the foot of the steps in the darkness—here—at Guildford,

waiting. A Dunpool police-inspector here in Guildford. *The*
Dunpool police-inspector here in Guildford—waiting to look at
him the moment he got out of the carriage.

But at once an obvious explanation suggested itself—became
the only possible explanation. Naturally the Dunpool police
would hope that the Prossips might be able to furnish some
information concerning Agatha Judd which would help them—
and naturally the Dunpool inspector in charge of the affair
would come up to Guildford where the Prossips were. Whalley
decided completely that the encounter had been a mere coincidence. By no possibility could anyone have known that he
himself was coming to Guildford. The man had looked at him
attentively, but, he felt sure, had not recognised him. Probably
he was merely waiting for a train to take him back to Dunpool.
Certainly, if he was not already on his way back there, he would
return there in a day or two. There would be nothing to keep
him in Guildford once he had interviewed the Prossips. For a
day or two it would be necessary to expect to meet him unexpectedly. But he was a big man. One would recognise him easily
some little distance off.

He waited near the wicket, pretending absorption in the
time-tables, and saw the two men shake hands and separate.
The Dunpool inspector disappeared down a subway, reappeared on another platform, and was carried away in a train
from which he waved a farewell to his friend. Whalley picked
up his suit-case and left the station, smiling grimly. What was
it the fellow had said? '. . . I don't think you can help me . . .'

He decided to postpone the selection of lodgings until the
exact position of the Deepford had been ascertained. When he
had engaged a room at a small hotel in North Street, he hurried
out again, anxious to avail himself of the last chill light of the
afternoon; but the roads along which he strayed, unwilling to
ask direction, were absolutely familiar. When at last he found
the Deepford, standing at one angle of a busy cross-roads,
darkness had fallen and two powerful arc-lamps guarded the

gate-pillars of its entrance. Two more guarded the wide steps leading up to a revolving door inside which a liveried hall-porter stood in a blaze of light. The short drive and the strips of bare lawn that flanked it were flooded with light. All the four rows of windows were lighted up. In the bay of the drive a noisy party of young people stood clustered by two large cars whose headlamps glared out at him defiantly. There were lights everywhere. From the brightly-lighted cross-roads four brightly-lighted roads ran away, bordered on either side by small new houses of the villa type, whose lighted windows made of them avenues of cheerful, confident vigilance. The pathways were not crowded, but there were always figures arriving at all the angles of the cross-roads, pausing, looking to right and left, and then hurrying to escape from the lights of a car. A policeman passed the gates of the Deepford, looked in, went on to stand at the angle to watch the crossing of the traffic. Whalley turned away and went back to his hotel, disconcerted. The Prossips lived in the town—in daylight.

Next morning he transferred himself to lodgings near the London Road station and began the difficult task of keeping the Deepford under observation. It was a fatiguing and monotonous business, involving an immense amount of walking and, for some days, complete disappointment. Twenty times a day he passed the entrance of the hotel, halted a little way up the road, then went on slowly to stray along the adjoining roads until he judged his last passing forgotten by anyone who might have noticed it. Too frequent goings and comings would have aroused the curiosity of his landlady; he was on his feet for hours at a stretch, returning to his lodgings too exhausted to eat the tepid chops which a slatternly maid slapped down in a dingy table-cloth with a curt 'Yer dinner.' At the end of a week he had discovered merely that Prossip went off most mornings about ten o'clock in the direction of the town and returned to the hotel a little before two. Of Mrs Prossip and her daughter he had seen nothing.

Then, however, a slight alteration in the hour at which he returned to his uninviting midday meal brought Marjory Prossip into view. He had breakfasted late that morning and it was a quarter-past two when he reached the entrance of the Deepford for what he had decided should be the last time that day. Marjory Prossip drove out through the gates in a small car, passing suddenly so close to him that he could have touched her. Her attention was divided, however, between the traffic of the road and her violin-case, which stood upright on the seat beside her. She had not seen him.

On three afternoons during the following week he saw her drive off at the same hour towards the town, always with her violin. He arrived at the conclusion that these regular departures pointed to some regular objective—presumably at some distance away. Possibly, he conjectured, she was giving violin lessons somewhere in the neighbourhood. He decided to return to Rockwood and bring up his own car. His plan had now abandoned the Deepford and was following a blue Baby Austin with a crumpled wing, which went off towards the town on alternate afternoons a little after two o'clock and returned a little before half-past seven.

And in a car one could wait anywhere, sitting.

In a chemist's shop one morning a hand touched his sleeve and a voice said, 'Mr Whalley, isn't it?' He had given the name 'Webster' at his lodgings and the sound 'Whalley' whirred an alarm. But in the end he decided to turn. It was the buxom, cheerful landlady of the lodgings of ten years ago, so shrunken and so forlorn that only her timid 'Mrs Rankin' enabled him to recognise her. Probably he had passed many people who had remembered him, but whom he had failed to recognise. Twice, between his lodgings and the Deepford he met the man who had seen the Dunpool inspector off at the station. And in the High Street, one afternoon, outside a tobacconist's shop, he had a curious meeting with Prossip.

He was standing, looking in at the gay window-display,

debating the purchase of a pipe, when an alteration in the light reflected from a long mirror attached to the wall beside the door of the shop attracted his attention to it. Prossip's image stood there, attired in a new, tightly-waisted overcoat, smoking a cigar as if he hated it, and regarding him with an intent scowl. He had been aware that someone had stopped outside the window, just behind him but, it had seemed to him, casually; but now, as he realised that it was Prossip who had stopped, the stopping appeared suddenly to have been deliberate and of definite purpose. For a long time Prossip's reflection glared and then the strip of mirror was empty and bright again. There had been no sign of recognition in the glare; but the incident was disquieting. The doubt would always remain.

In half an hour he was completely certain that Prossip had not recognised him. His purpose was a Juggernaut which rolled over all doubts and left them behind, flattened and squeezed of all threat. No one was aware of him, or knew what his curli-macews were planning and patting into shape. Sometimes he smiled at the stupidity of the people who jostled him along the narrow, crowded footpaths of the High Street.

He went out to Puttiford that afternoon by 'bus, timing his arrival so as to reach the cottage just after darkness had fallen. The little red-curtained windows might be lighted up; a stout motherly figure might stand silhouetted in the porch. But the lane which had led to Myrtle Cottage was now a road and a row of ugly little houses passed over the place where, astound-ingly, it was no longer. It had been burnt down, he heard in the village, a good bit back—getting on for two years now.

Another encounter which disquieted him a little occurred on the last afternoon of his stay in Guildford. He had gone up on to Merrow Down by the Leatherhead Road and struck across the golf-links towards a seat on which Elsa and he had often sat and discussed their plans for a future which had already begun to threaten. The seat stood at a high viewpoint on the crest of a long slope, some distance off the fairway of the course and sheltered by a high hedge which enclosed it on three sides; no one had disturbed their talks. They had sat there, he remembered vividly, the morning on which it had been decided definitely that he should abandon play-writing and try his luck with a novel; his tongue had been very sore just then and he hadn't been able to smoke. As he neared the seat—it had stood there all those days of those years—a young woman came along the path which passed in front of it and, after a frigid glance in his direction, sat down on it.

His feet stopped in the long, coarse grass for the time of a step. She was there—not ten yards from him—at his mercy. Three strides would reach her. He glanced swiftly back along the long bare slope which he had just ascended. Far away, down by the road, the houses were already indistinct. No one in sight there. No one along the last hole. No one to the left, back along the path. No one to the right. What was beyond the hedge at the other side of the path? A field of some sort. Elsa and he had looked through the hedge . . . cabbages . . . There would be no one in a cabbage-field at this hour.

But he turned away from the seat. Nothing was ready. There must be no hurry this time—no botching. Fifty yards from the seat, round a curve of the path, he met two farm labourers clumping home. Each of them carried a muddy cabbage tucked under his arm.

2

When Marjory Prossip had one of her headaches, her left eye kept twitching. It was twitching now as she sat looking down the slope towards the little distant houses along the Leatherhead Road. It had been twitching, on and off, ever since the last time she had sat on this seat. For a whole fortnight she had had a headache—nothing but a headache. That was all that had been left behind by the most extraordinary, terrible, enthralling, untellable thing that had ever happened her—a headache as dull as ditchwater and a twitch under her left eye. What rotten little houses those were down there—smelly little backyards where hens picked at old cabbage-stalks . . .

A Mr Chappell—he had been the first Claude she had ever known—had come to stay at the Deepford two weeks before—a quiet, middle-aged man with a limp and a charming voice which had been able to say quite extraordinary and—well uncomfortable—things in a detached, casual, cultured way which had made them seem the most ordinary things in the world to talk about. His voice had been the most noticeable thing about him. He had been rather plain, though his smile, in profile, had sometimes been quite attractive, and a little out of it at the Deepford on account of his limp—the result, he had said, of a shooting-accident in Burmah where he had owned plantations of some sort. They had had a long talk in a quiet corner of the lounge one evening, about all sort of things—Freud and birth-control and homosexualism and totemism and infinity and things of that sort—and he had promised to lend her a novel by someone called D. H. Lawrence. Next day he had proposed an afternoon walk, and after tea they had come up on to the Down by the back roads, slowly on account of his limp, talking about something called the Mendelian Theory and the Berlin night-clubs. It had been quite dark when they had arrived at the seat.

She had been telling him about her mother's heart-attacks when, suddenly, he had gone mad. Mad was the only word she could find for it—ferocious, panting, grunting, glaring-eyed mad. His arms had grabbed her and pulled her off the seat down on to the grass and there, while they struggled in the darkness, he had grunted and panted insane, crude, beastly things which, after a while, had made her feel vile and debased and willing to surrender. He had torn her clothes and bitten her—she had nearly stopped struggling then. But she had kept her head and jabbed both her thumbs into his eyes. That had ended the affair. He had uttered a little childish, frightened cry and let her go. She had left him there, sitting on the grass in the darkness, and, somehow, got back to her bedroom at the hotel, with a violent headache and a twitch under her left eye.

Mr Chappell had gone away next day. She had not seen him again—probably never would see him again—never wanted to see him again. He had come into her life to do that to her and leave her with the worst headache she had had for years. He was simply a part of the headache.

And yet it had certainly been a most extraordinary, terrible, exciting thing while it had lasted. It seemed impossible that it could have happened for no purpose—with no result. That sort of thing had never come near her before. There had been no necessity to keep it away; men's eyes had always told her that they had no use for her. That man who had come up across the grass just now had turned his back after a glance at her. These two working men coming up the path—they would glance at her, tell her that she was no use for that sort of thing, and look away at once. A curious thing that one man should appear, try to do that sort of thing to her, and disappear.

That sort of thing had often happened on that seat, she supposed. Dreadful, gawky, smirking young men from the town and dreadful squealing little shopgirls must often come up there in the evenings and maul and carry on . . . Disgusting.

She thought of her violin lying in its nest of amber velvet, the rich, soft brown gleam of its varnish, the clean, sharp strings, the familiar smell of resin and varnish when she opened the case. Dear old friend—always there to go back to; honest, clean, pure; far, far away from all that sort of thing. *It* knew what poor old plain, pasty, lumpy Marjory really was.

Her walk had done her headache no good—if anything the headache was a little worse. She didn't know why she had come up to this beastly old seat. Heaven knew who had sat on it last—some tramp perhaps; she had passed the workhouse on her way up.

She sprang up, brushed her broad stern vigorously with both

hands, shook herself, and hurried off down the slope towards the road to catch a 'bus which would bring her back to the Deepford in time for an hour's practice before dinner. She *would* practise in her bedroom. They might kick up a fuss, but they wouldn't stop her. They wouldn't silence that one dear old, kind, trusty friend.

Mr Prossip had been having a hell of a time of it for the past three weeks or so. The police had been pestering the life out of him about Agatha Judd and that trip of his to Rockwood. He had had to tell them that he had been thrashed and that he had been drinking in public-houses and that he had spent the night with the girl with the cough. They had treated him, not at all as a sahib, but as a liar and a drunkard and a seducer of servant-maids. They had conveyed to him that, if they came back to the Deepford and asked him the same questions often enough, they would be able to treat him as a murderer. They had come in plain clothes and he had smuggled them up to his bedroom, but he had felt, and felt now, perfectly sure that the whole hotel knew that they had been policemen. The manager had become distant and he had found difficulty in getting a game of bridge. In the end he had had to tell Emma who those queer-looking men had been and what they had come pestering him about. That had been a hell of a thing to have to do. Emma hadn't spoken to him since. Marjory hadn't spoken a word to him either for days. It was the very devil to have to sit opposite their two glum faces all through dinner and feel that everyone in the dining-room knew why they didn't speak to him.

He was standing by his dressing-table, scowling at his thoughts and wondering whether he wouldn't run up to town for a show, when he heard Marjory's violin. For the past three weeks he had felt cowed and bullied, and now a savage impulse to cow and bully someone else sent him pounding along the corridor and into Marjory's bedroom. He snatched her violin away from her chin, wrested it from her hand, and threw it on the bed.

'Now, damn you,' he snarled. 'Will you stop it? Do you want to have us turned out of the hotel? Do you? Do you, I say?'

For a moment Marjory stared at the violin, then she turned, picked up the carafe from the washstand and threw it at him. It missed him, passed out through the open door, and crashed against the opposite wall of the corridor. The crash excited her to bare-gummed fury and she followed the carafe with the soap-dish and the tooth-glass. They were struggling for the possession of the slop-pail-cover when the boots intervened.

3

Mr Knayle hadn't been able to settle down. The weather since his return had been depressing—a succession of grey, damp days on which he hadn't felt inclined to do anything in particular. His time had been frittered away in visits to his dentist, his oculist and his optician, his bank-manager, his stock-broker, and his tailor, and almost every day, at an inconvenient hour, he had had to keep some appointment which had involved waiting in more or less depressing surroundings and produced more or less depressing results. There had been no time to do anything of any real pleasure or interest.

A curious and rather sinister thing had been happening to him since his return. As if they had lain in wait for his home-coming, several causes had suddenly combined to compel him to an uneasy interest in his body.

It had been necessary to get another new plate and have three teeth stopped. The dentist had been gloomy about the failure of his first effort and had attempted to lay the blame for it on Mr Knayle's mouth. After fifty, he had said, everyone must expect that his mouth would change and keep on changing—shrinking processes set in. Mr Knayle had been depressed by the idea of his gums keeping on shrinking indefinitely and by the prospect of never being able to eat again with complete comfort and grace. The dentist had observed his depression and becoming cheerfully vindictive, had tapped two back teeth and said they would probably have to come out very shortly. That, of course, would involve another new plate.

The oculist had also been depressing. He, too, had spoken of changes which must be expected when a man reached fifty, and had not only prescribed more powerful lenses for reading purposes, but, to Mr Knayle's consternation, had told him that the wearing of glasses for long-distance ranges would be henceforward an imperative necessity. He had been quite exultant over his discovery that Mr Knayle's astigmatism had grown much more pronounced since he had last examined it, two years before, and had used the ominous word 'atrophy.' It had never occurred to Mr Knayle before that his eye-muscles, or any of his muscles could atrophy and keep on atrophying quietly without his being able to do anything to stop them.

His tailor had been rather familiarly jocose concerning an increase of an inch and a half in his waist measurement. His hair-dresser had found some dandruff in his hair, advised him to part it in a new place, and, without asking permission, had snipped away the hairs in his ears—a thing which no hair-dresser had ever done or offered to do to Mr Knayle's ears before. A 'bus conductor had helped him on to the step of a 'bus—another thing which had never happened to him before. He had discovered a small patch of eczema under one of his eyebrows. And, suddenly, one morning in his bath, he had noticed his toe-nails. He had always taken meticulous care of his toe-nails, but, in the course of a few weeks, in which he had not been able to pay so much attention as usual to them, they had gone utterly to seed. Some of them had split, others had begun to grow into the skin of the toe, most of them had turned yellow, all of them had developed a hard, chalky inner growth which had forced them outwards and twisted them in the most repulsive way. It had not been possible to dislodge this unpleasant substance with any degree of satisfactoriness. He had thought of going to a pedicurist, but had been able to discover no male pedicurist in

Rockwood. The exhibition of those distorted yellow ruins to a female of any sort had appeared to him out of the question.

His body had always conducted its affairs satisfactorily; he had never had to think about it. But now it had suddenly become unreliable and treacherous. He thought about it at night in bed—of all the complicated, disagreeable things that were hidden under the deceptive envelope of his skin—any of them liable to break down at any moment. The discovery of definite symptoms of decay had merged themselves into and pointed the vague dissatisfaction with himself awakened by close contact for three weeks with a number of healthy, vigorous, quick-minded young people. He had thought about those young people on the ship a great deal since—about their smooth skins, their tireless limbs, their elastic movements, their gay indifference to risks, the quick play of their minds, their capacity for liking and disliking strongly and vividly. There was no doubt about it, they had thought of him as old. They had been quite nice and jolly about it, but they had decided at once that he was done with it and out of it—something between a nuisance and a joke—something that was merely in their way. It was useless to argue that they had been merely thoughtless, stupid young people; he knew that their thoughts had been as clear as crystal, their judgment unerring. They, who owned life, had told him that he was old and would have no more share in it. He was, and always would be now, old and out of it. Eyes going, teeth going, toe-nails going, hair going from where it should be and coming where it shouldn't be, a pot sticking out in front. Good God! What an old scarecrow—falling to pieces . . .

Then a most distressing thing had happened at the club. He had been talking to Charlie Housall and some other men in the smoking-room about the extraordinary number of well-known people who had died in the neighbourhood that year. Poor old Charlie (he had been at Winchester with Mr Knayle) had said 'Good-night,' walked out into the hall, and dropped dead while a waiter had been helping him into his overcoat.

His income tax for 1932 had already become an anxiety. He had never overdrawn his bank-account since he had had one; but a very considerable overdraft would be absolutely necessary in January unless he sold some of his securities—at a very serious loss. His stockbroker, on the whole, had been of opinion that securities would continue to depreciate gradually until the crash came—perhaps at the end of February.

And so, as he sat in his sitting-room, Mr Knayle's thoughts had darkened. When they looked out on the world through the *Morning Post* they saw only a ghastly mess. When they looked at Mr Knayle they saw only his toe-nails. And when they looked up at the ceiling they saw only a ceiling.

Not a pang had fallen from it—only a gentle, painless regret, like the regret one felt when one thought of steady, cold rain pattering down on some place that one had known in sunshine. Some times it was quite impossible to remember what she had actually looked like—what the total effect of her face had been. And there was always the feeling that one had forgotten a little more of her—that it was safer not to tease and test what one still remembered.

Well . . . one could think of others . . .

A sprinkling of elderly people, contemporaries and friends of his parents, many of them invalids and most of them in reduced circumstances, still lived in Rockwood. He found them out in their lodgings and boarding-houses, brought them boxes of chocolates and magazines, and drank their washy tea while they maundered on of people and things which he had forgotten for thirty years. When he discovered that Charlie Housall's widow was in difficulties over the payment of succession duties and probate fees, he sold some of his stock and lent her three hundred pounds. Meeting Whalley in the garden on the day after his return from Bournemouth, he had another kindly thought. There was room in his garage for a second car, and no sense whatever in Whalley's paying ten shillings a week unnecessarily. He was extremely glad that he had thought of making this little suggestion. Whalley had been wearing a most deplorable old pair of shoes.

Old Ridgeway . . . What little kindly thing could one think of for him?

Mr Knayle bought a set of chessmen and a board and a book of the rules and invited Mr Ridgeway up for a game. Neither of them had played chess for forty years. It was a massacre. They made wrong moves, recalled moves, forgot where they had moved from, upset the pieces and put them back on the wrong squares. Their knights sprang round corners like boomerangs. For a long time Mr Knayle used his bishops as queens, and at one point, in a moment of excitement, took Mr Ridgeway's king with his own. Ultimately only the two kings were left stalking round the board, and they began afresh with portentous caution, considering each move with paralysed intentness, losing in the end all notion of what they were attempting to do, and subsiding into drowsy boredom. They gave it up finally and seated themselves by the fire and Mr Knayle talked for a while about his trip and the National Government, which he considered doomed to failure.

'Had any more visits from the police?' Mr Ridgeway asked presently, as he refilled his gurgling pipe.

Mr Knayle laughed. 'No. They've been worrying Chidgey a bit, but I think they've given him up as a bad job now. He was able to produce some friends who saw him in a cinema that night. And they had a violent disappointment over his garage-boots.'

'Garage-boots?' Mr Ridgeway repeated, yawning. 'I didn't read the accounts. What had Chidgey's garage-boots to do with it?'

'Oh, they found a lot of footprints. Whoever did the job wore an out-size in boots, apparently, and so my friend, Inspector Bride, had a bright idea and made a bee-line for Chidgey's garage-boots. Unfortunately, however, they didn't fit the footprints, so I rather think he's decided to leave poor old

Chidgey in peace.' Mr Knayle poked the fire. 'No. I must say this whole question of war debts and reparations is extraordinarily difficult. Of course, one can quite understand France's attitude, looking at it as a Frenchman would look at it . . .'

Mr Ridgeway lighted his pipe and threw the match into the fire. Extraordinary jumpy little chap, Knayle, always changing the subject that way . . . What on earth did anyone ever want to play chess for? . . . Big boots? What had he thought about big boots lately? Where had he seen big boots lately? Or had he seen them—or only heard them—and thought that they must be very heavy, big boots? What was Knayle chattering about now. Unemployment in America. Well, let him chatter away. All one had to do was to say 'yes' and 'I suppose so.' . . . Big boots? Bo—the sound of big boots, going up . . .

Then Mr Ridgeway remembered. It had been that night that he had gone up to the top of his little flight of steps to smoke another pipe before he smoked another pipe and went to bed. Whalley had come into the garden from the road and passed him and gone up the outside staircase, and his boots had made a large, heavy, clumping noise as they had gone up. Mr Ridgeway remembered that he had looked up the steps after them and thought that they must be a very large, heavy pair of boots. A curious thing—that must have been the night of the murder. It had been the night before the night on which Knayle had come down and told him about the murder and about a police-inspector having come bothering him—What on earth was Knayle talking about *now?* What did it matter what he was talking about? It wasn't even necessary to say 'yes' and 'I suppose so.' *He* hadn't known what shame and fear and searing, hopeless remorse were. *He* hadn't skulked in the ashpits of hell for eleven years. Let him chatter away. A grunt would do.

'Whalley's going away again, he tells me,' said Mr Knayle, eyeing Mr Ridgeway's pipe and trying to think that others were entitled to smoke gurgling pipes if it helped to make their lives a little happier. 'Going to Bournemouth.'

'Um,' grunted Mr Ridgeway.

'A very tragic thing happened at the club,' said Mr Knayle. 'I don't think I've seen you since. A very intimate friend of mine—a man called Housall—dropped dead—well, practically at my feet. Quite a young man—my own age. A charming chap. Gave us all a tremendous shock, I needn't tell you. Though, of course, if they had the choice, I suppose most people would be glad to die that way. I've often wondered—the majority of people who die in the ordinary ways—pneumonia or cancer or diabetes, or so on—at the last moment, do they . . . er . . . do they realise that they're going to die—or are they usually unconscious?'

'Oh, usually,' yawned Mr Ridgeway.

'It's the pass-over that's such a curious thing to think about,' said Mr Knayle. 'The sudden change. Now, Charlie Housall was putting his arm into the sleeve of his overcoat when he died. I suppose he was thinking about putting his arm into the sleeve of his overcoat—and then he was dead. One . . . er . . . one can't imagine the actual pass-over. I mean—have you ever thought about—about what's on the other side, Ridgeway?'

Mr Ridgeway laughed harshly.

'Thought about it? I've thought about it for eleven years, anyhow. Nothing, I think personally.' His fingers groped in a waistcoat pocket and took out a little metal case. He shook it, looked at it, and then replaced it in its pocket. 'Some day, or some night, I hope I'll feel sure about it. I always keep these little beggars handy, in case— But, it's funny—at the last moment I always funk it. Why? You're quite satisfied with Harvey Knayle, aren't you? I'll bet you can't think of anything you'd sooner be.'

Mr Knayle's blue eyes had remained fixed up on his guest's waistcoat speculatively. 'What is it?' he asked at length.

'Cyanide of potassium.'

'Oh. Very quick, isn't it?'

'A minute or so. A long time, a minute, though, Knayle. And you *might* have to start all over again at the end of it.'

'Well,' smiled Mr Knayle, 'I hope I shall start with a new set of toenails. Mine have got into a perfectly horrible state. Gout, I suppose.'

They talked about toenails and Mr Ridgeway yawned and suggested linseed oil and shambled towards the door, picking up the 'Rules of Chess' as he passed, opening it, and dropping it on the table again. He halted at the head of his little flight of steps when Mr Knayle's hall-door had shut with a bright 'Good-night,' and looked up at the stars.

They were very large and bright and they had come nearer to watch. They seemed to him to be quivering with impatience for some ending. It came into his mind suddenly that he would set off into the darkness as he was, in his slippers and without a hat, and walk out along those long miles of road to Camphill and do it there, in company, with the impatient stars watching him. He would never do it alone; he knew that now. But she was out there. The air that held her dust would envelope him with her forgiveness until he fell. He would find courage for that minute—think of nothing whatever—just count 'One—two—three—four—'

But he could never walk ten miles now. And when he got out there he would take out his little case and funk it again, as he had always done. And then there would be ten miles to walk back—in slippers and without a hat. He might meet a policeman and have to answer questions—say who he was and where he lived.

As he turned slowly to go down to his hall-door, feeling for his keys, the outside staircase passed across his view. Big boots—Rather curious that he should have noticed the bigness of a pair of boots on that particular night. Maddening little chap, Knayle—always changing the subject. Begun to think about having to die evidently—wondering if there wouldn't be some way to dodge it. Ah well, the stoat would get him in the end, fasten on his little neck and pull him down.

But not a bad little chap in his way.

*

Mr Knayle sighed faintly as he returned to his sitting-room; thinking of others was rather uphill work. He came to a pause before his writing-desk and picked up a letter which he had received that morning.

> Deepford Residential Hotel,
> Guildford,
> Nov. 17, 1931.

DEAR HARVEY,—Many thanks for the birds which arrived quite safely. Your friends the Prossips have left, under a cloud of some sort. No one seems to know exactly what the cloud was made of, but some of the hotel's crockery was mixed up in it. We all miss Mr Prossip's eyeglass so much. Tolly Duckett's widow is living in Guildford; she comes up to feed with us sometimes. A perfectly sweet thing; everyone here adores her. Not a red, and a small boy—the very image of poor old Tolly. A lot of the people we met here last winter have come back this year, and we shall probably stay on until the spring. Do run up for a weekend some time. Bill says do, too.—Yrs., GRACE FARNOLD.

Mr Knayle put down the letter and looked round the sitting-room. It was filled with the reek of Mr Ridgeway's pipe and held no comfort or significance whatever. He was simply standing there, boxed up by four walls—a funny little two-legged thing decaying under its funny little clothes, without use or purpose.

Why not run up to Guildford for a week? The place was evidently quite cheerful and comfortable; the Farnolds wouldn't have gone back there if it hadn't been. And the Prossips had left. There would be a lot of young people there, of course—but one would have to learn not to flinch—to accept the fact that life was theirs. Mr Knayle decided to turn the matter over, wrote the words 'Linseed oil' on a memorandum block and went to bed. It would be interesting to see if linseed oil would loosen that hard stuff.

Hopgood was also thinking of oil just then. He was sitting on the edge of his bed, pulling off his socks and looking at a photograph which stood on his mantelpiece beside the alarm clock and which he had found in Mr Whalley's rubbish-bin that afternoon. He still carried the bin down to the front garden on Mondays and Thursdays, because he had felt that he would like to go on doing it, and that afternoon it had been so full of torn paper that the lid wouldn't sit down properly. When he had raised the lid he had seen the photograph lying on top of the papers and had slipped it into his pocket, though it wasn't at all a good likeness of poor little Mrs Whalley and was badly stained with oil of some sort in one corner. When he wound up his alarm clock at night it would remind him of the good old days down at Whanton when half-crowns were plentiful. He was wondering whether methylated spirit would remove the oil in the corner.

The photograph was actually an enlarged snapshot of one of Mrs Whalley's fellow V.A.D.'s at Ducey Court, and Hopgood failed to get the oil off it. But for quite a long time he thought about half-crowns every night while he undressed.

CHAPTER XI

1

THE little old car took ten hours to do the journey to Guildford, going by Odiham and Farnham. There was not a square inch of it without its own tireless squeak or squeal or rattle or jingle, each with its own tempo, indifferent to the chattering growl and grind of the engine. Everything passed it. Uphill it stood still while everything leaped over the crest. But it churned on and on, hour after hour milestone after milestone, bent on its work relentlessly. Good little old car—on and on and on. No hurry—let them go by, swishing and swooping. Whalley sang snatches of war songs sometimes. Another milestone—fifty-three miles more. Fifty-three miles more to churn and churn—steadily, steadily, round the curve, up the hill, down the hill, through the village, past the post-office, under the bridge, round the curve. Another milestone—good little old car.

At two o'clock on the following afternoon the car took up position some fifty yards from the entrance of the Deepford against the kerb at the opposite side of the road. Whalley sat in it at his ease, reading and lighting cigarette after cigarette. But at half-past three he folded his newspaper and drove away with a cluck of impatience. It was a Tuesday and the Blue Baby Austin had failed to come out through the gateway. Now it would not come until Thursday.

But it would come on Thursday.

On Thursday he waited until four o'clock. It was raining heavily and the dilapidated hood split while he was putting it up. His newspaper was a sodden rag when at last its advertisements became intolerable. But she would come on Saturday.

At three o'clock on Saturday a policeman passed close beside the car, glancing back at its front number plate, and paused at the cross-roads to make an entry in his note-book. Whalley's nerves whirred an alarm. But the policeman had not passed previously since the car had taken up its station and could not have known how long it had stood there. The entry in his note-book had had no reference to the car whatever. Whalley resumed his newspaper tranquilly.

It was not until the Thursday of the following week that a growing suspicion became a certainty. He rang up the Deepford and inquired whether Mr Prossip was in.

'Mr Prossip and his family went away last week,' a curt voice answered.

'Oh? Have they left Guildford?'

'I've no idea.'

A violent attack of dizziness assailed him as he replaced the receiver and for some minutes he stood leaning against the side of the call-box, mustering up sufficient self-control to face the bustling street again. His plan had crumbled. The last traces of that quiet road had vanished and there was no new picture to go round and round with an outline always a little blacker and clearer and surer. He had had his chance and he had botched it—failed, as he had always failed, except by the merest accident. And now, what? Which way to turn when he shut the door of the call-box and had to decide whether to go up the street or down it? It was impossible that, in over a week, he should have seen none of the Prossips if they were still in Guildford. He had seen none of them; they had escaped.

But, as he neared the little hotel in North Street where he had stayed the first night of his previous visit, he saw Prossip come out, insert his monocle in his eye solemnly, and walk very slowly towards the head of the street. Prossip had evidently been refreshing himself somewhat incautiously in the bar of the hotel and swayed from side to side of the footpath as he walked. Finally he decided to leave the footpath and walk in the gutter, completely absorbed in the effort to keep a straight line. There was no difficulty in keeping his orange-hued tweeds in sight. Whalley became incautious and was only some ten yards behind him when Mrs Prossip came round a corner and, after a swift glance, grabbed her husband by the arm and endeavoured to pull him on to the footpath. There was no time to stop or cross to the other side of the road. As Whalley passed them, looking straight before him, he was aware that the two figures in the gutter had ceased to struggle petulantly and had turned towards him. Prossip's booming growl said, 'Well, I'm damned.'

But in twenty steps he was completely sure that the Prossips had paid no attention whatever to his passing. Their arms had simply ceased to struggle just then and Prossip had decided to return to the footpath of his own free will. He had said, 'Well, I'm damned,' simply because his wife had grabbed at his arm in the street and attempted to make him walk on the footpath so that people wouldn't notice that he was tight. Whalley looked back and saw the orange tweeds following Mrs Prossip sulkily down the side-road from which she had emerged. They had not seen him.

A little distance down the road—its name, he saw, was Burford Avenue—they entered one of the respectable, dull little two-storeyed houses, when Prossip had dropped his walking-stick twice in the effort to find his key. Whalley went past the house presently and saw the name 'Hindhead' on a plate affixed to the gate of the little dank front garden. A violin was wailing in one of the upper rooms. They were all in there, safe again.

A dull, ugly little road of little stupid, useless people. Thousands and thousands of roads like that in thousands of dull, ugly towns and cities. Ugly respectable women strealing to the town and strealing back with parcels. Husbands in offices in office coats and cuff-protectors. Perambulators in front gardens. Bird cages in windows. Imitation lace curtains. A smell of cabbage and cat and furniture polish in the hall. All useless—no plan.

Lodgings . . . Perhaps some poor devil in there with a writing-block—lifting, lifting, lifting, lifting, lifting. He was still thinking of lifting little heavy weights. But there had been a gap . . . A rather pretty woman with a slight squint had come out of the lodging-house and was looking at him while she opened the garden gate. But he hadn't seen her come out of the house or come down the garden, though he was looking into the garden. And he wasn't moving—he had stopped and was holding on to the railings. He went on uneasily. That sort of thing wouldn't do.

By the end of the following week his new picture was quite definite. Some fifty yards below 'Hindhead' a short narrow lane-way ran back from Burford Avenue between high walls, and led to a little cul-de-sac which turned off at a right-angle to it at its further end. In there, in a small rectangular space, shut in from all view by the walls of the surrounding gardens, a diminutive shed of corrugated iron stood amidst a collection of evil-smelling rubbish heaps. No one went up the lane except Marjory Prossip. A little before half-past seven on Tuesday and Thursday and Saturday evenings, her Baby Austin had turned into it from the road and disappeared at its further end. One could hear it stop—hear the padlock of the shed being unlocked—hear the Baby being driven in. One would run up the lane, then, while she was switching off the lights, turning off the petrol, and getting out, penned in in the narrow space between the car and the side of the shed. One would reach the doors of the shed just as she leaned into the car to take out her violin-case—pull them to as one crept in. Her ugly white face would come out from beneath the hood. Her torch would swing up and see—

But every sound must be timed—every move reduced to exact schedule—everything as sure as the snap of a lock. He decided to take his car back to Rockwood; there was no necessity to follow the Blue Baby now, and without a car to think about . . . afterwards . . . everything would be simpler and safer.

The Guildford police took a disquieting interest in noisy engines.

The simplicity and compactness of his new setting gave him satisfaction; it was all seen in a glance and confused by no distracting irrelevance. Each sound, too, was sharply definite— each move a matter of seconds.

The little old car churned back, squeaking and rattling and growling—mile after mile—round the curve—under the railway-bridge—past the post-office—up the hill—through the village—down the hill—another milestone. Good little old car—a mile nearer.

The garage at which the car had been stabled hitherto had been at an inconvenient distance from the flat and, having decided to accept Knayle's offer and the key which had accompanied it, he had closed his account there before his departure for Guildford. Knayle's garage was empty and, as he drove into it, his lamps lighted up a shallow box which lay in one of its inner corners. He got out and stood considering its contents for a little space before he picked up a heavy, short-handled hammer, whose battered head stuck out from a jumble of rusty tyre-levers, old spoke-brushes, discarded oil rags and other miscellaneous rubbish.

In that narrow space between the wall and the Baby's hood one would have very little room; one would want something that would do its work with a half-swing. He swung the hammer tentatively and then held it to a lamp to examine the name stamped on its head. 'Vulc—' and a blur. Oh yes—Vulcan. Evidently not used. And in any case it would go back into the box. Gloves—there were some old gloves in the . . .

Krank . . . Gelump.

He was leaning over, looking down. Gradually his dizziness gathered swimming planes of dimness into recognition. He was bending over the railing of the outside staircase, looking down into the little area of the basement flat, and holding his suitcase between his body and the rail. Perplexity held him motionless while he strove to understand how he had come there, and why he was leaning over the rail. It was only when the suitcase slipped a little that one of his hands told him that it had just dropped something.

A robed figure appeared below him, silhouetted against the light of a hurriedly opened door.

'Hullo, Whalley,' said Mr Ridgeway. 'I thought I heard you going up. Dropped some of your property into my area?'

'Yes,' Whalley replied, and began to descend towards him. 'Don't bother to come out.'

'No bother, no bother,' Mr Ridgeway yawned, striking a match. 'I've got it.'

When he had shambled up his little flight of steps and handed over Whalley's hammer, he turned and shambled down them again quickly because he had left a saucepan of milk on the kitchen gas-ring and he was afraid that it might boil over.

'You've been away, haven't you?' he asked before he shut his hall-door. There was no reply from above. But he knew that Whalley had been away and, shutting the door, shambled on to the kitchen, where he discovered to his annoyance that the saucepan had boiled over. Whenever he boiled anything in a saucepan something always took his mind off it and it boiled over.

Whalley left his suitcase and the hammer in the flat and then went back to the garage. The doors stood open and, inside, the little old car was churning with all its lights on.

2

Mr Knayle went up to Guildford by road on a very raw day and caught a slight chill during the journey. As he crossed the Deepford's lounge towards the fireplace at which Mrs Farnold sat toasting her hands, he sneezed loudly and very nearly ejected his plate. Every head turned sharply; a hostile and condemning silence fell, and after a moment someone tittered. He was a little pink when he reached Mrs Farnold's armchair.

She flapped a handkerchief at him and enveloped him in an atmosphere of eucalyptus—a smell which he had always disliked acutely.

'Wretch. Don't come near me. There. Sit there and breathe towards the fire. Good Heavens—you've gone into blinkers. Do take them off. They make you look like a professor of phrenology. And what on earth have you done to your mouth? It's all fallen in or something. You look about fifty years older than the last time I saw you.'

With a final desperate effort Mr Knayle restored his plate to its rightful place and mustered up a philosophic smile.

'Ah, well,' he said rather hurriedly. 'We can't all hope to remain young and beautiful for ever.'

Mrs Farnold had just shaken off a slight attack of influenza and was aware that she was looking her full forty-seven. 'Well, there's no necessity to be pathetic about it,' she said rather tartly. 'How unfortunate that you selected this week to come up. Billy's away. He's had to go up to Yorkshire. His uncle's dying again—he does it every November. Oh, by the way, I'm awfully sorry, but I could only get you a room on the top floor. The hotel's full up. I told you that the Prossips had left, didn't I? Why on earth did you send them here? Of course they claimed us at once as friends of their dear old pal Harvey Knayle. Billy was awfully put out. Fortunately I got influenza and retired to bed.'

She talked about influenza. Someone had brought it back from London and it had spread through the Deepford like wildfire. Everyone in the hotel had had it or was having it or lived in dread of having it. Two of the guests had retired to nursing-homes with pneumonia, half the staff were on the sick list; influenza, it became clear, was the Deepford's all-engrossing interest. Mr Knayle understood why the sneeze which had

announced his arrival had attracted such uncomfortable attention. But he couldn't persuade himself that there had not been
some special personal absurdity connected with his entry. That
titter still made him a little pink. He looked round the lounge
and formed the conclusion that the people staying at the
Deepford were rather a cheap-looking lot. Gracie Farnold, too,
had become exceedingly plain and—well—vulgar. That semi-hu-
morous bluntness of hers had become downright rudeness. It
had been all very well fifteen or twenty years ago. But now she
was simply a rude, fattish elderly woman with a reddish nose—
like everything else, falling to pieces. Billy away, too, and the
hotel full of 'flu. Mr Knayle decided that he wasn't going to
find the Deepford at all amusing.

He never recovered from that unsuccessful *debut*. There were
no opportunities to play the part of the resigned old buffer; he
was one. From the first, disconcertingly, the Deepford decided
that he was a resigned old buffer and left him to make the best
of it. The elderly bores of the smoke-room and the bar accepted
him simply as another elderly bore. The younger people took
no notice of him whatever. Suspecting that Mrs Farnold's bluntness had spoken truth and that his new glasses really did give
him rather an air of professordom, he left them off for a couple
of days. No one, however, seemed to notice any difference in
his appearance and, remembering the oculist's warnings, he
began to wear them again. This newly-developed self-conscious-
ness made him pettish. He refused to play bridge, although he
wanted to play bridge; he refused to dance, although he wanted
to dance. The uncle in Yorkshire died and Mrs Farnold went
up for the funeral. He was left absolutely alone amidst the indifferent clatter of some seventy or eighty people who bored him
to extinction.

The fact that he had been relegated to the top floor increased
his sense of isolation. He was the only guest who slept up there,
the other bedrooms on that floor being occupied by the hotel
staff. The partition walls were very thin and his neighbour on

one side was a waiter who muttered all night and at intervals uttered a blood-curdling groan. Every night Mr Knayle had to leave the cheerful brightness of the third floor and disappear up a dark, narrow staircase without a carpet. This nightly eclipse began to worry him a good deal. The people who were saying good-night on the third floor looked at him with faint amusement.

Then a rather annoying thing happened about Chidgey. One morning he found Chidgey waiting for him in the hall with a puffed cheek and a badly scratched nose.

'Hullo, Chidgey,' he asked. 'What have you been doing to your face?'

'I'm sorry to say, sir, I've had some more trouble. I thought I'd better let you know at once what happened, in case anything should come of it. It was this way, sir: I happened to turn into the Castle Hotel in North Street for a drink last night, and who should I find there but that old swine Prossip—'

'Mr Prossip,' corrected Mr Knayle. 'Well?'

'Well, sir, him and me had some words.'

'Words? What about?'

'About that Agatha, sir. It was him as set the police on to me about her—I know it was—trying to put off his own dirty work on me. I told him so to his face, before the whole bar.'

'Well?'

'Well, the long and the short of it is, sir, I let him have it in the jaw, and then we had a bit of a scrap. They turned us out into the street and a crowd got round us, and the end of it was a bobby came across from the station opposite and took our names. I suppose I'll be summonsed. Just my luck—out of one trouble into another.'

The Deepford's office was unable to supply any information as to Mr Prossip's new address, and Mr Knayle's first impulse to write a little note of personal regret was put aside from day to day and eventually abandoned. Chidgey had received no summons and the Deepford had at last provided Mr Knayle with an interest. He had been introduced to Tolly Duckett's widow.

The Farnolds had returned from Yorkshire and one after-noon Mrs Duckett came up to tea. She was a dainty, still girlish little thing with a bright, sweet smile and rather long grey eyes which were sometimes almost green. There was something in the smile and the shape and colour of the eyes that called up other eyes and another smile. Her voice was very quiet with an undertone of brave loneliness, which somehow excluded the Farnolds but at once admitted Mr Knayle to intimacy. After tea the Farnolds joined some friends at the other end of the lounge and he was left alone with her. When he moved his chair so that her eyes and smile faced him directly, he discovered that the smile was sometimes a little twisted and that one eye had sometimes a slight cast. But the cast and the twist came and went. They were not there when he lighted her cigarette for her and touched her little cool hand. Something warm and eager stirred in him when, after a long, silent scrutiny of him, she said, 'You know, you are exactly as I've always thought you must be.'

Afterwards he escorted her to her lodgings in Burford Avenue and in the darkness she talked of her unhappy married life. As he went back along Burford Avenue he was a little glad that it had been unhappy.

He was still endeavouring to appraise the exact quality of Mrs Duckett's soft 'Good-night' when he reached the mouth of a laneway which ran back from the avenue at some little distance from her lodgings. To his surprise, Whalley came out of the lane, looking at his watch, and after a hasty glance in his direction, hurried away before him. Mr Knayle's surprise was so great that he came to a stop for a moment. There was at first no doubt whatever in his mind that he had seen Whalley. But almost at once his first certain impression began to break up. Whalley was at Bournemouth. If he had been able to recognise Whalley, Whalley would have been able to recognise him and would have stopped. Of course he was wearing his new glasses—and Whalley had never seen him wearing them. But had he recognised Whalley? It was too dark to recognise a face at nearly ten yards distance—he had merely had a general impression that the figure and walk were Whalley's. He decided that he had been mistaken and went on, quickening his step as a clock in the town struck a half-hour. Half-past seven. Mr Knayle always shaved for dinner, and there were still shades of that soft 'Good-night' to explore.

Mrs Duckett came up to tea with the Farnolds several times and one day brought her little boy Cyril, a silent elf of five, whose large, wistful eyes still looked back at another world. Mr Knayle plied him with cakes and took him on his knee and told him stories by the fire. Cyril's little warm, fragile hand held his tightly during the walk to Burford Avenue and at parting he held up his face to be kissed. Mrs Duckett's laugh was mysteriously soft and tender. Fleeting visions of tranquil domesticity strayed through Mr Knayle's thoughts as he went back to the hotel. Here was a purpose and a usefulness. Dear little chap— That little nestling hand had asked for protection—those wistful eyes knew the cruelties and treacheries that lay ahead. One could do so much—form that little soul—prepare it for its battle. And there would always be something to go back to . . .

Cyril came again with his mother two days later and again Mr Knayle was left alone with them by the fire. He realised suddenly that the Farnolds always left him alone with her, and his blue eyes fixed themselves upon her with uneasy speculation. The cast and the twist were very noticeable today. There was no resemblance at all really—just something that was a little annoying because it was nearly a resemblance.

And why on earth did she keep on about Tolly Duckett and the discomfort of living in lodgings and the difficulties as to Cyril's future and then back to Tolly again?

Cyril began to play. He crept round one side of Mr Knayle's armchair and jabbed him in the ribs and then crept round the other side of the chair and did the same thing. He went on doing this and when Mr Knayle said, 'That'll do, old chap,' he put out an immense tongue and squawked, 'That'll do, old chap. That'll do, old chap.' For half an hour he punched Mr Knayle's ribs, and each time he punched he screamed, 'That'll do, old chap.' Then, fortunately, Mrs Farnold returned and, pleading some letters to write, Mr Knayle made his escape.

There was no one in the writing-room and he stood for some time before its fire, surveying the hearthrug blankly and retracing, step by step, the alarming path along which he had been led towards catastrophe. It was now perfectly clear that Grace Farnold had set a deliberate trap for him. She had inveigled him up to Guildford for the purpose of marrying him to this hard-up friend of hers with a cast and a crooked mouth and a loathsome little beast of a boy. It amazed him that such crude, audacious cunning should have been able to trick him so easily. Grace Farnold's perfidy shocked him. And worse than the knowledge that he had made a consummate ass of himself was the feeling that he had been disloyal. That thought twisted his face into a grimace. 'Oh you little old cad,' he said aloud.

The hearth-rug failing to supply any consolation, he arranged at the office to give up his room next morning, and then went up to town to see *The White Horse Inn*.

3

It was raining heavily when he got back to Guildford that night a little after midnight, and, as he opened his umbrella outside the station, he looked about for a taxi. There was only one in sight, already engaged by a heavily-built man who was endeavouring to climb into it on his hands and knees while the driver watched him from his seat with a sardonic grin. As Mr Knayle neared him, he abandoned this attempt and, subsiding slowly backwards, came to rest in a sitting position on the muddy footpath. It was Mr Prossip, very drunk and very blasphemous.

Aided by the driver, Mr Knayle at length got him into the taxi and then got in himself. Having given his address, Mr

Prossip fell asleep and left Mr Knayle to muse a little over the fact that he must have frequently passed the Prossips' new residence. From this thought he passed on to Mrs Duckett and he was still thinking of her twisted smile as he rang the bell of 'Hindhead's' hall-door.

Mrs Prossip, in a dressing-gown and a state of irritable anxiety, opened it. Her eyes took in Mr Knayle in surprise and then fastened themselves on her husband contemptuously.

'Oh it's you, is it? Here's a nice business. Marjory hasn't come back.'

'Hasencomeback?' repeated Mr Prossip. 'Wharyoumean?'

'I mean that she hasn't come back.'

'Oh, she'll comeback, allri',' said Mr Prossip with bitter confidence. 'Mawjory'll comebackallri'. Donyouworry.'

'You drunken brute,' exploded Mrs Prossip. 'How dare you talk that way of your own daughter, when she may be lying dead at this moment?'

'Tha'lldo, tha'lldo,' retorted Mr Prossip, waving his muddy hand. 'Dongetsited. No use standing here in the rain anyhow.'

They went in and Mrs Prossip explained the cause of her anxiety. Her daughter Marjory had gone to Farnham that after-noon in her car to see some friends named Reid. As she had not returned by nine o'clock Mrs Prossip had telephoned to the Reids and ascertained that Marjory had left them a little before seven. At latest she should have reached 'Hindhead' at half-past seven. But it was now getting on towards one o'clock in the morning and Marjory had not appeared.

'Oh, she'llcomeallri',' said Mr Prossip again. 'Donyou worry, Emma. I know. Ringupospil.'

But Mrs Prossip had already rung up both Guildford and Farnham hospitals. Mr Knayle had an idea while he strove not to yawn.

'Perhaps your daughter has gone somewhere in Guildford. She may have put up her car. Where does she garage?'

'Round in a lane off this road. It's only just a little shed.' Mrs

Prossip was silent for a moment while she scratched the back of her neck. 'The funny thing is that I thought I heard the car about half-past seven from my bedroom, going up the lane. I wonder, Mr Knayle, if you'd mind going round and looking through the window. If I gave you a torch you'd be able to see whether the car was inside. You can't mistake the lane. It's only a little way down the road—to your right from our gate.'

'I believe I know it,' said Mr Knayle, thinking that it was a little curious that he should have thought that he had seen Whalley coming out of a lane in which Marjory Prossip garaged her car.

But he was merely bored sleepiness, when he reached the little shed and, as he flashed his torch over its doors, stumbled a little over some object with which both his feet had collided. When he lowered the beam of the torch to the ground he saw that he had walked on a hammer, the head of which was bound about with a thick winding of, he thought, insulation-tape. It was very muddy and wet and he left it there, concluding that it was Marjory Prossip's property and that it was no affair of his if she left her tools lying about outside her garage. There was nothing to be seen through the window of the shed which was curtained on the inside with a piece of sacking. When he had reported his failure to Mrs Prossip, he went off in the taxi thinking that it had been rather cool of her to send him up a muddy, smelly lane for nothing.

His thoughts became drowsy and disconnected. Out of Burford Avenue now—done with the Prossips—he would never come across the Prossips again, please God. Done with Mrs Twisty-lips. Tomorrow done with the Farnolds and the little dark staircase and the muttering waiter. Done with all the Deepford tomorrow and going back—going back to what? What *was* he going back to? To sit and brood and fall to pieces. And nothing to bring back, now—nothing of her left—the last of that sacred, secret wonder sullied and trampled under foot. Nothing of her left anywhere, except in a bloodless fish and a fusty old abortioner—

He cancelled that last thought hurriedly. It had not been a thought. Those savage, ugly little labels had merely sprung into his mind and sprung out again. They had never been his—merely things that other people with unpleasant minds might have said or thought about Whalley and Ridgeway—but not he. He had never thought of ugly, savage little labels for people. He knew that beneath Whalley's cold curtness lay a grief that could find no help or use in words or friendship—that beneath Ridgeway's old dressing-gown lay beauty.

When the taxi stopped at the Deepford he was planning a long, low, snug house—somewhere in the Cotswolds, perhaps, but within reach of a good butcher—with three little bachelor suites. There would be a cosy common sitting-room with three big armchairs. They would sit there awhile in the evenings—not talking much, but together. The fire would crackle and the wind would sigh outside the windows. Sometimes they would talk about her and keep her—

Hopelessly impracticable, of course. That overdraft in January. Perhaps everything going smash in a few months. The world in ruins and fury—guns roaring and searchlights flickering and wheeling—Harvey Knayle scrambling for a place in a food-queue. Still, it was something to have thought of. He resolved, somehow, to get closer to Whalley and Ridgeway.

CHAPTER XII

1

MR RIDGEWAY was scraping a muddy pair of boots in front of his subterranean hall-door one foggy Thursday morning when someone addressed him by name. Raising his eyes, he was momentarily surprised to see Knayle standing looking down at him with a newspaper in his hand. The voice had not sounded like Knayle's.

'Hullo,' he yawned. 'You've got back, then?'

'Yesterday afternoon,' replied Mr Knayle. 'I say, Ridgeway—'

'Had a pleasant time?'

'Oh, so-so. I say, Ridgeway—have you seen the paper this morning? The Prossip girl's been murdered.'

'Oh,' said Mr Ridgeway, when he had picked up the other shoe.

'A most extraordinary thing,' went on Mr Knayle. 'I very nearly found her. As a matter of fact, I did find the hammer she was murdered with.'

'Oh?' said Mr Ridgeway.

Fortunately Whalley came down the outside staircase just then. Mr Knayle felt that his adventure deserved at least intelligent attention.

'Good morning, Whalley. When did you get back?'

'On Monday.'

'Have *you* seen the paper this morning?'

'No.'

'The Prossip girl's been murdered. A most shocking business, poor creature. Battered to death with a hammer. I was just telling Ridgeway—a most extraordinary thing—I very nearly found her—I actually did find the hammer. That is to say, I saw it. Of course I didn't know at the time that it was the hammer. But I actually saw it lying outside the shed. She was actually lying dead in the shed when I—'

'Well, but where did all this happen, Knayle?' asked Mr Ridgeway. 'Why can't you tell the thing consecutively? Don't jump about that way. Where was she murdered? Where was this shed you're talking about?'

'In Guildford,' replied Mr Knayle. 'You know Guildford, Whalley—'

'I used to know it.'

'Well, the Prossips are living in a road called Burford Avenue—perhaps you know it. The shed was in a lane off the road. The unfortunate girl kept her car there.'

'Good,' said Mr Ridgeway. 'Well, then, she was murdered in a shed in a lane off a road called Burford Avenue in Guildford. Who murdered her?'

'Oh, well,' expostulated Mr Knayle. 'I can't tell you that. But as I say, the extraordinary thing—'

'When was she murdered?'

'The evening before last—some time round half-past seven, they seem to think. Of course, when I—'

'Wait now. Don't jump. She was murdered with a hammer, and you saw the hammer. When did you see the hammer?'

'Oh, much later—about one o'clock that night.'

'So you were in a lane off Burford Avenue in Guildford at one o'clock that night. And you saw the hammer lying outside a shed, and the Prossip girl was in the shed, murdered. Well?'

'I don't think it's a matter for facetiousness, Ridgeway,' protested Mr Knayle severely. 'It's really a most shocking business. After all, you knew the poor girl—well, you knew her by sight.'

'I did,' said Mr Ridgeway dryly. 'And now that I think of it, I always thought she was the sort of person someone would murder with a hammer.'

'I didn't know that the Prossips were living in Guildford,' said Whalley after a silence.

'Oh?' said Mr Knayle. 'I thought I had told you. Yes. They've been living there since they left Rockwood. Oh—by the way—you weren't in Guildford last week, were you?'

'I?' Whalley repeated in surprise. 'No. Why?'

'Oh, I thought I saw you one night—curiously enough—coming out of the very lane where this thing happened.'

Whalley shook his head. 'I see you're wearing glasses now.'

'Yes. I've got some little trouble. Nothing at all serious; but I've got to wear these confounded things. They make me feel like a professor of phrenology.'

'What I want to know, Knayle,' demanded Mr Ridgeway from his little area, 'is, what were you doing in this lane at one o'clock in the morning? It seems devilish fishy to me, the whole business. You were there, and the Prossip girl was there—dead or alive, I'm not clear yet which—and now you say Whalley was there. Was I there?'

'Oh don't be an ass, Ridgeway,' said Mr Knayle a little acidly. He opened his newspaper and began to re-read the account of the murder, endeavouring to find the thread of his narrative; but Mr Ridgeway's hall door shut and Whalley had already reached the garden gate. There was nothing to do but shut up the newspaper and go back to a second cup of coffee which was now undrinkable.

His extraordinary adventure had gone quite flat; Ridgeway's tomfoolery had turned it into the silliest of jokes. There had been nothing at all extraordinary about it. The whole thing had happened in a perfectly ordinary and uninteresting sequence. He had seen Prossip home because there had been no other taxi, and Mrs Prossip had asked him to go round to the shed and he had gone and seen the hammer. He hadn't even found the hammer. He had simply seen it and left it there. Not only that—but it had been stupid of him to leave it there and not guess that there was something wrong. He had known that

Marjory Prossip had not come home and that Mrs Prossip had been anxious about her for several hours. Anyone with a spark of intelligence, seeing a hammer lying near the shed, would have guessed that there was something wrong. And he had simply left it there—with the result that the murder hadn't been discovered until ten hours later. The police would want to know why he had left the hammer lying there and given the murderer another ten hours, instead of telling the Prossips that he had found a hammer lying outside the shed—or doing something of some sort about the hammer. Everybody would want to know. He had had no extraordinary adventure. He had simply done something infernally stupid.

And yet Mr Knayle's adventure had appeared to him the most extraordinary when he had jumped up from his breakfast-table with the intention of going down to tell Ridgeway about it. He was a little upset because his story had fallen flat and he groped about for justification of the impulse which had sent him hurrying out in search of someone to tell it to. He was still sure that there had been something extraordinary in his adventure and after a little time he decided that the extraordinary thing about it was, not that he had seen the hammer, but that it was *he* who had seen the hammer. He had gone up to Guildford—a hundred and twenty miles away—and by an extraordinary chance had—well, very nearly discovered the murdered body of someone who had lived in the same flat with him in Rockwood.

But no—that was not quite it. Mr Knayle's mind groped on and suddenly rounded a rather startling corner. That maid of the Prossips . . . His visit to Guildford had obliterated Agatha Judd as completely as it had obliterated his dining-room carpet. But now he remembered that that girl who had been the Prossips' maid had been murdered. Hopgood came in just then to say that the car was outside and Mr Knayle raised abstracted eyes from his newspaper.

'You know, Hopgood, this is rather an extraordinary affair—this about Miss Prossip.'

'Extraordinary, sir?'

'I mean—well, it's only a few weeks ago that that girl—that maid of the Prossips—was murdered. I only thought of that just now.'

'It is a bit queer, sir,' Hopgood agreed. 'That very thought came into my own head when I was reading about it. I was saying to Chidgey just now that it was a bit strange. A funny thing that you should have been in Guildford when it happened, sir—'

'Funny?' repeated Mr Knayle sharply. 'Why funny?'

'Oh, well, I don't mean funny, sir, of course—'

'I don't think it's funny at all.'

Hopgood, however, continued to look as if he thought it funny.

'I forgot to tell you, sir, that that police-inspector called here yesterday wanting to see Chidgey.'

'Oh, confound him,' snapped Mr Knayle testily, picking up his newspaper and putting it down again.

'I told him that Chidgey had gone up to Guildford with you, sir. I hope that was right.'

'Right? Of course.' Mr Knayle's tone became elaborately casual. 'Er—tell Chidgey I want to see him, will you?'

Chidgey's hands became a little fidgety when he realised what the guv'nor wanted to see him about. But he was able to account satisfactorily for his last afternoon in Guildford. He had felt a bit seedy and thought that he was in for a go of 'flu. Mr Knayle had said that he wouldn't want the car that day, so he had gone to bed and stayed there until the following morning. The people at his lodgings, he was sure, would be able to say that he hadn't stirred out after one o'clock.

This was a relief.

Mr Knayle hadn't really thought for a moment that because Chidgey had assaulted Mr Prossip he had also beaten Mr Prossip's daughter to death with a hammer. That idea was, of course, ridiculous. Still, Chidgey had already been suspected of battering someone to death—and that someone had been the Prossips' maid. It was certainly a bit awkward that Chidgey should have been in Guildford and had that row with Prossip. And Hopgood had looked mysterious in that idiotic, owlish way of his. It had seemed to Mr Knayle just as well to find out where Chidgey had been that evening; he had had quite enough trouble about Chidgey and told him so.

'What does this confounded police-inspector want to see you about?'

'I don't know, sir,' replied Chidgey nervously. His face had grown steadily whiter and thinner during the interview and his hands refused to keep still. Mr Knayle eyed them over his glasses and found himself on the very point of saying, 'Blast you, why can't you keep your hands quiet?'

'Has Mr Whalley put his car in the garage yet?' he asked, picking up his newspaper again.

'Yes sir.'

'Look after it for him, will you? I shan't take the car out this morning. It's too foggy. That will do.'

Mr Knayle went off to see his dentist about his new plate and in the fog was nearly run over by a confectioner's van, the driver of which shouted a most objectionable remark at him. When he tried to tell the dentist about a most extraordinary experience which he had had in Guildford the dentist kept saying: 'Heh. Wid-ah,' and he had to give it up. At the club everyone was talking gloomily about some rather alarming rioting which had taken place in Dunpool on the preceding day. Six thousand unemployed had overwhelmed the police, set a factory on fire and invaded the City Council Hall. When at length he succeeded in telling how he had found the hammer a man whom he disliked extremely said: 'Well, I think you showed uncommon presence of mind, Knayle.' He lunched alone at a small table in a remote corner and no one seemed to care whether he did or not. His waiter, who was wondering whether he was going to win ten bob on the three-thirty, forgot him several times and it was necessary to speak rather sharply about the condition of the cruets.

During lunch, however, he decided to go round to the garage on his way home and say a soothing word or two to Chidgey. Chidgey had looked rather like a small lost dog.

2

When Mr Ridgeway had arranged his scraped shoes before his sitting-room fire to dry, he stood looking down at them meditatively with his fine, tired eyes. They were a large, heavily-soled pair of shoes which he used for his early walks on the Downs in wet weather, and he was thinking about the noise they made on his little flight of steps when his charwoman, Mrs Dings, brought in his breakfast from the kitchen.

'I've just heard a rather interesting bit of news, Mrs Dings,' he said, turning.

Mrs Dings sniffed. 'What's that, sir?'

'Your friend Miss Prossip has been murdered.'

'Murdered, sir?' Mrs Dings put down her tray and sniffed three times rapidly. 'Well, I never. Murdered? Well, that's a queer thing.'

There was only vivid interest in Mrs Dings' battered little face; in her heart was a vague stirring of faith that in the end God always dealt with people as they deserved. She had complained to Miss Prossip one day in the garden that that Aggie called her 'Sniffy' when they met at the rubbish-bins, and Miss Prossip had treated her like dirt.

'Well, I never. Don't let your haddock get cold, sir. Well that *is* a queer thing. Why, it's not a month ago since that Aggie was murdered.'

'You think it's a queer thing, Mrs Dings?' Mr Ridgeway asked.

'Well, you can't deny of it, sir,' replied Mrs Dings.

Mr Ridgeway contemplated his charwoman's little shiny,

bumpy forehead for some moments before he turned again to the fire. Behind it lay the brain of a rabbit. But Mrs Dings had instantly made that connection and thought it a queer thing.

Of late Mr Ridgeway had grown a little doubtful that things which appeared queer to him were really queer.

Mrs Dings knew his little ways and had a lot to do before she went away at one o'clock with her half-crown. She left him looking at his boots and sniffed back to the kitchen. She knew that she sniffed. But she had always sniffed and it was a great help.

3

Very slowly Whalley went down the garden and crossed the road. His legs moved with the rigidity of steel stilts, yet they trembled and sagged with their hate and fury. All his body was an aching passion to turn and rush back to that little dapper mannikin with the newspaper and catch him by his little babbling throat and choke his life out. Ten yards in on the grass of the Downs the houses were mere blurs, hardly darker than the fog. He shook his fist towards them ragingly and whispered:

'Mannikin. Mannikin.'

The Irish terrier from number 48 came out of the fog, shied violently away from his gesture, and disappeared, uttering little rumbles of alarm. He laughed boisterously at its sudden swerve and went on muttering.

'Mannikin. Mannikin. Puny Mannikin. Puny smirker—'

As his feet strayed on his eyes glanced from side to side restlessly with an uneasy vigilance that in two days had already become habitual to them. For now it was always necessary to keep watch. Every bush and every tree on the Downs were familiar to him, seen in relation to other bushes and trees. But this morning there were no points of reference. The world was a small circle of wet grass capped by a dome of sightless silence that moved with him. A tree loomed up alone, and had never been seen before. He stopped, turned about, could not tell in what direction he faced or from which direction he had come, and broke into a hobbling trot until he reached a seat which he recognised at length by its broken back. The icy clamminess of its iron arm was safety. He stood holding on to it, panting from his short run, furious that he had yielded to panic. Had it been panic—or had he lost himself again? Was he standing by this broken seat, holding on to its arm and panting. Was it he—and did he know that it was he? What was there to tell him?

Gradually his bewildered alarm allayed itself and he began to pace in narrow circles round the seat, unwilling to part from its anchorage. His eyes clung to its broken back, as to an established fact by which all other facts could be recovered and rearranged. All this about Knayle—that would all arrange itself in a clear, solving thought—cease to be a rain of dancing spots that ran together and made a little mannikin with a newspaper and then broke up into dancing spots again.

Think—think . . . A clear thought. The mannikin and the hammer in the lane together. Just a cunning, smirking trick, that—not a blinding flame that turned to ice. Full of tricks, the mannikin—coming and going. But think and confuse him and talk about his glasses. That had been very clever— very quick. Only a very clever, subtle mind could have thought of that—a mind altogether different from Mannikin's—keen and quick as rapier—dancing about Mannikin and confusing him.

He lighted a cigarette and sat down, reassured. His anger had passed and left behind thoughts—two thoughts that did not slide and melt. Somehow Knayle had seen him in the lane—a danger so incredible that his mind still refused to deal with it as a reality. But this was a new anxiety that would gnaw and fret the hours to come. For now—for this little space in which he sat there, smoking safely in the fog—an old anxiety was gone.

For countless centuries it had lived with him, a torment of doubt. But now he knew that he had left the hammer outside the shed.

Had he meant to leave it there—or had he forgotten it? He would never know now.

For the millionth time he strove to remember. It was all clear until he reached the turning of the lane and began to unwrap the brown paper. Her keys jingled—she was unlocking the padlock. And then nothing—until the subway at Guildford station. He had been dabbing his chin with his handkerchief when, suddenly, he had missed something.

He hobbled up the lane again and unwrapped the brown paper, crouching against the wall. Her keys jingled . . . No—nothing. Ten million times he might crouch against the wall, but he would never know. Not he, but someone else, had turned the corner.

But the hammer had been left—not carried through the streets. No need to worry about that.

Botched again, though. Always a botch in the end. And now, always, that other one to watch—the one who stole away round the corner and forgot. Churn, churn, rattle and squeak and jingle—the good old faithful noise; but who would hold the steering wheel?

And Knayle—little dapper, pop-eyed Knayle—suddenly dangerous. Puny but cunning, coming and going and watching and finding the hammer . . . Mad, mad—mad as a hatter. But he would have to be watched and thought about. Think about Knayle, not dancing spots falling like rain—

Mr Ridgeway came out of the fog, wheezing, and halted by the seat while he refilled his pipe.

'A bit too thick for me this morning. I shouldn't stay out in it, Whalley, if I were you. What are you rubbing that eye for? Got something in it?'

'Cigarette ash, I expect,' Whalley replied without interest. When he had looked at the eye for a moment or two, Mr

Ridgeway took out a pocket-lens and examined it more attentively.

'Umph,' he said, putting away the lens. 'You've got an ulcer
there. Better get a shade over that eye and see an oculist at
once.'

'An ulcer?' Whalley repeated sharply.

'Yes. A fairly common symptom with your trouble. Well, I'll
get in, I think.'

Mr Ridgeway was not greatly surprised when Whalley broke
into a fit of hysterical sobbing. He smoked his pipe until the
paroxysm had passed, and then went away, yawning. You got
that sort of thing, too, very frequently in pernicious anæmia
cases. And his chilblains were bad that morning.

4

Inspector Bride read the report of the Guildford murder at
breakfast and immediately connected it with the murder in
Abbey Road. The Abbey Road murder had given him a lot of
trouble for nothing. Every clue had petered out, and he was
beginning to feel rather fed-up with it. But the name Prossip
awoke his interest. It seemed to him queer that Prossip should
have been so intimately connected with two murders.

Almost instantly he thought of Chidgey. He still didn't think
that there was anything in Chidgey, but he had never been quite
satisfied about him. For one thing, one of the friends who had
stated that he had seen Chidgey in the picture-house that night
had since admitted that he hadn't seen him and that he had
said that he had seen him merely because Chidgey had asked
him to do so. Inspector Bride had called at Mr Knayle's flat to
see Chidgey about this, but had been informed that Chidgey
was away with Mr Knayle. He recollected now that Mr Knayle's
man had said that Mr Knayle had gone to Guildford, and it
seemed to him queer that Chidgey should have been in
Guildford at the time of a second murder connected with

Prossip. Nothing in it probably, but he thought he'd take a stroll up towards Downview Road that afternoon and see if Chidgey had come back.

5

To his annoyance, when he arrived at his garage Mr Knayle found Inspector Bride there, note-book in hand and holding Chidgey imprisoned against a wall with his glassy stare.

'Well, well,' demanded Mr Knayle, 'what's the matter now? I can't have this sort of thing, Inspector. You can't come here interrupting this man in his work constantly like this.'

'I've got to do my duty, sir. This man has committed a serious offence. He has incited another person to give false information to the police. I've come here in pursuance of my duty to ascertain—'

'False information? What about?'

Inspector Bride referred to his notebook.

'I have information that he called at the house of a person named Eustace Shawley on the night of November 11th and asked him to state to the police that he had seen him in the Rockwood Palace Cinema on the night of November 5th, knowing at the time that he had not seen him—'

'Oh—he—him!' exclaimed Mr Knayle impatiently. 'Why the devil don't they teach you chaps to speak English? What's all this, Chidgey? Did you ask this man to say that he saw you?'

'Yes, sir,' Chidgey replied miserably.

'Did he see you?'

'No, sir. But he might have done. He was in the Palace that night.'

'Oh, dammit,' said Mr Knayle. 'I'm sick of this, Chidgey.'

Inspector Bride put away his note-book very carefully and allowed a little silence to pass before he took Mr Knayle down another peg. He knew the effect of little silences.

'There's another matter, sir. I believe you've been away in Guildford for the past fortnight or so, and that you took your car with you. Am I right in supposing that you were in Guildford on the evening of last Tuesday? I mean the Tuesday of this week—the evening before last?'

'Quite right. And if you want to know where Chidgey was, he was in his lodgings—in bed. You were in bed ill, Chidgey, weren't you?'

'Yes, sir. I went to bed after me dinner, Inspector, and stayed there till the next morning. The people at the lodgings will tell you that.'

'I see,' said Inspector Bride, taking out his notebook again. 'Now, where might these lodgings be in Guildford?'

'32 Springfield Road.'

The stumpy pencil wrote the address with ominous deliberation and Chidgey's voice wilted into a cowed whimper.

'If you're going to make inquiries about me, I'd better tell you I had a row with Prossip in Guildford.'

'I see,' said Inspector Bride, after another little silence. 'A row, eh? What was the row about?'

'Now this is quite irregular, Inspector,' interrupted Mr Knayle. 'I won't have my servants bullied and cross-examined in this way. What is the object of these questions about Chidgey's having been in Guildford?'

'I must ask you, sir—' began the inspector.

His voice checked and, turning to discover the cause, Mr Knayle saw that Whalley had entered the garage. He was very much annoyed because he had lost his temper in a weak, ineffectual sort of way and because he had said too much. Chidgey had suddenly become a serious anxiety again; the note-book and the stumpy pencil and the glassy stare had made him look like a cornered rat. Mr Knayle had an abrupt impression that he didn't like Whalley's appearance—didn't like his shabby overcoat and his old shoes and his faded hat and his white face and his bloodshot eye and that raw scrape on his chin. He

collected these unpleasing details into a whole which he removed
from himself. He felt that he didn't want shabby-looking
people—of whom, really, he knew nothing—walking into his
garage and taking their shabby little cars out, at awkward
moments. He decided to light a cigarette to avoid the necessity
of speaking.

As Whalley passed on to his car Chidgey moved to lean into
it and take a pair of oil-stained gloves from the driving-seat.

'I found those in your car, sir, when I was cleaning it this
morning. I left them there, thinking you might have wanted
them for some purpose.'

Whalley stared blankly. 'They're not mine.'

'I know that, sir. They're an old pair I used to use for oily
jobs. Then you don't want them for anything, sir?'

'No. I don't know how they got into my car. I didn't put
them there.'

Not a word of thanks to Chidgey for having cleaned the car,
thought Mr Knayle. Ungracious, shabby writer of novels that
no one had ever heard of. Bloodshot eye. Driving out a shabby,
noisy little car, saying, 'Pretty thick now, isn't it?' as if one knew
all about him. Just drawl 'Yes,' without looking at him.

Inspector Bride had stood outside looking up and down
the road. It was a side-road, and there was nothing to see
except the fog, but to right and to left he found placid satisfaction. It looked to him now as if there might be something
in Chidgey after all. And he had taken cocky little Mr Knayle
down a peg. His tone was quite genial as he turned, straightening his tie.

'A funny thing, sir—as we were talking about Guildford—I
saw that gentleman at Guildford station a couple of weeks
ago—no, three weeks ago it must be, now. It's the gentleman
that has the flat above you, isn't it? A Mr Whalley, I think?'

'Yes, yes,' replied Mr Knayle abstractedly. 'He—er—I allow
him to use my garage. Er—is there anything more that I can
tell you?'

'Not for the present, sir—not for the present, thank you,' chanted Inspector Bride pleasantly and disappeared into the fog with a salute that was not quite a salute.

Two hours later Inspector Strong of the Surrey Constabulary called in person at 32 Springfield Road and interviewed the landlady and her maid. On the evening of the preceding Tuesday the landlady had taken Chidgey's supper into his room at half-past six and had then seen him in bed. She had gone out a little later and had not seen him again until the following morning. The maid had not seen him at any time that evening, though she had heard him moving about in his room between nine and ten o'clock. Inspector Strong had another conversation with Inspector Bride over the telephone and arranged to lunch with him at the Imperial Hotel in Rockwood on the following day.

6

When Hopgood brought in his tea-tray that afternoon Mr Knayle looked up from the almanac of his pocket-diary.

'Can you remember, Hopgood—what day was it that I went up to Guildford? Monday the 23rd, wasn't it?'

'It was a Monday, sir, anyhow.'

'Monday. I thought so. Monday the 23rd, then. Yes. When did Mr Whalley go away, can you remember?'

'Which time, sir?'

'Why?' asked Mr Knayle, turning, 'has Mr Whalley been away more than once, then?'

'Oh yes, sir. He's been away a lot. He went away the week before you went to Guildford—that was the first time.'

'Yes. Well?'

'Well, then, he came back the day after you left and went away again the next day. Then he came back last Monday night, very late, and the next day, I think, he was away again all day. There was no light up in his flat all the evening.'

'So he didn't come back on Tuesday night?'

'I can't say as to that, sir. I thought I heard him going up his steps late that night—getting on for twelve, it must have been. But I couldn't say for sure.'

'No scones,' exclaimed Mr Knayle, putting away his diary and turning to the tea-tray. 'Dear, dear. And I've been looking forward to your scones for a fortnight.'

It was too foggy to do anything after tea. He fidgetted about his sitting-room for a little space and then went down and rang Mr Ridgeway's bell. After some delay the door opened and Mr Ridgeway appeared, carrying a toasting-fork on which was impaled a large, untidy slice of bread.

He stood in silence and for a moment Mr Knayle, too, stood in silence and looked at him, wondering why he had come down and rung his bell and made him appear in his dirty old dressing-gown, carrying a revolting hunk of bread on a toasting-fork. The dressing-gown was appalling—stained, faded, frayed, burst at the armpits. Mr Knayle felt sure that it smelt and that beneath it lay no beauty at all, but horrors of uncleanliness. Only a ravening animal could eat a hunk of bread like that. And what a face—what a travesty of a face—sagging and loose, with heavy, sensual lips and a double chin that creased like india-rubber. Everything crooked and uneven—ears sticking out at different angles; one eye lower than the other—

'You look very mysterious, Knayle,' said Mr Ridgeway at length. 'You're not trying to ask me to go up and play chess, are you?'

'No, no,' laughed Mr Knayle.

'Oh, then that's all right,' yawned Mr Ridgeway.

'Though I do feel a little mysterious, as a matter of fact,' said Mr Knayle, grasping at the opening. 'You know, there *is* something queer about this business, Ridgeway.'

'What business?'

'This—this murder. I mean—the Prossips' maid was murdered only a few weeks ago—and now Miss Prossip has

been murdered—almost in the same way. I mean, you know—
it *is* quite a curious thing. Of course, I suppose I'm a little
thrilled because I was on the spot, so to speak; but quite apart
from that—I mean, doesn't it strike *you* as being a little
curious?'

'Oh, I don't think so,' replied Mr Ridgeway. 'That girl—what
was her name?—Rudd or Judd or something—she wasn't the
Prossips' maid when she was murdered. You never open the
paper now without finding that two or three women have been
knocked on the head.'

'Ah, yes,' urged Mr Knayle. 'But there's no connection
between them. There is a connection in this case. You must
admit there is. And it's quite clear that Miss Prossip wasn't
murdered in a haphazard way. The thing was evidently deliberately planned. It seems that she was in the habit of going to
Farnham several times a week and that she always got back at
the same hour—about half-past seven. Besides, you can't
imagine anyone going about with a hammer looking for someone
to murder.'

'Oh, yes, I can.'

'Oh, nonsense. This must have been a deliberate business.
According to the report, Miss Prossip always got back at half-
past seven—and she was murdered between seven and eight.
Someone must have watched the lane.' Mr Knayle lowered his
voice. 'I'll tell you a curious thing, Ridgeway. Er—you heard
me ask Whalley this morning if I had seen him in Guildford
last week?'

'Yes.'

'Well, he said I hadn't. Or rather, he didn't say anything,
now that I come to think of it, but he shook his head. Yes, that
was it—he shook his head and made some remark about my
glasses. At any rate I feel sure that he gave me to understand
that I hadn't seen him. But I did see him. I know for a fact that
he was in Guildford three weeks ago—and I'm perfectly certain
that I saw him there one night last week. And the curious thing

is that I saw him coming out of the lane where Miss Prossip was murdered.'

'That was the lane where you didn't find the hammer at one o'clock in the morning?' asked Mr Ridgeway.

'Oh, well—' said Mr Knayle, turning away rather huffily. Before he could turn again, Mr Ridgeway laughed and shut his hall-door.

It shut quickly but quietly and the effect produced in Mr Knayle's mind was that it had shut on something foolish which could be left outside with impunity. He felt foolish and somewhat alarmed by what he had done. He had put into words a most appalling and grotesque suspicion—deliberately coupled the fact that he had seen Whalley in the lane with the fact that Miss Prossip had been murdered by someone who had watched her movements for some time beforehand. There had been no previous intention whatever in his mind to couple them. But suddenly something—something quite apart from Ridgeway's sardonic amusement at his interest in the affair—had aroused an eager, savage little desire to connect them—in a lowered voice, too, not in the casual way in which he had meant to refer to the fact that he had seen Whalley. He felt that he had done something extremely serious and imprudent. After all, Ridgeway was almost an entire stranger. He was quite capable of repeating the whole conversation to Whalley—garbling it, and making it appear still more serious.

However, the hall-door was shut and Mr Knayle didn't see how he could very well ring again and ask Ridgeway not to repeat what he had said about Whalley. Besides, of course, it would be utterly ridiculous to couple the two things—grotesque. Ridgeway had laughed. He had seen at once that it would be utterly ridiculous to couple them. The whole conversation would fade from his fusty brain in a quarter of an hour.

Utterly absurd—grotesque.

But Mr Knayle was now quite sure that he had seen Whalley

come out of the lane. And he couldn't understand why Whalley should deny having been in Guildford when he had been in Guildford. He regretted very much that his voice had lowered itself and made an absurd and most indiscreet connection, between the fact that the lane had probably been watched for some time beforehand and the fact that he had seen Whalley in the lane at night during the week preceding Miss Prossip's murder. But the connection had been made, and he took it back to his sitting-room with him.

During the past few months the range of his thoughts had contracted steadily and his mind had grown accustomed to short views. A number of small stresses had soured his outlook and made him feel restless and a little undignified and peevish. When he had stared at the fire for a little space he remembered that, just after Whalley had come out of the lane he had heard a clock somewhere towards the town, strike the half-hour, and that it had occurred to him that there might possibly not be time to shave before dinner. Half-past seven—a curious coincidence. Supposing that someone had been keeping watch.

Presently he took out his pocket-diary again. As he opened it he remembered that he had noticed a long, raw scrape on Whalley's chin that morning.

While Mr Knayle sat busy by his fireside the little old car was climbing the long rise between Calne and Marlborough, edging along the bank, and making heavy weather of it on bottom gear. It had taken four hours to crawl thirty miles and its back-axle was knocking ominously. The black pallor of the fog bulged forward to meet it and blind it and thrust it down the hill again. About it whispered silences that drowned its labouring clamour and mocked its faltering. Its churning was dubious and treacherous Mannikin—mannikin—mannikin—ikin—mannikin—ikin . . .

7

At six o'clock next morning Mrs Prossip awoke and uttered a long, groaning yawn because, once more, she hadn't died during the night. Ever since she had begun to have her attacks she had hoped that she might have one during the night and die. Not that she wanted in the least to die, or really believed that she ever would die. But she wanted Lionel to come in and be the first to find her cold and dead and get a terrible fright and feel terrible remorse for the way he had always treated her. As there was now no chance of his doing so that morning, she switched on the light over her bed, scratched her legs enjoyably for a little while, wiped her face with a towel, and then threw back the bedclothes. The air about the bed was piercingly cold and for a moment she was tempted to draw the bedclothes back again and not go to early service.

Everything urged her not to go. Two days of shock and strain had lowered her vitality and made her slack and disinclined for physical movement. There was the inquest at eleven—Lionel to be watched all the morning so that he wouldn't get drunk and make a show of himself again—mourning to be tried on—telegrams from relatives about the funeral to be answered. She had felt very comfortable and warm scratching her legs under the bedclothes and the bedroom was very cold and filled with fog. She hated cold and she hated cycling in fog and her hands itched to pull the bedclothes up again.

But it had always annoyed Lionel when she went out to early service—annoyed him because she went out regularly two mornings in the week without ever missing, and because he never went, and because the noise she made dressing woke him up an hour and a half too soon. The infliction of this annoyance had given her acute pleasure for over thirty years and on bad mornings had always afforded her the additional satisfaction of self-sacrifice. The desire to preserve the

unbroken regularity of its infliction tightened her bluish lips
to resolution. She sprang out of bed and, hurrying to the
windows, shut them violently.

In the adjoining bedroom Lionel boomed wrathfully and
forgetting that Marjory had been murdered and was dead, she
hummed contentedly as she opened the door of the wardrobe
and shut it again with a bang. He might boom and pound his
pillows and bury his head under the sheets, but he would lie
awake now, growling and clearing his throat and trying to think
of some way to get his own back and not being able to think
of any way.

As she pushed her bicycle towards the gate of the garden
she hesitated again. The fog was so thick that nothing could
be seen of the houses at the other side of the avenue and the
street-lamp outside the gate was a glow-worm poised on a
shadow. But she had pumped up the tyres of her bicycle and
lighted its lamp and she didn't want to have taken so much
trouble for nothing. She wobbled off up the avenue, rumbling
windily, and keeping the kerb of the footpath within quick reach
of her left foot.

She made an effort to think of Marjory sadly as she went
along. But the wobbling of her bicycle made thought of any
kind disjointed and diffuse. Marjory, who had been trying in
life, had been extremely trying in death. Mrs Prossip felt that
she didn't want to think of her at all just then—that she had
done enough thinking about her during the past two days, and
that she was entitled to a little rest from her before she faced
the inquest. Some little distance behind her—a distance too
short to be altogether comfortable—a car was following slowly
and noisily. She turned her head a little, endeavouring to calculate its nearness and its speed.

Suddenly its grinding growl rose to uproar and the glare of
its lamps was close behind her. She uttered a cry of frightened
anger and, letting go the handlebars, flung herself sideways
towards the footpath.

The car had disappeared when she raised her head and, after some moments, saw her bicycle lying in the gutter a few yards away, crumpled and twisted ludicrously. She felt that she was going to have one of her attacks and lay down again.

CHAPTER XIII

1

MR KNAYLE was frowning over his bank-book towards five o'clock that evening when Hopgood came in to say that Mr Whalley was outside.

'Outside? What do you mean?'

'I think he must have met with an accident, sir. There's a policeman with him wanting to know if he lives here.'

At the hall-door Mr Knayle found a fresh-faced young constable who saluted him with cheerful smartness and then glanced towards the silent figure which stood at the foot of the steps, facing towards the road.

'Good evening, sir. This is a man named Whalley who was found lying under a car on the Hog's Back at seven-thirty this morning. I come from Guildford, sir. I've been detailed to bring him back. Your servant tells me that he lives in the flat above yours, but that there's no one up there to take charge of him. It's a bit awkward. Might I ask if you're a friend of his?'

Take charge of him—?

'Oh, well,' replied Mr Knayle, 'I know him, of course. He lives above me. Is he injured?'

'Not exactly injured, sir. There's something the matter with one of his eyes, but the police doctor in Guildford said that it wasn't due to the accident. He's had a bad shock, though, seemingly. He hasn't opened his lips since he was taken out from under the car. I suppose he has friends living in this neighbourhood?'

'Well—no. I—I don't think he has any friends living here.'

The policeman laughed placidly. 'Is that so, sir? That makes it a bit awkward, doesn't it?'

Mr Knayle hesitated. The situation had presented itself to him with such suddenness that he had not yet had time to grasp its chief significance securely. 'Take charge of him—' He took off his glasses to weigh that. The hatless figure at the foot of the steps had not moved and now that his eyes had grown accustomed to the darkness, he saw that its head was bandaged with a handkerchief. Its immobility and its averted face made it dubious and apart. Why did it turn its face away? Why didn't it move and speak? Why didn't it go up to its own flat? Why should he take it in and accept responsibility for it?

'What happened?' he asked. 'A collision?'

'No, sir. The car ran into the ditch and turned over. The fog was very bad up Guildford way this morning.'

The Hog's Back—Guildford. What on earth had taken him all the way up to Guildford in a fog like yesterday's?

'Do I understand that he's—that he's not able to look after himself?'

'Well, that's about it, sir. The doctor didn't know what to make of him. There's no mark on his head or his body, but he's dazed-like. He won't talk and he hasn't eaten anything all day. I don't know what to do with him now. The way it is, sir, I've got to get back to Guildford; but my instructions are to find whoever belongs to him and hand him over to them. And now you say there's no one here belonging to him.'

'So far as I know, no one.'

So the matter hung for some moments while Mr Knayle's good nature struggled with his doubts. Finally he went down the steps and, taking Whalley's arm, led him into the sitting-room. In the light his face was ghastly white and set in a desperate apathy. The bandage covered one eye and left the other in shadow—an enigma—the eye of a private-theatricals pirate. His clothes were torn and, though some effort had been made to clean them, caked with half-dried mudstains. Mr Knayle looked at him in distaste for a little while, pushed him down into an arm-chair and went back to the hall-door. But there was nothing more to learn concerning the accident. The policeman went away, disappointed that it hadn't worked out at a drink, and, after a little reflection, Mr Knayle sent Hopgood down to ask if Mr Ridgeway would kindly come up for a few minutes.

While he waited he returned to the sitting-room and rear-ranged Whalley more comfortably in his chair.

'Well, old chap. Don't you know me? Knayle? What about a cigarette? No? Something to eat? Eat?' His jaws and teeth performed the motions of eating, exaggerating them. His voice diminished itself to wheedling cajolement. 'Come, now, now—you must be hungry. You haven't eaten anything all day, you know. What's the matter with your eye?'

But there was no reply, no movement. It might have been some figure from a waxworks that sat in his arm-chair, neither seeing him nor hearing him. He stood staring at it, a little contemptuous of its helplessness, a little interested in its dead-ness, more than a little resentful of its intrusion. When Mr Ridgeway shambled in with his gurgling pipe, he waved his hand silently towards it as something which had no business in his sitting-room.

'Chidgey wants to know if you could see him for a moment, sir,' said Hopgood from the door.

'What does he want?'

'I don't know, sir.'

'Tell him to come in.'

Chidgey's eyes became uneasy when he discovered that the guv'nor was not alone. But Mr Knayle's 'Well, what is it now?' was peremptory.

'It was just to tell you, sir, that that police-inspector has been round to the garage again—him and another—an inspector from Guildford.'

'Very well,' said Mr Knayle with tightened lips. 'I'll write to the Chief Constable about it. What did they want to see you about?'

'About a hammer, sir. They showed me a hammer and asked me if I knew anything about it. They didn't say what hammer it was, but, of course, I guessed.'

'Well?'

'Well, they kept at me, sir, the two of them, asking me the same thing over again. Of course, all I could say was that I knew nothing about it.'

Mr Knayle's tone sharpened.

'Keep still, can't you. You don't know anything about it, do you?'

'Well, I don't know whether I do or not, sir—now. I told them I didn't, and they went away in the end. But it's a funny thing, sir, there's a hammer missing from our garage.'

'Missing?'

'Yes, sir. It was an old hammer the man you had before me used to use. It was too heavy for me, so I never used it. I kept it in a box with some other old tools and things, and when I looked in the box after they'd gone away, it wasn't there, sir— and it isn't anywhere about the garage, either.'

'What made you look? Was it like the hammer they showed you?'

'It was, sir, I think. That's what made me look in the box afterwards, when I thought about it. It was very much the same class of hammer.'

'When you say, like, what do you mean? Do you mean that the hammer they showed you might have been the hammer you kept in the box?'

'I wouldn't go so far as to say that, sir. But it was very much like it.'

'When did you see this hammer that's missing?'

'About a fortnight ago, sir, when I was tidying the box.' Chidgey's restless eyes flitted across the room. 'I was wondering if Mr Whalley could have borrowed it, sir.'

'Most unlikely,' said Mr Knayle, after a moment.

'Well, he took a pair of old gloves from the box, sir. I found them in his car. You were in the garage yesterday morning when I spoke to him about them.'

'Yes. I remember. But Mr Whalley said he hadn't put them into his car.'

'He did say that, sir. But I think he must have done, and forgotten about it.'

'Well, well,' said Mr Knayle, after another pause. 'It comes to this, Chidgey—Do you believe that the hammer that was shown you is the hammer that is missing?'

'No, sir,' Chidgey replied with convulsive loudness.

'Then, why the devil do you come to me with all this rigmarole?'

Mr Ridgeway asked for some hot water and some salt just then and Chidgey made his escape. 'Salt?' repeated Mr Knayle, when the door had closed behind him.

'I thought of bathing Whalley's eyes,' Mr Ridgeway explained. 'However, I suppose we had better get him into bed first. By the way, the bed ought to be well warmed before he gets into it. You've got some hot-water bottles, I suppose?'

This was a little too much for Mr Knayle. He walked slowly to the hearthrug and took up a definite position on it.

'You propose, apparently, that Whalley should remain in my flat and that I should take care of him?'

Mr Ridgeway shrugged, after a quick glance. 'Someone will have to look after him. Unfortunately I've only one bed.'

'What's the matter with him?'

'Oh—quite a number of things. It's rather an interesting case. You don't want him here, then?'

'Oh, well,' said Mr Knayle, 'that's rather an unreasonable way to put it. This may be a very serious business, you know, Ridgeway. He appears to me to be—well, to put it plainly, his mind seems to me to be affected. I—I really can't accept such a responsibility. I think we had better take him up to his own flat. Or if you'll do that, I'll ring up and get a nurse.'

'Cost you twopence,' smiled Mr Ridgeway. 'Don't worry. I'll look after him.'

The dingy arms of his dressing-gown encircled Whalley and raised him to his feet. Their movements seemed ostentatiously gentle and protective, and Mr Knayle turned his back on them. When at length the hall-door shut he called in Hopgood and made him brush some crumbs of mud from the seat of one of the arm-chairs.

'Would you like me to go up and give Mr Ridgeway a hand, sir?' Hopgood asked before he withdrew.

'I don't think it's at all necessary,' Mr Knayle replied frigidly. 'Get me some tea, now, will you.'

2

The next three days were wet and Mr Knayle spent the greater part of them before his fire. The occupation of his mind was not so much thought of any definition as the repeated asking of a few questions to which the fire supplied no answers. They were always the same; he could find no means to vary them or expand them. One long wet day had made him weary of their abortive monotony; three had robbed them of almost all relation to realities. But they refused to be shut out, and they had taken such complete possession of him that he could think of nothing else.

He shook his head to dislodge them, leaned forward to poke the fire, picked up a novel, and recrossed his legs. But the novel dropped to his lap and his eyes returned to the fire. Had Chidgey really lost a hammer? If he had, was it really like the hammer which had been shown to him? Was it the hammer which had been shown to him? Supposing that it was, had Whalley taken it from the box, with the gloves? Had Whalley taken the gloves from the box, or had Chidgey taken them and left them in Whalley's car and forgotten that he had done so? Had Chidgey made up a story about losing a hammer, or had

he really done so? If he had . . . Mr Knayle's questions slid past
ceaselessly on an endless chain, always detached, yet always
linked in the same order. He frowned, picked up his book again,
and saw Chidgey slide up over the edge of the page, bent over
a box, looking for a missing hammer.

Sometimes he made an effort to stop the chain. Chidgey . . .
Why not question Chidgey more closely? If his story was a
made-up one he would stick to it, of course. But if it wasn't—
Chidgey was a careful chap—very careful about his tools—very
unlikely to mislay a hammer—especially a hammer which he
didn't use. Suppose it, then. Suppose that a hammer was really
missing from a box in the garage. How like had it been to the
hammer which had been shown to Chidgey? Who could tell?
Not Chidgey himself.

From that uncertainty on everything was uncertainty. Mr
Knayle grew sick of his questions. They slid across the
hearthrug, the fire, the mantelpiece, the wall-paper, the ceiling.
They followed him when he got up, and slid across the carpet
and the windows. They slid across his plate while he ate, across
his mirror while he shaved, slid down the water of the geyser
while his bath filled, slid up the flex of the light over his bed
while he tried to read himself asleep. There was no escape from
them anywhere in the flat. He desired to escape from them, yet
found a perverse pleasure in surrendering to their obsession.
When Hopgood came into the room he watched him with a
raised eyebrow, impatient to be left with them again. Hopgood
grew a little nervous under this silent scrutiny and one day
upset the contents of an ashtray over the hearthrug. 'Leave it,'
said Mr Knayle, pettishly. 'Clean it up afterwards.'

The weather improved, but he could find no interest out of
doors. Only with the greatest difficulty could he persuade
himself to morning and afternoon constitutionals upon the
deserted Downs. He didn't want to go to the Club—he didn't
want to shoot—he didn't want to play bridge—he didn't want
to talk to people—he didn't want to do anything. It was alto-

gether unlike him and a little disquieting, but there it was. He didn't want to do anything, and there was nothing to make him do anything. It didn't matter in the least whether he did anything or not, and he didn't care whether it mattered or not. In his sitting-room he was his own and sufficient for himself, shut in from criticism, secure from slight and wounding indifference. It was always easier to go back to the arm-chair and think about Whalley.

Lack of fresh air staled his appetite quickly and made his sleep broken and irregular. He sat up late, got up late, changed the hours of his meals, smoked incessantly, and developed a slight but persistent dyspepsia. His temper became so irritable that Hopgood grew to dread the sitting-room door. But the fire had to be kept up. If it wasn't Mr Knayle sat looking at it and let it go out.

Curiously, although his thoughts concentrated themselves incessantly upon Whalley, they never directly faced the possibility that Whalley had committed murder. They were always sliding towards that possibility, skirting round it, and then retreating to make a fresh approach. The word murder and the idea murder had always repelled Mr Knayle. For him murder had always been an alien, abnormal thing which happened in the part of his newspaper which he never read. He had never had anything to do with murder, never conceived that he could ever have anything to do with it. His mind baulked at the thought that anyone whom he had known could commit a murder. It could suppose it possible that Whalley had taken the hammer from the garage—possible, even, that the hammer had actually been the hammer which had killed Miss Prossip. But it refused to suppose that Whalley had used it to kill her. There the chain always slid out of sight.

Suppose that Whalley's mind was affected—either by his wife's death or by the state of his health—or by money troubles and literary failures. But all that was too vague for Mr Knayle. Until this mysterious accident, Whalley had always appeared to him perfectly normal—a quiet, self-controlled figure going up or coming down his steps. He shied away from obscure aberrations, seeking for a deliberate, reasoned purpose. But what had Whalley ever had to do with the Prossip girl? There had been that ridiculous row over the gramophone, and apparently she had been chiefly responsible for its annoyance. But who could take that seriously? The fiddle? The flooding of the Whalley's flat? The complaints about that little dog—what was his name? Mr Knayle couldn't remember his name and couldn't imagine anyone killing a young woman because she had played a gramophone over his head six months before. He shook his head and lighted another cigarette.

Sometimes he raised his eyes to the ceiling, but they always returned to the fire quickly. The ceiling had become a reminder of a fatuousness of which he was now a little ashamed and which, he suspected, had been largely physiological—some late, feeble explosion of sex—no rose-scented rapture, but a whiff of musty decay. He didn't want to think about that sort of thing. His romance had become suspect—an elderly infatuation, of now uncertain ambitions, for another man's wife. He wanted to cancel all that and leave her in her original state—the wife of Whalley with whom he was now determined to have nothing to do.

Sometimes, too, he rose quickly from his armchair to peer through the window-curtains. But it was only to watch Ridgeway pass between his little flight of steps and the staircase leading to the upper flats. Ridgeway spent most of his time now in the first-floor flat, descending at intervals for meals, sometimes remaining up there all night. Mr Knayle kept watch upon his comings and goings and was always tempted to hurry out and ask him how Whalley was getting on, and whether his mind was right again, and whether it was likely that he had heard Chidgey's story about a missing hammer, and what Ridgeway himself thought about Chidgey's story. But, though his interest in Whalley had become an obsession, he was determined to have nothing to do with him, or with Ridgeway, who had taken charge of him. Ridgeway's remark about the telephone had been most offensive. When the sound of the slippered footsteps had died away Mr Knayle went back to the fire, remembering sometimes that he had peered through the curtains at Whalley's wife, and feeling a little furtive.

The grey days before Christmas passed. He was always sitting in his armchair before the fire, raising a cigarette slowly to his lips and taking it away again.

After lunch on Christmas Day his attention was attracted to the sound of footsteps pacing to and fro slowly above his head. They paced slowly and faintly, and when he had listened to them for some moments, expecting them to stop, his attention strayed from them. In a little while, however, it returned to them. They had not stopped, and they had grown louder.

For an hour and a half they paced, almost directly above his arm-chair. He got up to listen to them—listened to them from different positions about the room. Their sound grew louder and more distinct. When they ceased at length, he yawned with weariness of them.

Ten minutes later they began to pace again. They went on pacing all the afternoon, all the evening, stopping sometimes for a few minutes, sometimes for half an hour. They were audible everywhere in the flat—there was no way not to hear them. They were pacing when he fell asleep towards two o'clock, pacing when he woke at half-past three.

Next day they began towards midday. Mr Knayle swore at them and went for a walk. When he returned to lunch they were still pacing. They paced all the afternoon and all the evening. He got no sleep whatsoever that night.

When they began next day at half-past one he sprang up from the table and upset his coffee.

'Talk about the gramophone, sir—' said Hopgood, when they had stood for a little space looking upwards in silence.

It seemed impossible that they could continue and never grow weary. But they went on pacing all day long, all through the night. Actually their sound was scarcely louder than Mr Knayle's angry breathing, but his fretted nerves heard it as the trampling of a regiment. Its torture hammered on his smoothly-brushed head and beat it slowly into seething fury; it made his palms sweat and dug his finger-nails into them, made him writhe in his chair and batter the fire savagely. He tried various devices to deaden the sound—packed his ears with cotton-wool, wrapped a muffler round his head, turned on the wireless. Nothing was of any avail, however. In the end it was more satisfying to hear it clearly and hate it without interference.

He thought a great deal about this small, continuous noise which in a few days had made his life a poisoned agony.

'Can you remember, Hopgood,' he asked one day, 'how long used that gramophone of the Prossips to play—exactly?'

3

There was very little for Mr Ridgeway to do. He spent most of his time before the gas-fire in the dining-room, reading—got through Motley's *Dutch Republic*, James's *Varieties of Religious Experience*, *An Old Wives' Tale*, and some of Hardy's novels—dozed a good deal, and sometimes forgot to go down to his own flat for meals. Four times a day he attended to Whalley's eye; but the ulcer had now grown stagnant and there was really no necessity to trouble about it. At irregular intervals he made some tea and cut some slices of bread and butter. Whalley drank the tea greedily but sometimes left the bread and butter untouched. He refused all other food, and the liver which the butcher still delivered each morning went into the rubbish-bin. There was really no necessity to trouble about that either.

The pacing footsteps in the passage did not disturb Mr Ridgeway greatly; in the dining-room, with the portière drawn across the door, they were barely audible—no more than company. Sometimes he went out and stood for a while, watching and wondering when they would begin to tire. At first he had been a little interested by the fact that, as he paced to and fro, Whalley's face remained always raised towards the ceiling. But the pacing figure was always the same and its face always raised; Mr Ridgeway hardly thought about it at all now save to speculate as to how long it would go on pacing on a little tea and bread and butter. Not very long, he thought. Some weeks, perhaps. But there was no hurry.

Gradually the flat fell into disorder. At intervals Whalley interrupted his patrol abruptly and, hurrying into one of the rooms, resumed a process of dismantlement which had now been in progress for over a fortnight. It proceeded spasmodically, but with a persistency which had at first aroused a little speculation in Mr Ridgeway's mind, but had quickly become monotonous. Now a couple of pictures were taken down—now another strip of carpet was cleared, the furniture pushed into a corner, and the carpet rolled up. Now the contents of a bookcase were emptied on to the floor, or a shelf of the kitchen dresser cleared and the crockery stacked in the passage. These outbreaks of energy were, however, of brief duration; after a few minutes of feverish activity Whalley abandoned his labours as abruptly as he begun them, looked about him vacantly, and went back to resume his pacing again. Beyond keeping a clear approach to the gas-fire in the dining-room, Mr Ridgeway did not concern himself with this derangement. If its purpose was, as he surmised, an unusually elaborate spring-cleaning, he thought it extremely unlikely that it would ever be achieved. And even if one did walk on a picture or a Crown Derby saucer, it really didn't matter in the least.

One night he tried a little experiment. He brought up an aspirin tabloid and, just before he went away, opened Whalley's mouth gently and placed the tabloid on his tongue. Whalley swallowed it apathetically. No experiment could have been more satisfactory. After that the swallowing of an aspirin tabloid

became a nightly formality whose occasional omission appeared
to cause Whalley a vague disappointment.

His strength failed swiftly. Much more quickly even than Mr
Ridgeway had expected the pacing footsteps began to weary of
their sentry-go. Mr Ridgeway became restless and watchful and
left the door of the dining-room ajar a little while he tried to
finish *The Mayor of Casterbridge*.

CHAPTER XIV

1

On one windy night towards the middle of January Mr Knayle sat watching his sitting-room fire go out. For three hours he had sat there while its cheerful blaze had dwindled to a glow—faded—contracted—chilled to a grey heap of ashes whose pin-points of red were a mockery of warmth and comfort. His eyes watched the last phases of its death with stony bitterness and saw in it a symbol—an epitome of the disorder which had suddenly attacked his life. For the reason why the fire had gone out was that there was no coal in the coal-box. And the reason why there was no coal in the coal-box was that Hopgood had gone away at three o'clock that afternoon.

Mr Knayle was still too angry to think clearly how this malign and menacing thing had happened him. Hopgood's desertion confused itself with another malign and menacing thing which had happened earlier in the day. Shortly before lunchtime a mob of howling louts had passed up Downview Road, waving red flags and brandishing sticks and pieces of gas-piping. Suddenly a stone had crashed through one of the windows of the sitting-room. It had done no damage beyond breaking the window and sprinkling the carpet with glass; but Hopgood had been badly scared and, in his panic-stricken flight from the room, had pushed Mr Knayle violently out of his way. Mr Knayle had followed him out to the kitchen and said several things which he was now unable to remember but which he felt sure had been thoroughly deserved. There had been a most unpleasant scene in the kitchen. Hopgood had refused to gather up the broken glass, refused to get lunch ready, called Mr Knayle a bloody bully, shut himself up in his room, and ultimately gone off in a taxi without warning and without asking for his wages. It had all been so sudden and so sinister and so utterly contemptuous of Mr Knayle's dignity and comfort that he was still shaken by little hot quiverings of anger and apprehension—still quite unable to think clearly about it.

But he felt that a devastating catastrophe had befallen him. For nearly twenty years Hopgood had supplied the essential needs of every moment of the days smoothly and unfailingly that it had never been necessary to consider even the possibility of hitch or failure. Now, in a moment, all this tranquil, complicated security had collapsed into irreparable confusion. In his heart Mr Knayle knew that Hopgood could never be replaced. Another man could be found, no doubt, honest, intelligent, conscientious in the ordinary way—able to cook tolerably—able to keep things going fairly well. But there had been a hundred thousand small personal dexterities and understandings in Hopgood's service—a hundred thousand small knowledges which had supplied themselves to Mr Knayle's little ways with a loyalty which had been very nearly maternal affection. Mr Knayle knew that many of his little ways were rather unreasonable—some of them rather odd—some of them childish in their pettiness. He wanted no new hands to neglect them—no new eyes to watch them—no new tongue to gossip about them. Not in twenty years could any possible new man be taught to respect them and guard them as an honoured trust. Not in a lifetime could he be taught the devotion which with Hopgood had been a tradition. For Hopgood's forebears had served the Knayle family and its kindred for generations—a fact which lent to his desertion the baseness of a treachery. Mr Knayle's anger could not contemplate the task of training any possible new man to regard his little ways with maternal affection and to appreciate properly the honour of serving a member of the Knayle family. It was unable to look beyond the indignities and discomforts of the moment. It desired simply to defy them, not to think of remedies for them. He sat bolt upright, defying them.

It appeared to him incredible that he could find himself in such a position. He had had no food since breakfast. He was sitting in a room without a fire on a cold winter night. The carpet was covered with splintered glass and a desolating draught came in through the broken window-pane. Nothing would be ready in his bedroom. There would be no hot-water bottle in his bed. There would be no tea in the morning—no breakfast. These things appeared to him inconceivable and outrageous. He could have gone to the club or to a restaurant, but he had been determined not to go. He could have had the window mended, but he had been determined not to have it mended. He could have taken the coal-box out to the cellar and refilled it, but he had been determined that he would not refill the coal-box. He had never filled a coal-box in his life; nothing would compel him to fill a coal-box. He was resolved to endure cold and hunger and despise them proudly and angrily—not to yield an inch to them. He had yielded too much—allowed himself to be cowed and thrust aside—allowed his body to grow slack—his morale to slip into flabbiness. That must stop. A stand must be taken before it was too late.

He had had a bad headache since the scene in the kitchen that morning. It was not so much a headache as a sensation that his head was clamped in a vice which had compressed its contents into solidity. There was a persistent buzzing, too, in his ears which sometimes became the roar of swollen, rushing waters and blotted out everything except a desolating sense of imminent disaster. He could construct no definite thought about the discomforts of his position; they were all too sudden—too wanton in their senselessness. But they appeared to him of immense importance and significance—insults to order and justice and all sane purpose—manifestations of the sinister forces which had thrown all the world into confusion and alarm. The draught that came in through the broken window-pane was no mere current of cold air; it was an irruption of lawlessness, a spirit of brutal howling destruction. He saw that Hopgood's treacherous desertion typified the revolt of the masses—furtive cunning, insane in its lust to deface and pull down. It was that sort of thing that was undermining civilisation—idiotic rebellion against authority. His mind connected it with the disaffection of India—Bolshevism—the tyranny of the Trades Unions—chits of girls addressing men of fifty by nicknames—indecent films—litter left lying about the Downs—smash-and-grab raids—the swift breaking-up of the Empire. Everywhere revolt against order and tradition and superior intelligence. It was all confused and a little tremulous, but Mr Knayle was clear that it must be stopped. He saw himself—not as an individual, but as a class. It was the English gentleman, the guardian of honour and law and justice who sat by the dying fire and saw in it the threat of his extinction, and defied its threat contemptuously. There had been Knayles of Yelve Court since King's John's time—soldiers, sailors, lawyers governors, ministers, a Lord Chancellor, three judges, an admiral two generals, an ambassador and a bishop. They had all kept the trust. Mr Knayle's cleft chin tilted itself when he thought of them It was they and their kind that had always been the backbone of the country—the stable, stubborn spirit that had withstood all changes. What was there like them? He saw that there had never been anything in the world like them. And he was one of them He would fight the good fight—go down fighting . . .

Yes. He had allowed himself to weaken—shut himself up with his sickliness—brooded himself into cowardice. But that was done with now. Tomorrow, when the headache and the buzzing had gone, he would take steps to deal with all this—stop it—make a fresh start—get away from this sitting-room where his brain had thought itself into stupor—get away from that fellow Whalley and his pacing—get away from bleary, shambling Ridgeway—get away from rottenness and fear—get away from all the sickness of the past six months. A little place somewhere near Whanton—a bit of rough shooting—a garden—days in the fresh air—nights of sound sleep again—a couple of dogs. One would learn not to think again.

Tomorrow. Tonight everything trembled too much. A quarter to twelve.

But Mr Knayle was determined not to go to bed tonight.

2

The hall-door bell rang furiously and continued to ring while he made his way a little dizzily along the hall. When he opened the door Prossip lurched in, very white and oozing slightly at the corners of his lips. Mr Knayle stared at him in surprise and dislike—watched him shift a small suit-case to his left hand, and stepped back a little to avoid shaking hands with him.

'Hello, old chap,' said Prossip gloomily, moving his lips with great care. 'Sorry to knock you up at this hour.'

He stood, swaying a little, holding out his hand, looking so meanly bounderish in his new mourning that Mr Knayle remained determined not to shake hands with him. What was this boozing cad coming to his hall-door for at twelve o'clock at night, ringing the bell like a madman and slobbering at his lips? A mean, frightened-looking, drunken cad. What was he doing there? Shake hands with him? Mr Knayle was determined that he wouldn't

But something must be said to him—something about his daughter having been murdered. How would one begin it? 'I'm so sorry your daughter was murdered.' 'I'm so sorry that you have met with such a—' 'I'm so sorry—' Mr Knayle couldn't begin to think of something to say. Murder? Who wanted to talk about murder? Sick thoughts—footsteps pacing—pacing—pacing. Done with all that.

'I'm so sorry about your daughter, Mr Prossip,' he said at last, slowly and frigidly.

Prossip waved a hand. 'Don't, old man—' He darted a quick look of doubt. 'I've lost the poor Missus, too, you know.'

'The—your wife? Your wife? Do you mean that your wife is dead?'

Mr Prossip's head nodded gloomily. 'Gone. It's finished me, old chap. I'm through.'

3

It was late and Knayle looked damn unfriendly, but Mr Prossip decided to sit down on one of the very hard hall-chairs and tell how dear old Emma had gone from him. It was a long story because first it had to go back over his life with Emma and make it clear that they had always been the best of pals and had never had as much as an angry word between them. Then it had to make it clear that he had warned Emma hundreds and hundreds of times against riding a bicycle—done everything a man could do to prevent her riding a bicycle. All this took a lot of time because he had to move his lips very carefully so as not to be ill in Mr Knayle's hall. He had had a lot of whisky during the day and he knew that he was going to be ill as soon as he got up to his own flat; but he didn't want it to happen in Knayle's hall. It was an effort to keep his lips close together, and he was tired and Knayle kept on saying nothing and looking damn unfriendly. However he made it quite clear that he had always warned Emma against riding a bicycle. That was the important thing.

Then he told how Emma had gone off to church one morning and how a car had knocked her off her bicycle in the fog, and how she had been found by a postman lying dead on the foot-path. The postman had seen the whole thing from the other side of the road and had run after the car; but it had disappeared into the fog and he hadn't been able to see its number. A two-seater car, he had said, driven by a man with a bandage tied round his head. The bicycle, of course, had been smashed up, but Emma hadn't had a scratch on her. At any rate that was something to be thankful for.

Knayle kept on looking damn queer and unfriendly and, tiring of his story, Mr Prossip rose heavily to his feet and hiccupped loudly.

'Sorry,' he said. 'Can I have my key—the key of my flat, you know? I left it with you.'

'Key?' Knayle repeated. He opened his mouth, shut it again, dithered through a door, dithered out again, handed Mr Prossip a labelled key and opened the hall-door.

'When—?' he began, and shut his mouth again. Mr Prossip felt another hiccup coming on and lurched out into the safety of the windy darkness. The hall-door shut behind him immediately.

It was all damn odd and unfriendly, Mr Prossip thought as he climbed to the top flat with his suitcase. But everyone had been unfriendly towards him for some time back and he was beginning to expect it. No use worrying—just toddle along and take no notice. He sang as he fumbled with the latchkey.

'Pack all your troubles in your old kit-bag
And smile, smile, smile.'

The song died away abruptly when he discovered that the electric light had been cut off. After a long search he found a stump of candle in one of the kitchen drawers. But its wavering light cast uneasy shadows and never reached corners. Mr Prossip liked to be able to see corners distinctly now. Finding that Emma had stripped all the beds and locked away the bedclothes in a cupboard for which he had no key, he sat down and wept for a little while heavily. The thought that Emma would never unlock the cupboard again and take out the neatly-folded blankets and sheets and pillow-slips which she had put away so carefully strangled his heart. It was a reminder that all her untiring, ruthless efficiency was lost to him for ever; she died again while it choked him.

He had often wondered what it would be like if Emma died. It had seemed to him certain that, once rid of her watchful tyranny, his life would instantly expand into a splendid liberty—an unending series of eases and reliefs. But it hadn't worked out like that. The lonely weeks since Emma's death had opened his eyes and given him a new view of himself. He had discovered that all the comforts and conveniences of his life had depended upon her—that all his reputable friends had been hers, all his decent actions directed by her, all his facade of respectability maintained by her. It had been revealed to him that everything of him which had been at all presentable had died with her. What was left had not been agreeable company for Mr Prossip during the past five weeks. He had got through a lot of whisky in the effort not to think about it. But for some reason whisky had lost its kick since Emma's death. Mr Prossip merely got ill now, when he drank enough of it, and began to think about Emma's bicycle and Marjory's fiddle and the possibility of his ending in an inebriates' home. The wind howled and the shadows waved and he blubbered like a baby because he knew that he was just a helpless, boozing old blackguard and that there was now no one to care whether he was one or to prevent him from being one.

However, he felt better presently when he had taken a swig at a bottle of whisky which he had packed in his suitcase. Toddle along and take no notice. Scrape through. He would have to sleep in his clothes tonight, and there was a lot of troublesome business to be done with Emma's solicitors tomorrow. But in a couple of months he would be comfortably settled in a little flat in London, with an income of twelve hundred or so. No more nagging—no more going out to early service—no more scraping. Not so bad after all. Not so bad.

As he wandered towards the kitchen in search of another candle, his eyes fell on the gramophone standing in its old place with its lid open and a dusty record resting on its table. A little tune would liven things up a bit and get into all those dark corners. He set it going and stood listening, wondering if old what-was-his-name was still in the flat underneath, and whether he would have another swig before he looked for candles. After all, he didn't think he was going to be ill just yet.

4

Downstairs Mr Knayle paced to and fro fitfully, pursuing the irritation from which he fled. Sometimes the grinding smash of glass beneath his feet turned him aside in search of a new course for his restlessness. But the furniture baulked him and drove him back to the imprisonment of one short path. There was no escape from it; his buzzing, trembling mind must go, and turn and come back along it, always checked, always beginning again. When he stood still the swirling waters roared threateningly and the clamps tightened on his temples. He had become uneasy about his headache. the solid part of it had swollen and was pressing outwards against the clamps. It was safer to keep moving—safer not to let that roar become too loud. Blood-pressure, probably; something would have to be done about it tomorrow if it wasn't better. Tomorrow—today. Mr Knayle saw that it was nearly one o'clock and knew that far the wisest thing would have been to go to bed. The room had settled into grey aloofness and watched him with impatience. But he was determined not to be driven from it—determined that this—this—

He stopped, rubbed his forehead impatiently, then went on again, clicking his fingers impatiently. Strange this feeling that thoughts were solid, bursting heavinesses which it was exasperated weariness to move. But they must be moved—urged on before their weight became too heavy and too hated. Determined that this—this—

Turn again—begin again. Determined to what? Something about Mrs Prossip ... Determined to—to understand quite clearly about Mrs Prossip.

The old, weary, sick business beginning again—the infernal Prossips—Whalley—the lane—the hammer—Chidgey—Agatha Judd. The old exhausted, hated questions sliding by. No answers to them—only futility and nausea. What did it matter about that fellow Whalley? Let him pace. Why think of him or trouble about him? Why not leave him up there—escape from him tomorrow—today?

But no. Mr Knayle had done with escaping and shirking. This thing of Whalley must be faced and dealt with. He saw that he must face it and deal with it—that no one else could gather it together and piece it into certainty. Only he knew all about Whalley. For who knew—who knew that—that?

He turned and began again. The whole thing was there, tremblingly clear, buzzing with clearness. But the chain slid by too quickly; he couldn't select a piece and make it a beginning. Whalley in the lane . . . but a week before the murder. That proved nothing unless—unless one began with the hammer. But before one could begin with the hammer one had to begin with Chidgey. Had Chidgey really missed a hammer? Turn again. Begin with Whalley saying that he hadn't been in Guildford. But that began nothing unless one began with the lane, and the lane slid away until Chidgey slid up again. Agatha Judd—begin with her. But there was no beginning with her unless one began first with the Prossip girl—Whalley in the lane—Chidgey sliding up again.

Turn again. Face it and deal with it—gather up that fellow Whalley up there, drag him out of his hiding-place and finish him. Begin again. This about Mrs Prossip and her bicycle. A two-seater—a driver with a bandaged head—fog. But when—what foggy morning? What had killed her—her heart or the car? No beginning there—no proof unless those pieces fitted. Even then—even then—As he turned once more, Mr Knayle paused abruptly, looking upwards. A faint, new overtone had added itself to the mournful wailing of the wind—a sound whose improbability startled him, yet seemed to him expected —a dream-like, half-heard answer to his baulking thoughts. His nerves tightened as he listened to it. It was a prelude—a warning that filled the room with urgent danger. It came and went—swirled—died away in sickened weariness—shattered itself in an explosion which stunned the wind to silence. A splinter of glass dislodged itself from the broken window-pane and tinkled softly to the floor before a second report hurled him into furious action. Three more followed in rapid succession while he scuttled to the hall-door, snatching up a riding-crop as he went. Madness up there—murder broken loose. But *he* would deal with them. It was avenging justice that scuttled up the outside staircase and hammered savagely at a door that dared not open.

The wind was very loud up there and Mr Knayle had run up the steps so quickly that his ears roared like thunder. He heard a hiccup and knew that Prossip had come down and was standing beside him in the darkness, saying something about firing. But he didn't want to hear what Prossip was saying— Prossip who had brought back all this madness—who knew nothing—who was too drunk to understand anything. He turned a little, pushed him away with a thrust of his elbow and resumed his hammering until, at last, the door opened.

Ridgeway stood looking at him in an acrid mist that drifted sluggishly. His eyes were sly; Mr Knayle hated their narrow furtiveness and stormed in, twitching his crop.

'What's this?' he demanded. 'Who fired those—those—? Who fired?'

'Don't make a fuss,' Ridgeway replied hurriedly. 'It's all right.'

'All right? All right?' repeated Mr Knayle. 'All right?'

He hurried up the little staircase and stood looking about him in the narrow passage. It was blocked with chairs and tables, untidy heaps of crockery stood everywhere, mirrors and pictures lay smothered in the dust from an overturned coal-box. Its confusion confused him. For a moment he couldn't think why he was standing there looking at it.

'All right?' he said again, angrily. 'Who—who fired those shots?'

Ridgeway came up and passed him slowly, watching the twitching of the crop.

'Whalley.'

'Did he, by God?' said Prossip, coming up a step. 'Did he, by God?'

But Ridgeway was moving on slyly, creeping towards a door at the end of the passage, without seeming to move his feet.

'Wait—wait now,' commanded Mr Knayle. 'Stand still, you old fool. Why did he fire?'

'I don't know. I was asleep. It's all right. Don't shout.'

'Shout?'

Mr Knayle's voice slid up to shrillness and cracked so sharply that Ridgeway stopped to look back at him curiously. His eyes had risen to the ceiling and suddenly seen certainty. There it was, looking down at him, the answer to all his questions. The crudest of physical facts—a square of painted boardwork scarred by a ring of splintered gashes. Its crudity amazed him. It was merely a piece of splintered wood let into the plaster of the ceiling, altogether separated from significance. And yet he knew that it explained everything—that now he knew all about Whalley. The gramophone—that was it—that was the truth of it all. The gramophone—blaring—blaring—never stopping—torture like pacing footsteps. That was the beginning—the first piece—there, just within his grasp if he could stop its sliding and trembling.

He turned towards Prossip.

'The gramophone—' he said. 'He fired at the gramophone.'

But Prossip's face was white and trembling with fright—dribbling at the lips—going to be sick. Mr Knayle turned away from it in loathing. Who could explain to it?

'It was an accident,' said Ridgeway. 'He didn't know what he was doing. It's all right. Don't make a fuss.'

'Accident?' Mr Knayle repeated shrilly. 'Accident? It was murder—murder, do you hear? I warn you, Ridgeway. I know all about him. I know—'

Strange—he was standing there, opening and shutting his mouth and making no sound whatever. Ridgeway had slid through a door and shut it behind him. Whalley was in there, then—caught—cornered at last—the mad pacer—the evil, hiding thing that must be finished.

Strange though that there was no sound.

It was clear to Mr Knayle what he must do next. He must fling open that door, stride in, point his crop at Whalley and tell him all he knew about him. He must tell it all perfectly clearly, adding piece to piece, building it up to certainty, while Whalley listened in shame and fear. It was a fine, avenging entry and Mr Knayle's anger trembled on the point of making it—hung on the verge of movement. One more exhausted lifting—one more effort of torment—and then done with madness for ever.

The gramophone. Begin again. Torture—nausea—impotence. But begin again at Whalley—tear him out of it. Begin again. The gramophone—red scars—five of them in a circle—deliberate—

Suddenly Prossip was abominably ill. He had seated himself on the stairs and was leaning on his hands, vomiting with the gloomy abandonment of a disgorging ghoul. Mr Knayle stared at his heaving blackness for a moment in furious disgust, then rushed to the door at the end of the passage and hurled himself against it.

Another strange thing happened to him then—so suddenly that his perception of it clouded itself in acrid darkness. He knew that he was trying to open a door—that he desired to open it—that he had hurled himself against it in his desire to open it. But it refused to open—he had no power whatever to begin to open it. His body was a mere wisp of thistledown fluttering impotently against the battlements of a fortress—battlements of a weight and thickness for which there was no measurement. They towered above his feebleness—beat it back—scattered it in dizziness. Nothing would make them yield or surrender their secret. His fingers fumbled, lost the handle, found it again—could not begin the thought of turning it.

Strange. Dizzy as whirling thistledown. But it must be dealt with—finished.

The darkness cleared a little and Mr Knayle's determination

at last opened the door and carried him slowly into the room. Inside was silence and a confusion which bewildered him and deprived him of all sense of direction. At first he could see nothing except a barrier of furniture which occupied the central portion of the floor, collected, yet scattered as if some purpose had died in aimlessness. He edged along it, pushed a chair aside, stumbled over a rolled-up carpet, came to a pause before a bed which stood wedged between a wardrobe and a dressing-table. Its position stupefied him. It was a bed all ready for use—unruffled—immaculate in its crisp neatness and cleanness; and yet it stood there in the centre of the room, abandoned to the disorder which enclosed it. For a moment he stared at it vaguely, then moved on slowly until, rounding the side of the wardrobe, he saw another bed, standing awry in the angle of two walls.

But for Mr Knayle it was not a bed. It was a swirling torment of defeat which crushed his mind to nothingness. On it lay two figures interlocked in a frantic embrace which had the fixity of paralysis yet still struggled in delirious ferocity. But they had no significance—no thought. He knew that their struggling had ended. His questions would remain for ever unanswered. They were utter frustration.

His mind strove with them for an instant feebly, trying to disentangle them, trying to reach the thing which had baffled and eluded him and now lay hidden beneath a dingy dressing-gown. But Mr Ridgeway held his company fast; there was nothing that was Whalley except a twisted leg escaping from a rumpled eiderdown. Mr Knayle felt very weary of it suddenly and couldn't understand it. His ears roared painfully because its trembling deadness would never give an answer. It seemed to him safer to sit down until the pain had passed.

He made his way back to the other bed and seated himself on it with a little sigh of relief. It was very soft, very clean—without torment or question. After some moments his attention was attracted to a little case which rested on the pillows—a dainty thing of jade-coloured silk on which the name 'Elsa' was embroidered in a darker green. The letters trembled so violently that he bent his head to see them clearly. A faint perfume of roses assailed him dizzily—smiling—sunlit—dancing. Very slowly his head dropped to the pillows and lay quite still.

5

After a little while Mr Prossip felt much better. He was still badly frightened and he didn't think he'd bother to find out what was going on in that room at the end of the passage. The whole business struck him as damn queer. But everything was damn queer, when you thought about it. He ascended to his own flat in offended dignity, cheered himself up with another swig at his bottle, and then thought that he'd find out whether the gramophone had been damaged or had just stopped of its own accord.

To his satisfaction it was quite uninjured—much louder and jollier now that he had been ill.

THE END

THE DETECTIVE STORY CLUB

FOR DETECTIVE CONNOISSEURS

recommends

"The Man with the Gun."

THE BLACKMAILERS

By THE MASTER OF THE FRENCH CRIME STORY—EMILE GABORIAU

EMILE GABORIAU is France's greatest detective writer. *The Blackmailers* is one of his most thrilling novels, and is full of exciting surprises. The story opens with a sensational bank robbery in Paris, suspicion falling immediately upon Prosper Bertomy, the young cashier whose extravagant living has been the subject of talk among his friends. Further investigation, however, reveals a network of blackmail and villainy which seems as if it would inevitably close round Prosper and the beautiful Madeleine, who is deeply in love with him. Can he prove his innocence in the face of such damning evidence?

THE REAL THING *from* SCOTLAND YARD!

THE CRIME CLUB

By FRANK FRÖEST, Ex-Supt. C.I.D., Scotland Yard, and George Dilnot

YOU will seek in vain in any book of reference for the name of The Crime Club. Its watchword is secrecy. Its members wear the mask of mystery, but they form the most powerful organisation against master criminals ever known. The Crime Club is an international club composed of men who spend their lives studying crime and criminals. In its headquarters are to be found experts from Scotland Yard, many foreign detectives and secret service agents. This book tells of their greatest victories over crime, and is written in association with George Dilnot by a former member of the Criminal Investigation Department of Scotland Yard.

LOOK FOR THE MAN WITH THE GUN

THE DETECTIVE STORY CLUB

FOR DETECTIVE CONNOISSEURS

recommends

"The Man with the Gun."

MR. BALDWIN'S FAVOURITE

THE LEAVENWORTH CASE

By ANNA K. GREEN

THIS exciting detective story, published towards the end of last century, enjoyed an enormous success both in England and America. It seems to have been forgotten for nearly fifty years until Mr. Baldwin, speaking at a dinner of the American Society in London, remarked : " An American woman, a successor of Poe, Anna K. Green, gave us *The Leavenworth Case*, which I still think one of the best detective stories ever written." It is a remarkably clever story, a masterpiece of its kind, and in addition to an exciting murder mystery and the subsequent tracking down of the criminal, the writing and characterisation are excellent. *The Leavenworth Case* will not only grip the attention of the reader from beginning to end but will also be read again and again with increasing pleasure.

CALLED BACK

By HUGH CONWAY

BY the purest of accidents a man who is blind accidentally comes on the scene of a murder. He cannot see what is happening, but he can hear. He is seen by the assassin who, on discovering him to be blind, allows him to go without harming him. Soon afterwards he recovers his sight and falls in love with a mysterious woman who is in some way involved in the crime. . . . The mystery deepens, and only after a series of memorable thrills is the tangled skein unravelled.

LOOK FOR THE MAN WITH THE GUN

THE DETECTIVE STORY CLUB

FOR DETECTIVE CONNOISSEURS

recommends

"The Man with the Gun."

The Murder of Roger Ackroyd
By AGATHA CHRISTIE

THE MURDER OF ROGER ACKROYD is one of Mrs. Christie's most brilliant detective novels. As a play, under the title of *Alibi*, it enjoyed a long and successful run with Charles Laughton as the popular detective, Hercule Poirot. The novel has now been filmed, and its clever plot, skilful characterisation, and sparkling dialogue will make every one who sees the film want to read the book. M. Poirot, the hero of many brilliant pieces of detective deduction, comes out of his temporary retirement like a giant refreshed, to undertake the investigation of a peculiarly brutal and mysterious murder. Geniuses like Sherlock Holmes often find a use for faithful mediocrities like Dr. Watson, and by a coincidence it is the local doctor who follows Poirot round and himself tells the story. Furthermore, what seldom happens in these cases, he is instrumental in giving Poirot one of the most valuable clues to the mystery.

LOOK FOR THE MAN WITH THE GUN

THE DETECTIVE STORY CLUB

FOR DETECTIVE CONNOISSEURS

recommends

"The Man with the Gun."

Philip MacDonald

Author of Rynox, etc.

MURDER GONE MAD

MR. MacDonald, who has shown himself in *The Noose* and *The Rasp* to be a master of the crime novel of pure detection, has here told a story of a motiveless crime, or at least a crime prompted only by blood lust. The sure, clear thinking of the individual detective is useless and only wide, cleverly organised investigation can hope to succeed.

A long knife with a brilliant but perverted brain directing it is terrorising Holmdale; innocent people are being done to death under the very eyes of the law. Inspector Pyke of Scotland Yard, whom MacDonald readers will remember in previous cases, is put on the track of the butcher. He has nothing to go on but the evidence of the bodies themselves and the butcher's own bravado. After every murder a businesslike letter arrives announcing that another "removal has been carried out." But Pyke "gets there" with a certainty the very slowness of which will give the reader many breathless moments. In the novelty of its treatment, the humour of its dialogue, and the truth of its characterisation, *Murder Gone Mad* is equal to the best Mr. MacDonald has written.

LOOK FOR THE MAN WITH THE GUN

THE DETECTIVE STORY CLUB

FOR DETECTIVE CONNOISSEURS

"The Man with the Gun."

recommends

THE PERFECT CRIME

THE FILM STORY OF

ISRAEL ZANGWILL'S famous detective thriller, THE BIG BOW MYSTERY

A MAN is murdered for no apparent reason. He has no enemies, and there seemed to be no motive for any one murdering him. No clues remained, and the instrument with which the murder was committed could not be traced. The door of the room in which the body was discovered was locked and bolted on the inside, both windows were latched, and there was no trace of any intruder. The greatest detectives in the land were puzzled. Here indeed was the perfect crime, the work of a master mind. Can you solve the problem which baffled Scotland Yard for so long, until at last the missing link in the chain of evidence was revealed?

LOOK OUT
FOR FURTHER SELECTIONS FROM THE DETECTIVE STORY CLUB—READY SHORTLY

LOOK FOR THE MAN WITH THE GUN